Rodin's Debutante

Books by Ward Just

NOVELS
A Soldier of the Revolution 1970
Stringer 1974
Nicholson at Large 1975
A Family Trust 1978
In the City of Fear 1982
The American Blues 1984
The American Ambassador 1987
Jack Gance 1989
The Translator 1991
Ambition & Love 1994
Echo House 1997
A Dangerous Friend 1999
The Weather in Berlin 2002
An Unfinished Season 2004
Forgetfulness 2006
Exiles in the Garden 2009
Rodin's Debutante 2011

SHORT STORIES
The Congressman Who Loved Flaubert 1973
Honor, Power, Riches, Fame, and the Love of Women 1979
Twenty-one: Selected Stories 1990
(reissued in 1998 as The Congressman Who
Loved Flaubert: 21 Stories and Novellas)

NONFICTION
To What End 1968
Military Men 1970

PLAYS
Lowell Limpett 2001

Rodin's Debutante

Ward Just

Houghton Mifflin Harcourt

BOSTON • NEW YORK

2011

www.hmhbooks.com

Library of Congress Cataloging-in-Publication Data
Just, Ward S.
Rodin's debutante / Ward Just.
p. cm.
ISBN 978-0-547-50419-3
1. Coming of age—Fiction. 2. Boarding schools—Fiction.
3. Friendship—Fiction. 4. Maturation (Psychology)—Fiction. I. Title.
PS3560.U75R63   2011
813'.54—dc22   2010042695

Design by Robert Overholtzer, Boskydell Studio

Printed in the United States of America

DOC 10 9 8 7 6 5 4 3 2 1

As ever, to SARAH *and to*
TONY LEWIS *and* MARGIE MARSHALL

and in memory of
PAT THOMPSON

Part One

THIS IS A TRUE STORY, or true as far as it goes. Ogden Hall School for Boys never would have existed were it not for the journey that two Chicago girls made to Paris with their mother. The eldest girl had her head sculpted in marble by the great Rodin in his atelier at the Dépôt des Marbres, a bust from his own hand and chisel. The Chicago girl was eighteen and lovely, the bust a present on her birthday. Rodin was demanding, meticulous in his craft. His eyes glittered as he worked, his unruly head moving to some mysterious rhythm. The girl was a little bit afraid of Rodin, his glare almost predatory, his eyes black as lumps of coal. And when she mentioned this to her mother, the woman only smiled and said that such men were forces of nature but that did not mean they could not be tamed. Only one question: Was the taming worth the trouble? This Rodin, probably yes; but it would take time to find out. The finding-out would be the amusing part and naturally there was ambiguity as in any sentimental endeavor. Taming had its unfortunate side.

In any case, the girl's mother said, you are much too young for such an adventure. Wait two years.

The sitting took only a few days—Rodin wanted an additional day but that was out of the question owing to the travel schedule—and then the girls went on to Salzburg. Their mother was devoted to German opera. Then east to Vienna, south to Florence, and west to Nice, and when, one month later, they returned to Paris the bust was done and in due course sent by ship and installed in the hallway alcove of the Astor Street house, a beautiful work of art, most soulful, luminous in the yellow light from the new electric lamps, and a trenchant counterpoint to the soft Cézanne landscape on the wall opposite. All the newspapers took notice. The Art Institute took particular notice, though the curator privately thought that the bust showed signs of haste. Rodin's debutante was the talk of Chicago. The cost was trifling, a bagatelle. Mother paid francs, cash, on the spot. Two husky workmen were required to transport the wooden case to the brougham waiting at curbside.

THAT WAS MARIE'S POINT, made again and again to her husband Tommy, who was unimpressed, sawing away at his beefsteak, his head low to the plate. Who knew if he was even listening. Tommy Ogden, irascible at all times, disliked discussion of money at meals. The price, Marie went on, was barely more than a wretched automobile, one of Ford's small ones, a mere piece of machinery as opposed to a work of art that would endure forever and ever. The argument began at cocktails, continued through dinner, and did not end—well, in a sense it never ended. There were witnesses to it, the van Hornes and their daughter Trish and the Billingtons and Tommy's lawyer Bert Marks and the Italian servants, Francesca and Alana. Marie wanted her own head in marble and Tommy was too damned cheap to pay for it. Cheap, self-centered, and an egoist, concerned with himself alone. Tommy who thought only of shooting, shooting in Georgia, shooting in Arkansas, shooting in Scotland and Austria and the eastern shore of Maryland and Montana and East Africa and beyond. His set of matched Purdeys cost much more than Rodin's magnificent marble of the Chicago girl and that was consistent with his scale of values. Firearms figured mightily in Tommy

Ogden's scheme of things. So, Marie said, with Tommy or without him she intended to leave at once for the south of France, where she had engaged a pretty villa near Antibes. The route to Antibes led through Paris, where her destination was the atelier at Dépôt des Marbres.

Maître Rodin was said to be most engaging, a powerful presence, something of a roughneck, so French.

I have seen a photograph of the bust, Marie said. That girl's head is even larger than yours, Tommy.

Go to Paris and be damned, Tommy said at last. Under his breath he added, If you can get there. As was often the case, Tommy had confidential information.

I will, Marie said. I propose to leave tomorrow.

Good luck, Tommy said. Don't expect to find me here when you get back.

Steady on, Tommy, Bill van Horne said, but in the thickness of the atmosphere at table no one heard him.

And where are you going? Marie demanded.

Idaho, Tommy said. Pheasant.

Marie made a noise somewhere between a cluck and a growl and signaled Francesca to pass the wine. Tommy was drinking whiskey and now took a long swallow, draining his glass and replenishing it from the decanter on the table.

I've got news for you, Marie.

What's that, Tommy? What's your news?

I'm finished with this house.

What house?

This house, Tommy said. I'm getting rid of it.

You wouldn't dare, Marie said. Your father built this house.

Watch me, Tommy said.

Drew up the plans himself, Marie said. The bedrooms, the library, the re-cep-shun room. But it doesn't matter. No one wants this house. No one will buy it. It's a white elephant.

Think so?

Absolutely, she said.

I'm not selling it, Marie. Get that through your head. I'm giving it away. I'm *donating* it, you see. That's my decision and it's final. You better clear out your things before I get back from Idaho.

Tommy, Bill van Horne said, for God's sake—

You're crazy, Marie said. I've never heard of such a thing.

Bert has all the details, Tommy said. Isn't that right, Bert?

Of course, Tommy. Bert Marks had no idea what his client was talking about.

Your mother died in this house, Marie said.

Leave my mother out of it. My mother is none of your damned business.

Died in the bedroom just upstairs—

Damn sight more comfortable than any hospital, Tommy said.

When did you get this crazy idea?

I don't like that word, Marie.

Well, it's crazy.

Don't say that again.

Did you get your idea yesterday? This morning? Did it come at dusk like a bird on the wing? I'll bet it did.

Tommy pushed his chair from the table and crossed his legs with a show of nonchalance. His expression was vacant, as if he were alone at table, deep in thought. When he moved his body the chair creaked. It was much too small for him, a rosewood chair that looked as if it could be smashed into matchsticks by his huge fingers. His face was flushed but the company did not notice owing to the darkness of the room. Tommy's face was in shadow. They waited for him to speak and dreaded whatever it was he might say. Tommy Ogden was unpredictable to say the least of it and an atmosphere of violence followed him wherever he went. When he was shooting he was most excited at the kill itself. The beauty of the day or the natural surroundings had no

meaning for him. His shooting partners were ignored. Bloodlust
had meaning and he was a natural marksman. Now he took another swallow of whiskey and looked directly across the table
at Marie. He said, I've had the idea for a while. But I decided
definitely only ten minutes ago when you started mouthing off
about French sculptors and that damned Chicago girl. I'm sick
and tired of it. I'm sick and tired of you, so you'd better stop
mouthing off.

But that was not Marie's way. She and Tommy had been married just seven years and argument was their natural milieu. It
was how they got on day to day, arguments over small things,
large things, often nothing at all. They had both learned to make
their way in the world, Tommy because he was rich and Marie
because she wasn't. Marie once explained to Beth van Horne
that she looked on her husband as the tyrant of the city-state
next door; give him an inch and he'd take a mile and before
you knew it you were a province of his realm. Subject to whim.
Tommy's not sinister, Marie said to Beth, it's his nature. He can't
help it and there were times when he was quite sweet, really,
though those times had become rare lately. Marie wore a small
sarcastic smile and now she said, So you're *donating* my house.

That's right, Tommy said.

And in the meanwhile?

That's my business, Tommy said.

I'll just bet it is, Tommy. Let me guess. A cabin in Idaho? Your
Scottish lodge?

Her husband only looked at her, his foot tapping the parquet
floor.

And the donation? To whom? And for what? Marie began to
laugh, a harridan's cackle in the quiet of the vast room, its ceiling so high that it was invisible in candlelight. The Italian serving girls had disappeared. Trish van Horne had excused herself
and left the table. She was now waiting alone in her parents' car,
smoking a cigarette and wondering when she could go home.

Marie said, What do you have in mind, darling? An orphanage? An old folks' home? Perhaps an asylum, lunatics would feel at home in Ogden Hall. Or—a firearms museum. All your shotguns and rifles, even that wee revolver you carry in your jacket pocket when we go on the town. Your stuffed animals round and about, that bear carcass in the library? The antelope horns on the wall? An owl. Who's the lucky, lucky beneficiary? I can't wait.

Tommy wasn't listening. His eyes were far away. He had refilled his glass once again and remembered the estate as it was when he was a boy, the road through the iron gates, the gatekeeper's house to the right, the long run up the road and under the railroad trestle—a spur off the main line for his father's private car, a necessary convenience for the man who owned the railroad—with wide fields and thick stands of black oak either side of the road, two hundred and fifty acres in all. There were two barns and a dormitory for the farmhands. A quarter mile in, the road entered a dark space winding through white pines. Sunlight never penetrated the canopy and midday looked like dusk.

That was where, at age ten, Tommy found his love of the kill, roaming the estate with a .410-bore shotgun his father had given him on his birthday, an efficient piece, walnut stock, American made. It came with a leather slipcase, his initials on the case and the year, 1883. He always began the hunt in the copse of white pines, stalking squirrels and rabbits, muskrats on those few occasions they showed themselves. On the far side of the white pines was a field, and beyond the field a one-acre pond, habitat for the muskrats. Ugly beasts, bad-tempered, scavengers. At eleven years old Tommy shot his first mallard, the bird rising from the water in a frenzy of wings, gathering speed and in one second arrested in flight, its rhythm collapsed; and his whole life Tommy remembered bringing the .410 to his shoulder and the snap of the shot, the descent of the mallard and the heavy splash when it landed mid-pond, dead duck. The time was dusk, mid-November, cold enough so that ice had formed around the edges of the pond. But he stripped off his clothes and went in after the bird. He did not feel the cold, only a surge of—he supposed it was pride, a kind of mastery, certainly an unambiguous happiness along with great slowness, deathlike calm. He heard a voice behind him: Fine shooting, young man. Congratulations, you'll have a tasty meal tonight. It was the farm manager, a Scotsman sparing with compliments. But Tommy did not like it that he had appeared unannounced; something underhanded about it. Shooting was a private business. Tommy said, Do you know the name of a taxidermist? He spoke with his trademark sneer, a family property inherited from his mother. The farm manager replied that he would try to find the name of a taxidermist but a mallard made mighty fine eating.

Tommy turned his back and walked away, the duck's neck pinched between his icy fingers, its belly bumping against his thigh, reliving the moment when the bird crumpled and died, arrested action, utter stillness except for the echo in his ears. He liked to wait for windy days, the birds careering every which way. Tommy stationed himself at the eastern edge of the field waiting for the birds to come to him as he calculated the horizontal flight and the vertical shudder and the distance he was obliged to lead, a matter of geometry until geometry became instinct. On the windiest days he would lead the bird by three feet or more, swinging with it, and then by its flight guessing high or low—whether the wind would raise the bird or lower it. More exacting was the passing shot, the bird cruising from his left or right, appearing as a dot in the sky, and then he led it by four or five feet. The bird flew into a hail of lead. The more difficult the calculation, the more Tommy liked it, the test of skill. He thought of the winds as Homeric, a creature of the gods, gods heedless of consequence, gods who did anything they wished to do. Tommy's view of himself in the field, unobserved and unmonitored, was that he matched any god. At such moments he felt himself stretched to the breaking point, discovering a kind of perfection of equilibrium.

WHEN HE TURNED TWELVE years old his father gave him a side-by-side twenty-gauge shotgun, cherrywood stock, a British-made Boss, beautifully balanced and as light as a walking stick. He came to appreciate shooting in bad weather, in the hours following an electrical storm, the ground sodden underfoot, thick with leaves, the air carrying a scorched odor. Nothing moved in the dampness. Tommy stepped with caution, waiting for the stray target. Some creatures were obtuse and impatient, careless in their habits. Tommy was never impatient and sooner or later his discipline was rewarded with a sighting of a squirrel or mallard alone and defenseless, disoriented in the heavy silence. He often stood motionless for an hour at a time waiting for a creature to show itself, and it was in the stand of pines, one afternoon in the late fall, that he had a revelation. Something in his eyesight did not look quite right, a color he had never seen before in the woods. He was standing in the shadows of the white pines and staring dead ahead at a tawny patch where the woods gave onto a cornfield. With his usual deliberation he raised his binoculars to his eyes and found the tawny patch dissolving into a hunter's cap, the bill pulled low; and the cap moved, revealing a bearded face. No one was allowed on Ogden property, for hunting or for any other reason. Tommy believed his domain had been violated. There was no excuse for trespassing. When he raised the Boss he saw the hunter move his shoulders, and then the barrel and telescopic sight of a rifle came into view. So the trespasser was waiting for deer. Then Tommy saw a plume of smoke, indistinct in the gray air. The fool was smoking a cigarette, the one thing above all the other things that was forbidden when stalking deer. A deer would smell tobacco a mile away. The hunter rose to full height, the cigarette in his mouth, the rifle resting barrel-forward on his shoulder. Tommy had a clean shot if he wanted to take it. The range was fifty yards, too far for a twenty-gauge load to be fatal. But the wound would hurt and hurt badly and would not be forgotten, and that would put an end to trespassing.

The hunter's neck might as well have had a bull's-eye drawn on it. Tommy sighted the Boss, then paused at a distant rattle from the trestle followed by the shriek of a whistle, his father's train. When he looked again the trespasser had broken from cover and was running through the cornfield and in a moment was gone. Tommy began to laugh, the scene somehow reminiscent of a vaudeville act. He waited another minute before he turned to work his way through the copse to the great house, dark at dusk, a long Georgian silhouette against the black oaks beyond, trees that had first seen daylight when General Washington was a boy. Ogden Hall had forty-two rooms, including a vast library and a solarium, a garden room and a kitchen nearly the size of a tennis court; and there were two of those next to the swimming pool and the flagstone terrace at the rear of the house where the lawn rolled away to a muddy stream. The railroad had been very good to the Ogden family. Tommy entered by the front door, the house silent, dark within. His mother was somewhere about, knitting or writing letters. Standing in the foyer with its grand piano and six cane-backed chairs for the ensemble that gathered on Sunday for musical evenings, Tommy felt an inhabitant of an antique world that had begun long ago but was vital still, with breath to last at least until tomorrow or the day after. The hush of the room was spoiled only by the hiss of the radiators and the smell of beeswax.

Tommy took off his coat and dropped it on the piano bench and took the stairs two at a time to the second floor and went down the long corridor to his room, the Boss resting on his shoulder. Inside, the door closed, he cleaned and oiled the shotgun and returned it to its case in the corner. Then from his desk he took out the heavy sketchpad and sat on the window seat and began to draw, heavy black lines that described vegetation and soon a bearded face among the branches, difficult to see unless you looked closely and perhaps had an idea what you were looking for. The face had a furtive look, someone who was in a place he ought not to be. Present also was a rifle with a telescopic sight and in the far distance a railroad trestle. Tommy Ogden went long minutes without drawing anything at all, staring at his composition, then making one, two erasures. Twice he dropped the paper to the floor and began again. When the buzzer sounded for dinner he had almost finished the piece but put it aside now. He never hurried his work. He returned the sketchpad to the top shelf of his closet, put the sketch on top of it, and the pens and charcoal pencils on top of that, then closed and locked the door. No one knew of his fascination with drawing. He believed that to share it would be to lose it. Like so much in his life, Tommy's drawing was private.

Every year until he was twenty his father presented him with a firearm on his birthday, and when he turned twenty-one his father died and Tommy had no further need for anyone's largesse. Tommy bought the set of matched Purdeys at auction, staying dollar for dollar with a property developer who was twice his age but much less than half as rich. He asked his mother to come with him to the auction because he did not know the form of things, the signals, how the bidding progressed, and the percentage that went to the house. He did know enough to maintain a stony demeanor, the look that said to his competitors: I am in this forever if need be, so fold your hand now and save yourself the trouble. Lily Ogden explained the procedures and left him alone, moving to the rear of the chandeliered room to watch the bidding. And as she said later, it was thrilling to watch her son, a natural, natural aplomb, ice water in his veins, implacable. Chinoiserie, impressionist canvases, Fabergé eggs, Syrian carpets, and Biedermeier cabinets flew by as Tommy sat quietly, arms folded, his head bent forward as if he were stalking game, awaiting the presentation of the Purdeys. Quite frightening, Lily told a friend, how much her son loved the hunt—or, as he said, shooting and the game that made shooting worthwhile. He rarely spoke of his passion in company because it was no one else's business. The phrase he used was, It's nothing to do with them. I don't know where he came from, Lily said. He is nothing like his father and nothing like me. Then she laughed: Well, maybe a little like me and a little like his father, bless him, who always kept his cards close to his vest. I imagine shooting is what Tommy will do in his life and how fortunate he will never have to work for a living because he has no head for commerce.

This was mostly true. Shooting was Tommy's vocation and everything else in his life seemed incidental, schoolwork, games, the news of the day, even girls. Like his drawing, shooting was personal and he would no more confess to it than a priest would confess to vice, though probably not for the same reason. He believed that people—anyone, anywhere—were eager to take from him what was rightfully his. He believed it as a boy and believed it more strongly as he aged, no doubt the legacy of his father, who maintained that anyone, anywhere was after his money. Friendships were suspect for that reason. The railroad was most presciently sold by his father in the months before the Panic of 1893, the old man explaining to his son that he was uneasy about the capital markets, an orgy of ill-considered speculation with dubious characters in the vanguard. They were scoundrels, connoisseurs of swindle. They would ruin the economy and take the railroad down with it. Lily and Henry Ogden were exceptionally close and when Henry explained his suspicions, Lily urged him to consult her psychic. The psychic was never wrong. Henry followed his wife's advice and when Madame Hauska advised him to sell the railroad at once, without delay, he did so and not long after the market crashed. The old man told the story again and again to his son, proposing that the psychic was evidence of the existence of a spirit world that trumped Wall Street; and he never failed to add that he had persuaded the buyers of the railroad to lease him his private car for a dollar a year, ten-year minimum. They were happy to do it because they thought they had a bargain, even though the terms were cash, no notes, no bonds. The psychic had insisted on it, knowing very well that Mr. Ogden cherished his car and would be unhappy without it.

Tommy came to know every tree and trail on the estate, a monotonous terrain where the horizon was invisible. In that part of Illinois, well beyond the city's monstrous clamor, the land was flat as a plate, an anonymous kingdom of farms, small-holdings, and the one market town nearby that contained a restaurant, a movie house, and the station that served the Ogden railroad. A hardware store and a barber shop completed the ensemble. Ogden Hall was the only estate of note in the vicinity, the site deliberately chosen by Henry Ogden for its distance from the glitter of the horse country west of the city. He disliked horses almost as much as he disliked glitter. The Ogdens were seldom seen except for the boy Tommy—an impolite boy, badly mannered, abrupt—who stopped by the hardware store every few weeks to buy ammunition. Never a pleasantry. Never a hello, never a goodbye. He spoke two words only: Charge it. As time went by, his logbook filling up with his precise recording of creatures shot dead, the date and time, mallards, geese, deer, muskrats, squirrels, rabbits, and one German shepherd he had mistaken for a wolf, Tommy wondered what shooting would be like in the mountains or the high plains of the West or the equatorial jungles, dangerous ground, dangerous animals, perhaps a fairer test of the shooter's skills and nerve. But that was the future. For the time being he was content on the estate, familiar ground. At night you could see Chicago's sulfurous glow to the east. The market town, Jesper, had a rustic appeal, slow-moving, people going about their business normally. The barber gave an honest cut. The people in Jesper talked too much but that was a rural conceit and easily ignored. There were other small towns round and about, Hilling to the south and Quarterday to the north. Hilling was home to the German taxidermist, an old-world figure who spoke little English but was a wizard with fur and feathers. In Hilling the sidewalks were deserted at dusk. There was one peculiar attraction a few miles north of Jesper, a nightclub called Villa Siracusa. Incongruous place for a nightclub, in a cornfield an hour's drive from Chicago. The parking lot was crowded with black Packards and Cadillacs, many of them chauffeur-driven. In the spring and summer and early fall, when the weather was benign, the chauffeurs sat at an outside table that was reserved for them. A waiter was on call to fetch drinks. Patrons crossed a humpback bridge—an unsuccessful attempt to replicate the Ponte dei Sospiri in Venice—over a pond to reach Villa Siracusa, named for the ancestral city of the family that owned it. The façade was a gaudy marriage of stucco and steel and lit by red and yellow spotlights that could not be seen from the main road a half mile distant. Inside, the loggia gave way to a lounge with tables and a long oak bar. Villa Siracusa was notorious in the neighborhood, something mysterious and surreptitious about it, and one evening early in their acquaintance Bert Marks explained. Bert was an occasional patron. I'll call ahead, he said, let them know you're coming. The Villa is a kind of club and like most clubs they're suspicious of strangers. The bartender's name is Ed and he'll want a moment or two of conversation before he clues you in. Give him some money. The action doesn't start until ten or eleven and for God's sake eat before you go. The food's terrible. So at eleven on a Thursday night in October, Tommy Ogden installed himself at the long bar and waited for Ed to finish his conversation with a sheriff's deputy at one of the tables. The deputy was in uniform, a pearl-handled revolver in a holster on his hip. Ed was talking and the deputy was listening and nodding without enthusiasm; and when he saw Tommy at the bar he nodded stiffly and smiled, saying something to Ed. Tommy continued to stare at the deputy's back until he pushed his chair away from the table and hurried from the room. There were a dozen customers, all of them men, a few of them even larger than Tommy. However, none of them were dressed in a soft tweed Norfolk jacket and gray flannel trousers, tattersal vest, bow tie. None of them had blond hair and blue eyes. When Ed made his way at last to Tommy he found a twenty-dollar bill on the bar. Tommy said, Bert Marks sent me.

Ed said, You know Deputy Ralph?

I know him, Tommy said. We meet now and then on the highway.

That's what he said, Ed said.

My car is faster than his but sometimes I let him catch up.

Yes. That's what Ralph said.

In a moment Tommy was through the inconspicuous door at the far end of the room and inside the casino, tables of craps and blackjack, baccarat and roulette. The gaming tables were crowded with players, their conversation raucous and punctuated by the *ka-thump* of slot machines arrayed along one wall. Next to the slot machines was a caisse where chips were bought and cashed in. When Ed turned to leave, Tommy said, I don't want this room. I want the other room. You know the room I want. When Ed hesitated he found another twenty dollars in his palm and presently a curtain parted and Tommy found himself in a parlor, a trio of musicians playing quietly in an alcove. A bartender polished glasses behind a shiny steel bar. Young women were seated here and there on sofas and overstuffed leather chairs that looked as if they belonged at a downtown men's club. The women were staring at Tommy and smiling. He looked as if he had just arrived from a golf course or a racetrack and they knew at once that he could pay the freight, whatever the freight turned out to be.

Tommy took his time, inspecting each of the women in turn, attractive women, well turned out, big-boned country girls. Bert had told him that most of the girls were from farming communities in the immediate vicinity, two towns in particular that had been hard hit by falling prices and mediocre yields of corn and soybeans. The Midwest had been in a half drought for most of the past decade and in thrall to the brokers of the Board of Trade in Chicago. The towns were depressed, without life, and the girls were looking for a way out. Their parents had grown listless, worn down by hard work and discouraged at the prospects. All the boys had left home seeking work elsewhere, far downstate or in the West, the army. The way of the world, Bert said, not a damned thing to be done about it. One girl, almost thirty, was a sort of supervisor and talent scout for Villa Siracusa. She was from one of the distressed towns and had recruited others, friends from high school. Word had gone around and before long girls from the farming towns were sending messages asking if there was work "where you are." They always sent photographs of themselves, often in gowns made by their mothers for graduation day and the prom that night. Anything to get away from the farm. Many of them sent money home, like immigrants from Ireland or Italy, claiming they had found work as shop girls at Field's or Montgomery Ward and that business was good in Chicago. Tommy looked at them now, eight round-faced girls and one tall brunette in a black floor-length gown, a rope of pearls around her slender throat, smoking a cigarette and smiling nicely. She had a beautiful clear complexion, one Lily would have called peaches-and-cream. She looked city rather than country, not because of the dress and the pearls but because of the way she stood and the frankness of her look.

Tommy nodded at her and she was at his side at once, her arm through his. She said, Champagne? He said, You have champagne, I'll take whiskey. She stepped to the bar and returned bearing a tray with two glasses, an ice bucket, a bottle of champagne, and a bottle of Johnnie Walker. She indicated the stairs and preceded him to the second floor, where she paused. She asked Tommy if he would prefer the third-floor room, the best room in the house, most comfortable. It had been furnished by a client, a gentleman of the old world. Tommy said fine, it didn't matter to him. They continued up the stairs and through a soundproof door and into a spacious, dimly lit bedroom with three chairs, a sofa, a cocktail table, and the bed, appointed with red sheets and a white duvet and plump pillows. The furniture looked as if it had been assembled from the German-speaking world, Vienna or Berlin, bowed blond wood and steel, not a straight line anywhere you looked. The drawings on the wall were vaguely pornographic, big-haired women in corsets, their breasts exposed. Tommy was offended, he was no friend of the Hun, whether Austrian or German. The Kaiser was a scoundrel.

She said, Do you like it?

He said, I'll have to get used to it.

She poured a glass of whiskey for him and a glass of champagne for herself and gave her name as Claire, twenty-one going on twenty-two, working her way through the university seeking a degree in art history. Claire was well-spoken but nervous, perhaps daunted by Tommy's size and forbidding glower. Tommy, himself nearly thirty-five years old, guessed she was more like eighteen than twenty-one and perhaps younger than eighteen. He introduced himself as Tom Ogden, the closest he had ever come to assuming an alias. No one had ever called him anything but Tommy. They had one drink and another while, in a rare inquisitive moment, he asked her about herself. Was she one of the girls from a farm? No, she had never been on a farm. She came from downstate near Kankakee. Her father was a salesman but now he was gone, caught the flu and died, her mother too. Would you rather have a girl from a farm? No, Tommy said, I like you. Claire looked around the room and said it was her favorite. The client who furnished it was not her client but sometimes in the afternoon when it was quiet she and one of the other girls came up to listen to the phonograph and smoke.

Do you mind if I smoke? she asked.

Yes, Tommy said. I don't like tobacco.

Anyhow, Claire said, being in the third-floor room was like being in another world. It's far from Kankakee, Tommy said. No kidding, Claire replied. They sat quietly and then she began to describe her studies, utterly fascinating. Did he know that art authorities had drawn a direct line from Rembrandt to the French impressionists? Everybody steals from everybody else, Tommy said, and fifty years from now everyone will be stealing from the impressionists. Claire blushed and turned from him to hide her confusion. She giggled and admitted she knew nothing of art history. But the client who furnished this room had become a friend. He owned an art gallery and liked to talk about painters, how they were derivative of each other. Rembrandt was his specialty. Also, she went on, the university was a fiction. She was saving her money to buy a beauty parlor. She intended to return to Kankakee and open a beauty parlor, a place of her own where she was the boss. Later, telling the story, Claire said she had no idea what caused her to lie and then retract the lie. Probably she felt that Tom Ogden would find out somehow and be displeased. She had never met this Tom Ogden before and had no idea what he was capable of, but from the look of him he could break her neck with his bare hands. He had a tremendous stillness about him, as if there were no moving parts beneath his skin. He was very direct. Her own work had taught her to go slowly with clients and reveal nothing of her personal life. She had said Kankakee but actually her home was Moline and her late father was not a salesman but a druggist. Somehow Tom Ogden inspired trust, otherwise she would not have retracted her lie. He didn't seem to care, only asked her the name of the art dealer. When she hesitated he said to her that he had need of an art dealer, so she gave up the name. When Claire asked Tommy what he did for a living, his business, he said he didn't do anything for a living. He was not in business. He had no interest in business. She should not speak to him of business. He was a shooter, and when he saw the look of alarm in her eyes he sneered and assured her, not that kind. He shot animals. Pheasant, deer, duck, squirrel. Whatever animal was available. Elk. Tigers and lions. Elephant.

Sport, she said.

I suppose so, he replied.

Claire relaxed then and they undressed as if they had known each other for years. He was not rough at all, as she expected, but rather formal. He was limber for so large a man, and fit. The word for him was considerate and she was surprised at that. She could not say it was the most exciting evening of her life—there were few enough of those in any case—but she was not frightened, either. There was but one pause in the play that followed. Round about dawn Tom Ogden sat straight up in bed, turned his head, told Claire to shush, and put his palm to his ear in order to clearly hear the plaintive faraway sound of a train's whistle. Tom was silent a long moment and then began to laugh. When Claire asked him what was so funny he said that his father had paid them a call, first time he had heard from the old man in years and years.

What do you mean?

My father is dead, he said and made no further comment.

Tom Ogden did not leave Villa Siracusa until Sunday morning. Food and drink were brought to them. The arrangements were everything Bert Marks had promised and more. Claire was good-natured and willing. She never complained. Each morning around dawn Tommy heard the sound of the train's whistle, a signal of approval from his even-tempered father. And no wonder. Tommy was the happiest he had been and the amazement of it was the absence of complications. He made a date with Claire for the following Thursday, and the Thursday after that, and before long Thursday through Sunday was a permanent appointment unless Tommy was away shooting. A productive conversation with Herr Mackel, the owner of the gallery, transferred the lease of the third-floor room to Tommy; he became a silent partner in the Mackel Gallery, the better to display his sketches. He thought it time to move into the world a little bit, and Herr Mackel turned out to be a considerate German.

A year or so later, Villa Siracusa was raided by the sheriff's department, some question about the monthly stipend. After that was straightened out, federal agents arrived to close the place for good, a complaint about unpaid income taxes. The Siracusa family moved the business from its location north of Jesper to a more sympathetic jurisdiction but five years later there was more trouble from the county sheriff, who had been bought but refused to stay bought, a chronic problem in Illinois, though rarely in Chicago. At last, acknowledging defeat, the family returned to the big city, where the rules, once set, were scrupulously adhered to. Villa Siracusa—now Chez Siracusa—was established in a handsome brownstone on a tree-lined street on the South Side not far from the university. Once again Tommy was provided with a room of his own, furnished as before with a nice view: a private library of a scientific nature was situated across the street and over the rooftop of the library could be seen soaring church towers and the spires of the university and there was so little traffic you could believe you were in a small town downstate. Papa Siracusa himself assured Tommy that the trouble had gone away, vanished, because so many aldermen were clients. Chicago was a difficult environment, unforgiving, rough-edged. Costs were higher all around, he said, but there was peace of mind too, knowing that the rules, once set, were scrupulously adhered to. Tommy listened and concluded that the old man was losing his mind, believing he was back in Sicily. Rules endured only so long as they were convenient for everyone concerned, and when they ceased to be convenient they bent like giraffes in a hurricane. Watch yourself, Tommy, Bert Marks said, to which Tommy replied, Why should I? Susanna followed Claire, and Monica followed Susanna. Papa Siracusa died and was succeeded by his eldest son and everyone agreed that the apple had fallen far from the tree, the boy but a shadow of his father, a gentleman of the old school. The atmosphere Chez Siracusa became rowdier. One night a doctor was summoned to see to one of the girls who had become hysterical and on another night shots were fired and police actually entered the premises, weapons drawn. Tommy remained in his room on the top floor, well away from the unpleasantness, not that he cared.

He was a loner certainly and found repose Chez Siracusa. One of the girls compared Tom Ogden to a farm animal, content to remain at rest in a field chewing its cud until it felt hunger or some other manly urge. He would remain silent for hours at a time, deep in thought, often sketching—the roofline of the scientific library, the rooftops of the university high on the horizon, students in the street below, Claire, Monica, or Susanna reading or doing her toenails. The sketches were simple but took hours to complete because Tom was meticulous, never drawing a line until he had thought it out and the lines that would follow. He drew the way he shot, with patience and economy, and when he was finished he told the girls stories about his shooting adventures, the firearms he owned, and the correct manner to stalk game. Silence was the first trick, quick reaction the second. Third was composure, though surely composure was a function of silence. It's fair to say that the girls had never met anyone like Tom Ogden. Everything about him was a puzzle, including his courtesy in bed. He had only sporadic interest in knowing anything about them, and when Claire and Susanna moved on, he gave each girl a wad of money for whatever the future might bring. If asked, Tommy would have said that his happiest hours spent indoors were on the topmost floor of the brownstone, a view of the university rooftops beyond the scientific library across the street. In the autumn the colors were marvelous and in winter the roofs were stacked high with snow. Tommy had a massive lack of interest in the world around him, or that part of it unrelated to shooting, but he found consolation in the small-town feel of the

South Side. Naturally he was most at home in the country, his firearms within easy reach, the fields always filled with game. He was never lonely in the great house with its forty-two rooms, listening to the echo of his footsteps wherever he went.

He supposed that at some point he would marry. Most men did. Probably he would marry if he could find a suitable woman, a woman who liked her privacy as much as he liked his. When he asked Susanna what she thought about marriage she misunderstood—she was so startled by the question that she was unable to speak for a full minute—and thought he was proposing to her. Susanna's eyes grew wide and tear-filled and when she threw her arms around him he was obliged to say, No, not you, marriage in general. Marriage as an institution. Her feelings were hurt but Tommy did not grasp that; hurt feelings, his own or anyone else's, were not in his arsenal of sentiments. Susanna, furious, her mouth drawn in a thin line, said that in fact she believed in marriage despite appearances. She had a fiancé and in due course she intended to marry the fiancé and settle up near the Wisconsin Dells where the fiancé had business prospects. They aimed to have three children. Tommy had ceased to listen. He half suspected that marriage was a chore in the way that his father had decided that business was a chore and had visited the psychic Madame Hauska who gave sound advice, and his father never worked again. His father swore by her, maintaining that she was a wizard with a balance sheet along with being a prophet. Surely she would be no less deft with matrimony.

Meanwhile, Tommy had iron-hearted Chicago, its fearless clamor, its no-nonsense way of going about things, its license, meaning contempt for civic virtue. He felt Chicago was a city with a curled lip and chips on both shoulders, a remark an infuriated schoolteacher once made about him. Tommy Ogden felt he knew Chicago in his bones; they were the same bones. At any event, for the remainder of his days he made the detested journey from his estate near Jesper to the South Side brownstone where he was most favored customer Chez Siracusa. He had furnished the top-floor room to his own taste—it had the leather quality of a shooting lodge—and caused a fireplace to be installed. In the heavy armoire below the mirror he kept shirts and a change of linen, pens and sketchpads and a revolver in the event of mischief. Everyone respected Tom Ogden. Never made trouble, never complained, paid handsomely, a perfect gentleman. All the girls liked him even as they tended to tune out his lectures, the monologues about shooting that went on for so many, many minutes. But he did not notice that, either, because he was not looking at them as he talked. He was deep inside himself, an inaccessible, perhaps barren, region to which only he possessed a map. It was always pleasant for Tommy to talk to someone who did not talk back.

THE CANDLES GUTTERED. The Billingtons were on their feet, saying good night to Marie, such a lovely evening, we must do it again very soon. Sorry things got so out of hand, Susan Billington whispered to Marie, who only smiled and winked as if to say that the show was far from over. The worst was yet to come. Bert Marks yawned and touched Tommy's shoulder by way of farewell but Tommy did not respond except to nod in the direction of Bert's chair. Sit down a minute, Bert. I want you to hear this. Give me the benefit of your experience, let me know what you think about my plans. He did not look at the lawyer as he spoke, staring instead at the blank ceiling high above.

It's so damn late, Tommy—

Won't take long. Sit.

Bert returned wearily to his seat, knowing that he had one more hour at table. That was the minimum once Tommy got up a head of steam. Tommy's mind resembled a ponderous locomotive, the train of thought that went on for miles and miles, switchback following switchback with no end in sight. The Billingtons and the van Hornes—joined now by daughter Trish, yawning, a cigarette in her fingers until her mother told her to put it away, tobacco disallowed at Ogden Hall—took their seats once again. Why was dinner at the Ogdens' such a trial? It took so long to get there from the city and the way back was even longer.

Tommy poured a glass of whiskey and looked at each of them in turn, ending with Marie. Her face was in deep shadow, almost invisible. He sought her a moment but she was out of reach in the darkness.

He said, Listen carefully. I don't like to repeat myself. I have decided to found a school. First class, everything first class all the way. A school for boys, midwestern boys of good family to show those bastards in the East what a real school looks like and how it conducts its affairs. That school will be located on this property, in this house, and of course the surroundings. It will accept boys who have had trouble fitting in elsewhere, boys of ability who had been unable to find their place in the world. Or put another way: boys who know perfectly well their place in the world but find it denied to them. I know what I'm talking about. I went to seven boarding schools, three in one year. I was said to be unruly, not a team player. A rotten apple, out of sync. I was out of sync wherever I went but I didn't mind because I've always been out of sync. We Ogdens are different, you see. We have a different metabolism. My father may have minded because he had to read the snotty letters from the headmasters, their bills of particulars. One headmaster—a minister of God, no less, a Presbyterian from Ipswich—called me mutinous, as if his god damned school was a vessel on the high seas and I was Fletcher Christian. I laughed in his face. I threatened him. I frightened him, as a matter of fact, because I was big for my age and did not respond well to criticism. Naturally I always had a firearm with me, my little peashooter, the .410. They frowned on that. They did not permit firearms in the dorm. No firearms, no whiskey, no cigarettes, no girls, no visitors. These schools were penitentiaries. I have no use for them. My school will have a fine, open-minded headmaster and an open-minded staff, men who well understand the way the world works and can communicate this knowledge. Tommy thumped his fist on the table and fell silent.

What way is that, Tommy? Marie asked.

It isn't a god damned sailing ship, Tommy replied.

Yes, but explain how the world works. I've always wondered. Your view.

Tommy moved his shoulders, glowering. He said, If you have to ask you'll never understand, exactly like jazz music. He had heard the remark from a musician Chez Siracusa, an apt lesson for so many things in life. Not that Marie would get it. Getting it was not her long suit. Marie preferred argument.

I'm afraid I don't quite understand, Marie said with a little strangled laugh. She moved her head forward out of the shadow and into the bright bath of candlelight. Surely you can't be saying that your fine young men who've been cruelly denied their place in the world will be content with—enigma. That would never do, Tommy. You must do much, much better than that.

And now Tommy foundered. Marie was a scourge, a plague upon the earth. She was an agent of discord. He glared at her, her glittering eyes and her half smile. She threw her head back, looking down her nose at him, and he supposed she was practicing her pose for Maître Rodin. Hard to recollect now, but there was a time when Marie was a sport, easy mannered, easy to get on with, easily amused, comfortable with silence. She loved the field and was an excellent wing shot, really a beautiful shot and wonderful-looking in her high leather boots and canvas pants. She wore a green British army–issue sweater and a black beret, a teal-blue ascot at her throat, yellow-lensed French aviator glasses on her nose. He watched her take two pheasants in one pass, clean shots both, one second apart. That was in Scotland, a shooting party of twelve. Tommy was the stranger but Marie made him feel welcome, proposing that they pair up together, an idea that horrified him until he saw her shoot. She shot like a man and drank like one too.

Their first night together she told him that she preferred the company of men, their jokes and laughter, their rough edges, their camaraderie, their effortlessness. When he asked her what she meant by that, she said that men were extemporaneous; not all men, of course, some were swine. Still, she said, men were fun to be with. He was delighted when she said that she liked the smell of men, sweat and musk whatnot, a song of the earth. That first year they had wonderful times shooting in Africa and the American Far West. At night they relaxed with a drink and gin rummy, at which she was adept. Marie had a phenomenal memory for cards and much else. She never forgot a slight. She told him about growing up in Tucson, where her father was a successful prospector. Her mother died when Marie was young and she missed her every day, a woman of the frontier with a wild streak. She never forgot a slight, either. At that time Tucson was the frontier or close enough to it, a violent country of stark beauty. Marie killed her first rattler at age fifteen, a specimen diamondback six feet long. She and her father spent weekends on horseback, shooting rattlers and gila monsters and the buffoonish and harmless javelina. Marie knew how to take care of herself from a very young age. She said she wanted to be cared for just enough but not too much. There was a line Tommy must not cross. She had always been independent and that was why they must keep their money separate, separate accounts, different banks. She would handle the household expenses and the rest was his. She knew he would never do anything to harm her and that was important. He understood that she would disappear from time to time, not for long; and he had the same privilege.

Tommy listened to her with envy, this girl who was shooting rattlesnakes when he was shooting sparrows. What a life it must have been in the desert near Tucson, as unforgiving as any terrain on the face of the earth. They had driven through it on their way to Idaho, stopping once to walk into the desert at dusk. There was not a single plant that did not sport thorns or needles. Terrible country, dry and desolate, though not to Marie. After the wonderful time in Africa and the American Far West they returned to Jesper and Ogden Hall and things went sour because she never shut up about Tucson and the life she had led there, her heroic father and wandering mother fortified by the example of the noble yet put-upon redskin. Marie claimed her mother was part Apache. Marie's stories of her youth reminded him of Rudyard Kipling at his most florid, didactic, and hysterical. To Marie the West was a kind of Eden before the Fall. Tommy watched her now, tapping her finger on the tabletop as she awaited his reply.

He ignored her and turned to Bert. He said, My school will have all the finest equipment, scientific laboratories, a gymnasium, a splendid library. I have a few thousand volumes already in place, complete sets of Balzac and Dickens and Robert Louis Stevenson bound in leather. Why, the pages are uncut! The books are pristine, never read by anyone living or dead. You've seen the library, room enough for forty boys at least. There're rooms enough for thirty classrooms and an office suite for the headmaster. There's open land for football fields and a polo pitch, even a nine-hole golf course. Never cared much for golf myself but they say it's the coming thing in our area. The tennis courts are already in place. I'm thinking also of a regulation shooting range in the basement. I'll convert the useless stables into a dormitory. There isn't any good reason why a boy from Illinois or Indiana has to go to Massachusetts or New Hampshire to receive a brilliant education. I've thought it through, you see. And that's what I intend to do, establish the finest boys' preparatory school in the land. Assemble a faculty that's second to none. I mean men of the world who know the score. Men who've been through the mill themselves—and here Bert Marks and Harry Billington glanced at each other because the unspoken clause in the sentence was "as I have been." And what mill, exactly, would that be? If Tommy Ogden had ever experienced one misfortune in his life, they had never heard of it. Tommy Ogden had always done just as he pleased. The world's machinery had always been his for the taking, and when he chose a drill that displeased him he put it back or threw it away without hesitation or apology. Viewed dispassionately, Marie would qualify as a drill, and in time she too would find herself replaced. Not, from the look of things, that she would care overmuch. And not that she would fail to exact revenge. Marie was fed up with her dyspeptic husband, his selfishness and his eternal animal gloom. He so rarely appeared to be having a good time but that was difficult to know for certain because so much of that time was spent inside himself, a place that he, if no one else, evidently found a fascinating country. Of course Marie was aware of Tommy's situation Chez Siracusa. She was aware that he was well liked there, liked by the girls and by the management and not only for his generous wallet. Tommy had always been generous with money. But surely that was another matter entirely, the exception that proved the rule. Still, when she had first met him in Scotland he had been attractive. She was drawn to him at once. She found him quite shy and open to possibility. He was beautifully built. He moved with assurance. Other men made way for him, and Marie had liked that. But he had not aged well.

There's not a moment to lose! Tommy shouted. He took a swallow of whiskey and sat back in his chair, Marie forgotten. He was remembering the dinner table when his father and mother were alive, the identical china and Tiffany flatware and centered silver candelabrum, the heavy crystal. Dinner proceeded in a standoffish silence until his father made a comment about his day, something to do with business usually, the railroad, and when that was gone his many investments, the shape and disposition of the capital markets, their natural rhythm. Who was selling short and who was buying long and why. That was the reason he was leaving for New York in the morning. New York City was where the decisions were made, the customary processes of consultation among bankers in London and Boston as well. Money moved like the mysterious ocean currents and that knowledge was not available in Chicago. We are a colony, you see. We are Hong Kong or India and we do the bidding of others because we do not control our own assets. They are held in trust, as it were. Our assets are controlled for us and if we desire a slice for ourselves we can have it so long as fees and interest are paid; and that rate is set also in New York and London and, depending on the size and shape, in Boston. Here in our region we manufacture things, automobiles and heavy machinery and the food that feeds the nation. We do not own it, however. They own it, because they own the banks that supply the credit. Frequent visits to Wall Street were necessary in order to know who was buying long and who was selling short and why. Well, his father would add, you never knew why, precisely, beyond the obvious: someone invented a new machine or discovered a mine rich with ore. Someone identified a fad, the hoop skirt or the tulip. The way of things was that someone met someone else in the men's room of the yacht club or at a wedding or funeral and received a tip, bullish or bearish, it scarcely mattered which. But we do not have that information at the Chicago Club or that golf course out in Lake Forest.

Tommy remembered his father's gruff voice in the thick silence of the dining room, candles guttering then as they were now. Much of what his father said was swallowed up in that vast whale of a room; a tree crashed and no one heard. He spoke often of the mysteries of the balance sheet, numbers assigned arbitrarily to the left-hand column or the right, depending on whether you wanted to show assets or liabilities, mumble mumble, for the taxman or your shareholders or for other reasons. Depreciation was a black art. Then there was the psychology of the thing, the mood of the day, what the headlines said. What the headlines didn't say, mumble mumble. As for himself, he believed it wise to keep all his cards close to his vest until the specific moment when it was advantageous to allow someone a peek. One card only and usually not the relevant card. Keep that in mind, Tommy. You'll never go wrong. Money moves on the tide. Identify the tide quickly. Don't be the last boat launched or you'll be ruined.

And Tommy listened, without comprehension, his father's words somehow soothing even with the undertow of anger and resentment; he seemed to take such pleasure in explanation, and if the explanation was opaque, that was part of its charm. The fact was, his father knew things that other men did not and that gave him authority. He wished to pass along this authority to his son and that was why he was so patient; alas, everyone had a cross to bear. Meanwhile, Lily would be picking at her food, her mind far away, to come awake only when her husband commenced to complain about school, why Tommy couldn't do better, why Tommy was eternally on the wrong side of the headmaster. With just the slightest effort . . . Henry, his mother said, leave Tommy alone. Tommy's fine. We simply haven't been able to find the right place, with a congenial atmosphere among boys like himself and instructors who know how to give individual attention. Those schools are so cloistered, they're nunneries for boys. No wonder Tommy can't get on there. Who could? And what difference does it make? It isn't as if he has to go out and earn a living, starting off as a clerk somewhere. Tommy has his own métier. Tommy will find his way. I'll see to it.

But his father went on as if he hadn't heard, as perhaps he hadn't. The many valuable friendships one forms in boarding school, friendships that last a lifetime, boys helping one another as they moved onward in life, in business and so forth. Sports, even marriage. Whom do you turn to for advice but your oldest friend, and that would be the friend met in boarding school. And that's why boarding school is important. Once under way Henry

Ogden was difficult to divert. He was not amenable to diversion. Once he had a thought he pursued it to the ground. The Ogden dining room was suitable for thoughts expressed at length, its dark corners and invisible ceiling encouraged reflection. When his father fell silent at last, a servant would appear as if by magic and the plates were silently removed from sight.

Lily always had the definitive last words, not spoken so much as crooned: We'll see. On this occasion Lily ventured another thought: I wasn't aware you were so fond of your boarding school or your college, either, Henry dear. And I wasn't aware you had any help along the way. To that thought her husband had no reply but smiled as if he understood. The boy Tommy learned the way of the world in that room, and now he looked up to see the company staring at him.

Bert Marks cleared his throat and said, That's a marvelous idea, Tommy. Really generous and farsighted. Naturally it'll take some time, getting things started. Extensive renovations to the house and outbuildings, recruitment of a headmaster and faculty. Recruitment of boys. It can't happen overnight. Bert smiled gamely. His great skill as a lawyer was delay and obfuscation when an unmanageable, potentially dangerous problem presented itself. A problem he wanted to make go away. Amazing how many problems vanished when you drew them out, taking one baby step at a time, finding difficulties within difficulties, and all the while toiling away at out-of-town trips, depositions, and necessary fact-finding, a remorseless search for precedent. It wasn't called due diligence for nothing. Still, it was also a fact of life that Tommy, once settled on a course, was hard to divert.

Nonsense, Tommy said. I expect these matters to be completed by September, latest.

I'm not sure about that, Tommy, Bert said. It'll be hard getting all our ducks in a row . . . Bert wondered where in the world Tommy Ogden had hatched such a scheme. Only once had Bert ever heard him talk about education and that was this very evening, another context entirely, something about a headmaster—my God, how many schools had Tommy been to?—from Ipswich. He never went anywhere except for shooting expeditions and South Side Chicago for evenings Chez Siracusa. He never read a newspaper. He had no thirst whatever for information unless the information related to firearms or wild animals. He knew no educators or, for that matter, boys. And then Bert wondered if it was one of the tarts Chez Siracusa making mischief, talking sadly about opportunities that had come and gone owing to bad luck, bad cards, unreliable men, and a shabby education. Maybe one of them had said something about school, a nasty incident that had prevented a career on the stage or a Michigan Avenue dress shop.

You can have all the help you need, Tommy said.

Bert nodded.

You're in charge. I'm giving you an open checkbook.

Bravo, Tommy, Susan Billington said. A wonderful idea.

Are you going to be headmaster, Tommy? Marie's voice was a silky purr filtered through a cat's malicious grin. I can't wait, she went on. Headmaster Tommy Ogden. It's a simply thrilling idea. I'm especially looking forward to my duties as headmaster's wife. Are we going to give your boys afternoon tea?

That's idiotic, Tommy said. I'm giving them Ogden Hall. I'm giving them an endowment. I'm giving them Bert. And I'm walking away. I will have nothing more to do with Ogden Hall except make damned sure that it doesn't fail.

It's going to cost a lot of money, Bert said.

I've got a lot of money, Tommy said.

I don't think you realize—

Don't tell me what I can or can't realize. This school can't cost more than I've got. You worry about the school and I'll worry about the money.

Yoo-hoo, Tommy. I have a question, Marie said, raising her hand as if she were a student in a classroom eager to participate in the discussion. Who's "them"? Who exactly are you giving Ogden Hall to? Who are the lucky beneficiaries?

That's Bert's job, Tommy said.

What do you think, Bert? Are you going to put an ad in the *Trib*? Marie smiled brilliantly, false to the core. You'll need a board of trustees along with Tommy's second-to-none faculty and the wonderful wellborn boys who'll constitute the first class. Where do they come from? All those boys so hell-bent on discovering how the world works. Marie took a moment to look around the vast dining room with its portraits of Lily and Henry flanked by sporting scenes, men with firearms stalking elk, elephant, duck, and pheasant. One fine Indian miniature proposed a maharajah skewering a tiger with a ten-foot lance. She tried to imagine refectory tables and raucous adolescent voices, a solemn grace before meals. Boys throwing buns.

I will make inquiries, Bert said quietly.

Stay out of this, Marie. You don't know what you're talking about. Tommy reached again for the whiskey decanter.

It's a fine gesture, Susan Billington said.

Bert Marks coughed and said he had to be going.

Good luck, Tommy, Bill van Horne said.

You could be one of the trustees, Billy. Man of your experience and tact, you'd be a natural. Tommy and I would be grateful. Help us out in this way.

I'm retired, Bill van Horne said.

It's a retiree's job, Bert said.

Yes, Tommy added. It's time we all gave something back.

Back to what? Bill said.

Back, Tommy said and seemed to falter at giving further explanation. To Illinois, he said finally.

Well, Bill said, we can think about that later when everything's in order. When Bert has his ducks in a row.

Forget about the ducks, Tommy said.

What about me, Tommy? Marie's voice was seductive. Can't I

have a role? I could take charge as the school nurse, all decked out in a white uniform and a wimple. I took a course once in emergency medicine. Filthy boys, they pick up all manner of disease. They are unclean. They must be watched constantly.

Tommy looked sharply at Marie, believing she had said "washed," washed constantly, exactly the sort of coarse remark expected from one who had grown up among Indians. Tommy opened his mouth to reply but in the end said nothing, rising instead to signal that the evening was ended. The company was already in the hallway collecting coats from Francesca and retreating to the porch. The evening was chilly, unusual for the season. Feathery mist, white as a shroud, rose from the wet grass and hung in the heavy air. The night was still. Tommy stood in the doorway of the dining room, placidly sipping his drink, watching his friends file into the night. From his look there was one last thing he wished to say but did not know how to go about it. From somewhere in the forest came the cry of an owl, the sound reminiscent of a train's whistle.

Good night, Tommy. Good night, Marie.

Good luck with Rodin, Bert said.

Tommy barked a laugh. Forget it, he said loudly. There won't be any Rodin, not now and not a month from now. That's finished. I have news! I got word just before dinner, my agent in New York. Tommy stepped onto the porch, still holding his drink. Now he lit a cheroot and watched the flame and the smoke rising in the darkness. No one had ever seen him use tobacco. Tommy blew a thick smoke ring and said, There're troop movements all over Europe. The Hun is marching south to the Somme. He paused, allowing the news to register. He had followed events in Europe with care, paying attention to weapons and tactics, the order of battle, paying particular attention to regions he knew well—the Dordogne for boar, the Kleinwalsertal for mountain goat, the Pripet Marshes for duck, and now he decided to give his guests the benefit of his expertise. You see, first Germany declared war on Russia, already mobilizing to defend little Serbia. In support of Russia, France mobilized against Germany. Germany invaded Belgium. The British swine have declared war against Germany and the French have declared war on Austria-Hungary. Now everyone is mobilized and there's more to come, Italy and the Netherlands . . . And here Tommy foundered. Where exactly did Italy fit in? And Japan was somewhere in the mix, he couldn't remember where. Hard to keep them straight, the wretched nations of Europe. Tommy said, There's cheering in the streets of Berlin and Vienna. They're saying that the war will be over by Christmas, but it won't be over by Christmas this year or next, mark my words. The blood's up. The cat's among the pigeons.

Satisfied, Tommy stopped there, amused at the disbelieving faces of his dinner guests. This news was hard to credit on a quiet summer evening in Illinois. It was difficult to imagine armies on the march and the roar of cannon and harder still to understand public jubilation. My God, thought Bert Marks, did no one remember Antietam barely fifty years past, twenty-three thousand dead and wounded from sunup to dusk, the battle fought to a stalemate. But Europeans had no memory of anything outside their own orbit. They were obtuse, dumb as oxen. Perhaps Tommy had his facts scrambled. It wouldn't be the first time. The war had been predicted for so long that it was hard to take seriously now, and in any case it would be fought over there, Berlin, Brussels, Vienna, even Tokyo if Tommy was to be believed. And to think he had kept this news to himself all evening long, preferring instead to discuss his ridiculous boys' school. For a moment no one said anything and the party trooped to their cars amid tepid good-nights.

Tommy turned to Marie. So you can forget about your damned Rodin and your villa in the south of France. You can't get there from here, my pet. Europe's cut off. The boats won't be sailing.

You're crazy, Marie said. You're as crazy as that hoot owl. She turned and went back inside the house.

Bert Marks heard her and looked up to see Tommy Ogden standing alone on the porch of his vast domain. He seemed to savor the evening air, so soft, so seductive. The owl cried once again, a kind of swoon. Tommy cocked his head as if listening to distant gunfire. And then he wheeled and stepped inside, leaving the door ajar. Bert remained alone in the driveway, waiting for the denouement that was soon to come. He was thinking of Antietam but listening to the raised voices inside Ogden Hall, Tommy and Marie having at each other. Tommy's bass rumble, Marie's screech.

And the next sound was an explosion of splintered glass and a moment later Marie's wild laughter, rising and falling and rising again, laughter that went on and on. Bert did not linger. He had heard it before.

Part Two

THE TOWN OF New Jesper was located on the western shore of Lake Michigan north of Chicago, named for the same eighteenth-century French missionary who had founded the smaller Jesper downstate. A megalomaniacal missionary and sensualist, according to my father, probate judge and civic leader, and self-described amateur historian. The Abbé Jesper left his name wherever he went and he was widely traveled: farther west was Jesperville and other variations north into Wisconsin and Minnesota. Haut Jesper and Lac du Jesper were fashionable fishing camps north of Green Bay. Most of the settlements had long vanished. There was not much history in our New Jesper or around it for my father to explore. Indian tribes had roamed the region for a thousand years, but of them little was known. The Fox and the Sac were peaceable for the most part but after an uprising in the early nineteenth century were expelled from the territory, pushed west and north—and the trail ended there. They were not industrious Indians, leaving little account of themselves; or perhaps they were only discreet and suspicious, clannish like the Roma. They had no written language. They left no high art or architecture of the sort characteristic of the more flamboyant southwestern tribes. Nor had they any military skill. Here and there were burial grounds and odd bits of sculpture from religious sites, not much that was notable or collectible. The Sac and the Fox were presumed to have a nomadic civilization but evidence was scant; at least, not much came down. One thousand years of traveling but no souvenirs.

My father was not sentimental about the Indians—"damned savages"—but he was perplexed, spooked, as he said, by their mysterious history, how they organized themselves, their family life and religious beliefs, how they got on from day to day. Were there courts of law? My father had a fine appreciation of ambiguity, eccentricity, love, ambition, and spite, having dealt with wills and trusts for most of his adult life, but he could not figure out the Indians. In our part of Illinois they had left virtually nothing of themselves, only now and again an arrowhead or skull discovered in a farmer's field—and who knew if the skull was Sac or Fox or one of the violent pioneer homesteaders, even Abbé Jesper, whose fate was also unknown, though communities in both Wisconsin and Minnesota claimed him. *They were here first,* my father said—and he said it with the awe and respect a scientist might express in reference to a groundbreaking colleague, a Pasteur or a Newton. They were here first yet almost nothing was known for certain. Where is their Stonehenge? My father was a practical man, no way a romantic or friend of the occult. But he did believe that the wandering souls of the Indians were present in New Jesper and the surrounding countryside. The souls were not malevolent. They did not cause grief or misfortune. But they were disappointed and most watchful, especially in the autumn, Indian summer. My father believed they were souls in turmoil, unreconciled with themselves or their territory. This led him to suppose that New Jesper was like a game board with a piece missing, leading to the usual asymmetric results. My father believed our town was not quite whole.

NEW JESPER'S SITUATION was attractive. When the great glacier retreated in millennia past it left an escarpment straight as a ruler for twenty miles. Below the plateau—"down below the hill," we called it—were railroad tracks that ran from Chicago to Milwaukee and beyond. We thought of the tracks as bound north because they originated in Chicago and everything north of Chicago was wilderness, more or less. We stood with our backs to the wilderness, an open door with nothing behind it but lakes and forests and small towns like our own. The open door led nowhere with its terminus the Arctic. On clear nights we saw the white hell-born glow of Chicago, an unvirtuous city prodigious in its turbulence and variety, its dash, the capital of our region, at times magnet, at times repellent. Chicago was uncomfortable as the wilderness was uncomfortable. We in New Jesper were poised between two eternities, neither here nor there. My father believed we were superior to both, being small and therefore manageable. We charted our own course, taking care always to avoid Chicago's muscle to the south and the forbidding wilderness to the north.

This is what we had in New Jesper. Behind the railroad tracks were the steel mill and the auto parts plant and the Bing Company that made tennis rackets and the harbor that brought raw materials to those industries. And behind them was the vast gray lake with its befouled beach. The industries discharged waste directly into the lake, oil and chemicals and sludge that contaminated the water and caused fish to die. There was a suspiciously high incidence of cancer among the residents of New Jesper but that was not evident until much later. In any case, the lakeshore was littered with dead fish. New Jesper was a mill town, neither more nor less. Chicago was a mill town too, but its farsighted founders saw to it that the lakefront was kept pristine, conceiving of Lake Shore Drive as a kind of prairie corniche. The North Shore suburbs followed suit, their lakefront reserved for sandy beaches and above the beaches the sprawling mansions of meatpacking barons and merchant princes, even a cemetery or two.

Not so New Jesper. My father liked to explain that our town was built for heavy industry, a blue-collar town with blue-collar

values. Except for the Bing Company, these industries were
owned by men in Pittsburgh and Detroit and the local managers
were hired help along with the people who worked the assem-
bly lines. When World War II came, New Jesper prospered and
the population doubled to close to forty thousand. Puerto Ri-
cans and Negroes from the southern states arrived to find work,
and they were not always welcomed by the second-generation
Serbs, Poles, Germans, and Swedes, who thought of themselves
as guardians of New Jesper's hard-won way of life, God-fearing,
law-abiding, prideful, and strict. When the war ended, the town
began a long decline, a twilight that has lasted to the present moment. The steel mill closed. The auto parts factory moved south.
Lake commerce dwindled. The harbor was converted to a ma-
rina for the yachts of the North Shore rich; their own towns did
not allow marinas because they wished to keep their beaches
clean for swimming and the view from the bluff unspoiled. New
Jesper struggled to convert itself from heavy industry to a service
economy but with only marginal success. Its workers were not
trained in service and—well, it was not men's work, no sweat,
no heavy lifting, no union. The downtown continued to decay as
unemployment grew. None of this set New Jesper apart from any
of a hundred small mill towns of the Midwest and Northeast.
What was unique was the presence of the Bing Company, family-owned and staffed by men and women from the same small
town in Bohemia, where they had crafted musical instruments.
Bing prospered during the war, having converted to the manufacture of swagger sticks for the United States Army. And when
the war ended, Bing went back to tennis rackets and for a time
ran three shifts a day as the sport gained in popularity. From the
1920s until well into the Carter administration, wherever you
went in America and people asked where you were from and you
answered honestly, they would laugh and say, Ah! Where they
make the tennis racket! And recite the radio jingle, *Bing Bing
Bing, the Tennis Machine*. My father always found the reference

irritating and the jingle infuriating, as if New Jesper had no other claim to fame. But the truth was, it didn't. Hershey was where they made the candy bars and Milwaukee where they brewed the beer and New Jesper where they made tennis rackets. The Bing racket was high-end equipment, like a Balabushka pool cue or a Purdey shotgun. Old Walter Bing, who managed the company until well into his nineties, never changed the design or the materials that went into it. He disliked plastics and had even less use for aluminum, and so sales fell and by 1980 the company was out of business, a victim of technological progress. The only growth industry in New Jesper was the center of its civic life, the courthouse with its full complement of judges, clerks, and bailiffs, and the army of private lawyers, most of whom lived out of town. The courthouse and its annex was a turn-of-the-century stone pile of a building whose marble floors echoed like a tuning fork. The lights sometimes failed. The elevator was often out of service. My father didn't mind the inconvenience. The building had grandeur. For many years he tried without success to place the building on the National Register of Historic Places. That happened finally in 1999, but by then my father was long gone.

New Jesper was a fine place to grow up in, its streets lined with chestnut trees and elms and oaks. In the summertime you could ride your bike all over town and not see the full sun, only its shafts of light through branches thick with leaves, chestnuts scattered everywhere. At one time the downtown had an oak at each pedestrian intersection, but the merchants complained that they interfered with foot traffic so the city council ordered their removal. A women's group organized a protest, but the protest went nowhere and one by one the heavy trees were removed, leaving the downtown bare as a settlement in Arizona or Utah. Still, the public school system was excellent, staffed mostly by middle-aged women of frosty temperament and high expectations, though few of its high school graduates went on to college. College was not the normal aspiration for the sons and daughters of blue-collar mill workers for whom English was very much a second language. The sons followed their fathers into the mills, and the daughters their mothers into marriage, usually after a stint as a clerk in one of the two downtown department stores. This was before and during the war, in retrospect a dynamic parenthesis in the progress of things in the small towns of the Midwest. The war was much distant, present in newspaper headlines and the conversations of adults at the dinner table, unless a father or a son was away fighting in it, and that was not the case in my family. The terrible details of the struggle were known only to the combatants. Reversals were concealed by the authorities and meanwhile the place names flew by. Saipan. Ploieşti. My friends and I graduated from Cowboys and Indians to a game we called War, heroic leathernecks battling the sly Japanese, surely the main enemy. There were many German-speaking families in our town and no one wished to make their lives more uncomfortable than they already were. I suppose that was the reason, looking back on it. Bloodthirsty Tojo was the greater threat to domestic tranquillity. At any event, in those years New Jesper prospered, the factories running two and three shifts a day. Work was available to anyone who wanted it and wages were high. Everything changed after the war.

MOST DAYS AFTER SCHOOL my friend Dougie Henderson and I would scurry down below the hill looking for adventure that could not be found among the mowed lawns and shaded porches of the neighborhood. We carried air rifles for rabbits and the occasional raccoon. A ten-minute walk on the path through the underbrush at the base of the bluff took us to the railroad tracks. The path wound through a marsh, standing water that in summer was fetid, the water black and clammy as ink, boiling with mosquitoes. The underbrush was so tangled you could not see through it. The lay of the land down below the hill was a different country, untamed and unsupervised, and it was ours,

Dougie's and mine. Also, it was inhabited. Along the way we found empty whiskey bottles and crushed cigarette packs, evidence of adult life. We had a hilarious time imitating drunkards, weaving and stumbling incoherently. As we approached the tracks we threw away the bottles and moved with care, Indian fashion. In a thicket off the path was a concrete root cellar, origin unknown; there were no houses anywhere in sight. But we were always careful to look inside, pushing away the brambles that hid the entrance. The root cellar was usually undisturbed and that made it more mysterious still. We listened carefully for the freight train that lumbered by at slow speed, fifteen or twenty miles an hour. The trains came up without warning. The air seemed to stiffen and suddenly the engine surged by pulling a load of fifty freight cars with the red caboose bringing up the rear. Every few weeks a train came by bearing battle tanks on flatcars, causing us to wonder what need they had for tanks in Milwaukee. Soldiers lounged on the flatcars and when they saw us they would give a casual military salute, the sort of salute a professional soldier would give to a civilian. We tried to get to the tracks before four o'clock in the afternoon, in time to watch the passenger express from Chicago, bright yellow coaches and the steam engine in front. The express hurtled by at such speed that we could not see the passengers but always waved at them, imagining the day when we would be aboard, bound for Milwaukee or the Twin Cities on business, nonchalantly reading a newspaper and enjoying a cocktail and a cigarette. The train was there and gone in seconds.

There were tramps down below the hill, men riding the rails to get to somewhere else. Dougie and I were told never to approach them for any reason whatsoever, but when we saw a tramp, which was seldom, he looked harmless enough, always unshaven and badly clothed but not threatening in any way. They were not interested in children and seemed to inhabit a world of their own, always moving on. There was a kind of romance to it, men without women or families, waiting for something to turn up. The tramps we saw were old, at least as old as our parents and some much older. They had evidently led hard lives, though neither Dougie nor I could have said what a hard life constituted, beyond shabby clothing and an untrimmed beard and eyes that did not seem fully focused. Dougie said they looked uncoordinated, borrowing the expression from our gym teacher.

Once a month or so a tramp showed up at our back door and asked for food. My mother would give him fruit, apples or bananas, and when I delivered it to him he would invariably nod and thank me and walk slowly away, down below the hill in the direction of the railroad tracks, retracing his steps. Asking for food, he always held his cloth cap in his hand. These men were very much a part of our lives and at the same time invisible. We never saw the same tramp twice and yet we did not differentiate among them. Their threadbare clothes were a kind of uniform. Where had they come from? Where were they going? My father said you found tramps anywhere there was a railroad. He called them hard-luck cases. Broken homes, he explained, along with "early defeats" leading to a loss of purpose in life, aimlessness and dependence on whiskey, but all the same, subject to the identical laws and penalties as anyone else. In that way, my father said, justice was blind.

Along the railroad tracks were the remains of fires and always an empty bottle of whiskey nearby, along with cigarette stubs and apple cores and discarded bits of clothing. Looking at their camps, Dougie and I couldn't piece together the lives of these men, not that we tried very hard. They were beyond our understanding and certainly beyond our help, and they seemed very far away from the poise—I suppose the better word is coordination—of our own fathers, part of another world altogether, a respectable, successful world. The tramps were the inhabitants of the uncivilized country down below the hill, a small, mean world with the promise and variety of a set of railroad tracks—except, of course, to Dougie and me, who saw it as a form of liberty, release from the coat-and-tie milieu of our fathers.

When we reached the tracks we always paused for a cigarette, Old Golds for Dougie, Chesterfields for me, filched from cigarette packs at home. Something lawless about it, casually smoking a cigarette as freight trains lumbered by, and then snapping the butt at the rails and watching the shower of sparks. Often we would climb atop a switching box in order to see the lake a half mile distant, a sliver of blue beyond the bulk of the auto parts factory. Our terrain was so rough it was difficult reconciling it with the flash of color on the horizon. In summer we saw the sails of small boats and that was more incongruous still, the graceful lines of the vessels in sharp contrast to the underbrush and stunted trees around us, the clouds of mosquitoes and the dead campfires of the tramps. In the damp prairie cold of January and February ice built up along the lake, white replacing blue. The harbor was frozen all the way to the breakwater and sometimes beyond. The lakefront was out of reach because the auto parts factory stood in the way, the factory bounded by a chain-link fence with razor wire along the top. The rumor in town—vigorously denounced by my father—was that secret work was proceeding inside, something important to do with the war effort, and that New Jesper should be proud to be summoned to play a role. Once, standing at the fence and looking inside to see the secret work for ourselves, Dougie and I were shooed away by an indignant watchman. Goddamned kids, he shouted at us, but we thumbed our noses at him. The fence that kept us out also kept him in, though it took Dougie to notice that he was wearing a revolver in a holster and was carrying a two-foot-long billy club in his fist. We assumed that the fence was there to protect the factory and its secret work from the tramps and that set us to laughing because the tramps were so uncoordinated, as Dougie said. None of them had the cunning or initiative of Japanese spies. They were down and out.

I suppose Dougie and I were eight or nine years old when we saw our first tramp. He was asleep with his head resting on a discarded rail tie. He looked deflated, collapsed like a rag doll. I thought he was dead but said nothing about that to Dougie. We were twenty feet from him, staring at him as if he were an animal in a zoo. The tramp looked up, startled, and seeing we were boys and not rail agents, let out a high-pitched whoop and then smiled broadly.

You boys have a smoke for an old man?

Dougie and I looked at each other.

Give us a smoke, the tramp said.

I threw him a Chesterfield, underhanding it so that it bounced at his feet.

Match, he said sharply, so sharp it was almost a snarl.

I threw him a book of matches. He caught it, lit the cigarette, and sat Indian fashion, his arms on his knees. He put the matches in his shirt pocket.

Now where are you boys from? I'll bet you're from up there on the hill.

That's right, Dougie said.

Live in a fancy house, I'll bet.

We've got to be going, I said.

Stay awhile. Have a smoke.

We have to go home, Dougie said.

You just got here.

We said we would be home.

Up there on the hill, he said.

Dougie shrugged. Everyone lived on the hill.

Sit awhile, the tramp said. We can visit. What's your name?

Dougie and I took a step backward.

I got boys your age, the tramp said. But I don't know where they are. I don't know where they live. The tramp exhaled a great cloud of tobacco smoke and watched it disperse in the breeze. Last time I heard they was down south somewheres. But I can't remember the name of the town. I prefer riding the rails and one of these days I'll get back down south. I only need some money. I need some dollars.

Dougie and I nodded.

My name is Minning. Earl Minning. You boys got any dollars on you? I'll bet you do, coming from up there on the hill. The tramp smiled unpleasantly and when he began to struggle to his feet Dougie and I took another step backward and ran away like rabbits. He yelled after us, Come back, come back, you little bastards. But we ran and ran through the underbrush. I could hear Earl Minning behind us, his footfalls and heavy breathing, and when I stumbled and fell I expected his rough hand on my head, but when I turned he was not there. I sensed him nearby but I could not see him. Dougie was up ahead yelling at me to get up and run but I was frozen stiff, my knee bloody from the fall. A sour odor was in my nostrils and I knew it was Earl Minning and I had no money to give him. At last I was on my feet, and my fear vanished. I joined Dougie and we trotted up the hill until we reached my house. My mother was in her garden and when she saw us tumble out of the underbrush she asked us what was the matter, and we replied that we were footracing and nothing was the matter. I did not want her to know that we had come upon anyone down below the hill, certainly not a tramp. We regarded the place as private, our own domain, exclusive. We were not intruders; Earl Minning was the intruder. But I also knew for a certainty that he did not wish us well. From the expression on his face he did not wish anyone well. And all these years later I continue to wonder what brought him to that place, his children down south somewhere, he himself riding the rails.

LOOKING BACK on my childhood I am surprised that our parents allowed Dougie and me to roam unsupervised down below the hill. My father spent his childhood in the house we lived in and I do know that he had fond memories of the wild terrain and unexpected encounters with animals. My air rifle was a hand-me-down from him. It was my proudest possession, though I did not have it with me that day we met Earl Minning, and I am certain it would have made no difference if I had. My father wanted to believe that New Jesper had not changed since his own untroubled youth. And it was true that the iceman arrived with blocks of ice on his horse-drawn wagon and some of the streets on the north side of town were still gaslit. Every Friday morning the cutler arrived to sharpen our knives. The Victorian courthouse was unchanged. My father occupied the same chambers as his father when he was a probate court judge, and many of the same photographs hung on the walls and my grandfather's law books crowded the oak shelves on the dark side of the room. A six-foot-high grandfather clock occupied one corner and a hat rack of deer antlers another. He wrote his serious opinions in longhand at a standup desk, his routine ones spoken into a Dictaphone and transcribed by his clerk.

My father was forty years old when he married my mother. She was barely twenty, a downstate girl in New Jesper visiting her aunt. The aunt gave a dinner party, invited my father, and he and my mother were married one month later and I followed nine months after that. My mother was called Melody, most apt because she was always humming a tune. My father was a profoundly conservative man, sober perhaps to a fault. He avoided excitement and believed that unpleasantness should be kept out of sight, especially from women and children. In a sense his greatest wish was that tomorrow be much like today, or, better still, yesterday. Like many conservatives he was a pessimist. His business, supervising wills and trusts, did not discourage him in this view. He had watched people try to control their money from the grave, their hands reaching up to grandchildren and beyond. There were only four or five truly rich people in New Jesper and they all wanted a say after they'd gone. They made the money, they had the right to determine its distribution, hence wills that were bewildering in their complexity and too often a contradiction of human nature. Now and again my father would receive a will from one of the North Shore rich and be astounded at its size and labyrinthine byways and spiteful codicils. Their Chicago lawyers learned soon enough that they required local counsel to navigate the heavy weather in the chambers of Judge Erwin Goodell. My mother was always amused at my father's droll accounts of proceedings in his courtroom. When I came to know him as a man as well as a father he was already deep in middle age. He believed in home rule, the town, the neighborhood, the second-floor bedroom. I am bound to say that this cast of mind led to innocence as to the dangers of the world. His courtroom was not the world.

I am sure that in some sentimental region of his mind my father believed it would be wrong to declare the area down below the hill as off-limits to his son. It would be the same as declaring boyhood itself off-limits, an admission that New Jesper had become unmanageable and somehow sinister, barbarians in charge. New Jesper would be no different from Chicago, gang-ridden, absent of civic virtue, altogether corrupt. Certainly no place to raise a family in comfort and safety. Certainly no place to grow old among neighbors you had known your entire life. New Jesper would not go to the dogs on my father's watch and therefore his son and his son's friend could roam down below the hill as much as they liked. Be watchful, Lee, my father said. Take care. There were tramps in his day too, though perhaps not so many. My father customarily delivered his lectures in the early evening, often while listening to Sidney Bechet on the phonograph in his study. He was a devotee of blues music. Colored music, he called it. Soulful music. The genuine article.

THINGS CHANGED FOR GOOD after two incidents that occurred within one month of each other. The year was 1946. They were unrelated incidents but always spoken of together as if they were somehow linked, and a forecast of disorder. My father called it breakdown. A tramp was found dead near the railroad tracks not a quarter mile from our house. The tramp was badly beaten and, it seemed, tortured. The police had no leads, and the chief was quoted in the newspaper as saying it was the worst crime he had ever seen or heard of and he had spent a harrowing year in Europe with the airborne and was no stranger to atrocity. I read the paper avidly but understood that some details of the killing were being withheld. Indeed there was no mention of torture, a word my father had used in private conversation with my mother. The report of the killing in the *New Jesper World* was nothing like the reports of crime in the Chicago papers, one lurid particular after another. The Chicago papers did not cover the tramp killing because he was, after all, only a tramp and not a socialite or gangster. His name was unknown. No one knew where he came from. His destination was unknown. All that was certified was that he was male, Caucasian, brown-eyed, middle-aged. Our police chief admitted there were no suspects while at the same time vowing to clear New Jesper of tramps. Tramps were no longer welcome in the city, he said, as if it were all but certain that the killer himself was a tramp and that tramps generally constituted a threat to the good order of the community. The first duty of civil authority was to keep the town safe from lawless elements.

The story made the afternoon edition of the *World*. My father came home to dinner that evening much subdued. I could discern his mood by the way he closed the front door, softly, with barely a click of the latch. He was dressed in his usual courtroom uniform: a doubled-breasted blue suit, white shirt, and foulard bow tie. He looked exhausted, his gray hair mussed as if he had passed his hand through it again and again. I thought also that he looked defeated by the events of the day but I believe now that I had misapprehended things. My father was seething with anger. He collapsed into his big wing chair and accepted an old-fashioned from my mother; they always had one cocktail before dinner, which was served precisely at six-thirty. That night six-thirty came and went while they drank their cocktail and then had another. I always sat with them as they recounted their days and asked me about mine. But that night they sat in uncomfortable silence until my father turned to me.

Go upstairs, Lee. Finish your homework.

I've done my homework. I saw the story in the paper—

Check it again, son.

Always when there was an unusual or unexpected event in town I could count on my father to explain it to me. He seemed to know everything about politics and government and therefore he knew the story behind the story. There always was one, and it was rarely the version printed in the *World*. His idea was that we had a government of laws, not of men. But the men made the laws so—was there a difference? But from the look on his face I knew this story-behind-the-story would remain mysterious, at least to me.

Yes, sir, I said.

But I left my bedroom door open and tried to listen as my father related the day's events to my mother, his voice barely above a whisper. The facts were too shocking to speak out loud. I did manage to hear my mother gasp at what she was told and declare, That cannot be. What a terrible thing! Oh, that poor man. I wondered if the dead man was one of the tramps Dougie and I had come across on our afternoon adventures—the *World* did not publish a photograph—but I had no way of knowing. Of course the name that came to mind was Earl Minning, from the encounter years before, but surely he would have moved on. Tramps still arrived at our back door, hat in hand, to ask for food. My father's voice rose in anguish. This sort of thing did not happen in New Jesper except rarely in the colored section, always described in the *World* as a domestic dispute. And then my father used the word "torture" and another word whose definition I did not know but resolved to learn as soon as I could discreetly consult the dictionary in my father's study downstairs. They were quiet now, sipping drinks in the living room. I heard the tinkle of ice as my father refilled his glass, something he rarely did. I thought it safe to return, so I made a noise in my room and more noise as I came downstairs.

My mother and father were staring bleakly at each other.

My father turned to me and said, I assume you saw the paper.

Yes, I said. There was a killing.

The report in the paper was not complete.

It wasn't?

No. There was more to it. Quite a lot more. Now listen to me, my father said and steepled his fingers as he often did when rendering a verdict from the bench. His words: "rendering a verdict." I came to know his steepled fingers as well as I knew my own, for he often asked my mother to bring me to court when an especially important case was at its conclusion. He thought it important that I see how justice was done in New Jesper, the procedures and the precedence of things, the special language, and his own role at the center of events, for surely that would be my life too when the time came. He said now, You are not to go down below the hill ever again except in the company of an adult. Is that clear?

I was crushed. No more adventuring with Dougie Henderson. No more express trains thundering north. No more air rifle and, especially, no more inspections of the factory beyond the chain-link fence where secret work was still being done. For me at that moment New Jesper became like any other small midwestern town, a cliché—tiresome, narrow-minded, and boring. I said to my father, Yes, sir.

Ever, my father said again.

What happened? I said. I was miserable. I think I was near tears.

One of the tramps was killed, he said.

But I knew that. I said, How?

Murdered, he said. Never mind how.

It was a terrible killing, my mother said.

I spoke with Dougie's father this afternoon, my father said. We are in agreement. You boys are forbidden to leave the neighborhood. And if you see a tramp anywhere nearby you are to call me at once. I doubt that will happen. The tramps have been sent a message. This outrage has changed everything.

What message? I asked.

They are not welcome here, my father said.

But—where will they go?

Away, my father said. Not here.

I waited for him to say more, but he fell silent. My mother slipped away into the kitchen to finish dinner preparations. I could not see what any of this had to do with Dougie and me, but it was obvious that my father had said all he was prepared to say. The subject was closed. I asked him if he wanted to listen to the radio as we often did in the evenings. He liked to hear the political news from Lowell Thomas and Gabriel Heatter. But he only shook his head. We sat in silence a minute or more, my father pulling slowly at his drink. The ice had melted.

I know how much it means to you, he said at last.

Yes, it does.

It was always a special place, the railroad and the marsh. In my day there were muskrats, ugly animals. There was a herd of deer also, and pheasant. Johnnie Regan and I made the path that's there to this day, took us all fall and half the winter. It was a wilderness. I guess to Johnnie and me it represented the outside world, so mysterious and dangerous, although we could not have said what the danger was. All my life I've lived near the railroad tracks, the train whistles as familiar to me as an ambulance siren is to someone who lives in the city and come to think about it both the whistle and the siren gave a kind of warning. Watch out. Take care. My father smiled suddenly, a looking-backward smile that was almost boyish. Johnnie and I used to pretend there were panthers in the underbrush, huge black creatures that had escaped from a circus. They were so fleet that they appeared only as shadows. They were something, our imaginary panthers. Whenever we came across a dead animal we knew the panthers had killed it. And I'll tell you something else, Lee. Johnnie Regan and I used to smoke cigarettes down below the hill. We had a particular place we went to, near the—

Old root cellar, I said.

Things don't change much, my father said with a grunt.

We once saw a tramp sleeping in there.

You didn't bother him?

No, we went away. And when we came back he was gone.

Riding the rails, my father said.

I guess so. We met another tramp once, asked us for cigarettes and then he asked for money. We gave him a cigarette but we didn't give him the money.

What happened then?

He was angry. He came after us.

You should have told me, my father said.

We outran him. He was mean-looking, though. He told us his name and said he had children living down south. He needed money to see his children.

Did you believe him?

Yes I did. His name was Earl Minning.

When was this? my father asked.

A few years ago. We never saw him again. I'm going to miss our travels down below the hill. Dougie, too. I sure wish you'd change your mind. You had your panthers and we had Japanese spies. There's this, though. We don't go down there as much as we used to. But it's good knowing it's there. You once called New Jesper closed in.

Did I? Well, it is.

Everybody knows everybody else, I said.

They certainly do, he said.

Down below the hill you can be yourself.

Unsupervised, he said.

Yes, I said.

We had a nice town to grow up in, my father said after a moment. Nice for me and your mother, nice for you. I thought New Jesper would be nice also for your children, my grandchildren when they came along. Your mother and I have often spoken of it, the advantages of a small town where everyone was acquainted and things are on an even keel. Your family's nearby. You didn't have to lock your doors at night. You left the keys in the car. And if your neighbor was in distress you helped him out with a hamper of food or a donation. If there was illness you took the kids for a while, happy to do it. We had an expression, "Safe as houses." Now we're no better than that goddamned Chicago. I'm sick at heart that this sort of thing can happen here in New Jesper. My God, what have we come to?

As it happened, the word sodimmy was not in my father's dictionary. Dougie knew the meaning, though.

ONE MONTH LATER, almost to the day, another calamity struck our town. My father called from his chambers to tell my mother not to wait dinner for him. He would be along later, bringing some friends with him for a private meeting in his study. My mother said his voice sounded strange on the telephone. At first she did not recognize it. Your father sounded as if he were underwater, she said. I think he had people with him in chambers.

I've never known him to have a meeting at home.

But he didn't want to meet in the courthouse. Too public, he said.

I don't like the sound of it, my mother concluded.

Promptly at nine my father arrived, accompanied by Mayor Bannermann, the police chief, the owner of New Jesper Dry Goods, the president of the First National Bank of New Jesper, the publisher of the *World*, the principal of the high school, and Walter Bing. The corporation counsel for the city would have been present but he was out of town. Six of these eight men, known informally as "the Committee," were the ones who made New Jesper go, whose approval was essential for any civic undertaking, from a new bond issue to the removal of a tree. With them, anything was possible; without them, nothing was. They were second- and third-generation residents, married with families, golf partners; two of them were godfathers to each other's sons. Of course there were rivalries. The mayor and the publisher were at arm's length owing to political differences. The banker and the merchant were at odds because the banker's son and the merchant's daughter had recently divorced, an ugly divorce that went on for months with the usual airing of dirty linen. Still, in any important matter affecting the town they stood together in order to present a united front when the matter, whatever it was, had to be explained to the public. The idea, as I understood it, was to present a fait accompli disguised as a consensus; or perhaps it was the other way around. My father was the de facto chairman, admired for his integrity, even-handedness, and devotion to the town. It has to be said that the police chief and the principal of the high school would not normally be invited to such a gathering. My mother had never met them and had to be introduced. That chore done, the seven grim-faced men were ushered into the study by my father, the door closed behind them.

The night was warm for mid-September. My father opened his windows to admit what night breeze there was. And I, perched in my bedroom window directly above, strained to hear each word. In our community, as in every community large and small, there were the scenes and the behind-the-scenes. The latter was infinitely more interesting, and I was an inquisitive boy.

My father offered coffee or a drink to anyone who wanted one.

They all took coffee except for the police chief, who said he was not thirsty.

I heard the scrape of my father's chair as he moved it from behind his desk, a tactful assertion that for the purposes of this meeting, all men were equal.

There was an awkward silence before my father cleared his throat and said, Perhaps the chief can bring us up to date. What is known and what is not known. The investigation so far. And then he lowered his voice and the few words that followed were inaudible.

Then Chief Grosza gave an audible sigh and said, The girl is in St. Vincent's Hospital, the emergency ward. She's not in good shape. Her wounds are very serious and beyond that she seems to have suffered a nervous collapse. Her mother is with her. The precise whereabouts of the father are unknown. The mother and father are separated and have been for some little while. Some time elapsed before the girl was discovered, perhaps several hours. The timeline is not yet established. Perhaps our principal can speak to that point. At that, Chief Grosza fell silent.

The attack took place in the gym, the principal said. I should say an equipment room just off the gym. A little-used equipment room. There is no cause for anyone to go in there. Question is, what was the girl doing there? We don't know. The principal spoke rapidly and now he was silent, and the conversation became general, several questions at once. Did the equipment room have a lock on the door? Was the door in fact locked? Where precisely was the equipment room located in relation to the gym itself? The answers came quickly and they were longer than they needed to be. Even I understood this was a kind of ballet, a wordy prelude to the heart of the matter.

My father had not spoken.

The president of the bank, known for his brevity, said, What about suspects, Chief?

Our investigation continues, Chief Grosza said.

Are there leads, Chief?

Nothing solid, the chief said. We were not notified until at least two hours after the attack, perhaps longer.

After the rape, you mean.

Yes, it was rape.

Has the girl said anything?

She has not, the chief said.

She is not cooperative?

She is unable to speak. She has not uttered one word.

What is her name?

I would hope we could keep her name out of this for the moment, the principal said, until I have a better fix on what happened.

Her name is Magda Serra, the chief said.

Magda? the banker asked.

The mother is Serbian. The father is Puerto Rican.

And the father's whereabouts are unknown?

He is believed to have returned to Puerto Rico. Earlier this year.

There was once again a confusion of voices, the identity of the father, his employment, his age, his reputation. No one in the room had met the father, who was working as a gas station attendant before his return to Puerto Rico, address unknown. But I was not listening carefully because I knew the girl, a cheerful tenth-grader who had been kept behind one year. Magda was in my freshman math class, not a good student. She was overweight but didn't seem to care. Magda had thinning hair and at the beginning of the term wore a bandanna but the bandanna was in violation of school rules so she was asked to take it off. She always had a smile on her face and a musical lilt to her voice. Lee, will you help me with these equations? I donna unnerstan' equations. And I would walk her through quadratic equations and she always caught on eventually, even as she made plain that she didn't care for the sphere of math, equations or any other part of it. The point was that Magda was foreign and I always suspected she hid inside her language and her Serbian–Puerto Rican background in order to get on from day to day, and in that sense part of her remained invisible. I tried to imagine her in a hospital emergency room, raped and frightened, silent. Who could do such a thing? Everyone liked Magda Serra, even the teachers. Downstairs they were still talking about Magda's father's whereabouts when I heard my father clear his throat.

Can we return to the leads? I cannot believe there are no leads at all. Can you explain, Chief?

We are only at the beginning of the investigation, Chief Grosza said.

Nevertheless, my father said.

We must wait to speak to the girl.

That may take a while, my father said.

Yes, it may.

And in the meantime, you do have leads.

One lead, the chief said.

It would be helpful if you could discuss that lead with us, my father said.

But the chief did not reply. I leaned out the window and saw a yellow shaft of light on the lawn, my father's desk lamp. Now and again a car passed in the street and I heard music from the radio, the normal sounds of a summer night. Magda's face came to me again, round-cheeked, bright blue eyes. Her skin was brown. She was baffled by equations and always seemed to be laughing. Downstairs they knew none of this.

We're trying to help out, Chief, my father said.

The investigation has only just begun, Judge.

Nothing remotely like this has ever happened in New Jesper, my father said. Nothing even close . . .

The tramp, somebody said. Only weeks ago.

The tramp is not *this*. Something altogether different, *this*. In our own high school. The one I attended and most of us here attended, the one my son attends now. My father's voice rose in indignation. A girl goes to school in the morning and ends up raped in the afternoon. This is outrageous. So I would like to know what progress you've made, if any.

Tell him, the mayor said.

But still the chief was silent.

Or I will, the mayor said.

We have an interview, the chief said, and that was all he said.

With whom? my father asked.

A student, the chief said.

A *student?*

A classmate of the girl's, the chief said.

And what did the interview reveal?

The chief was silent a long moment, and when he spoke it was with obvious reluctance. He and the girl had been seeing each other. What he knows is unclear at this time.

Is he in your custody?

He is not.

And why not?

I have nothing to hold him on, the chief said.

So he is free.

Correct, the chief said.

Something in Chief Grosza's tone of voice, perhaps his guardedness, perhaps the look in his eyes, caused my father to pose an unexpected question: Is this boy represented by counsel?

In a manner of speaking, the chief said.

Well, is he or isn't he?

Tell him, the mayor said.

The boy's father is a lawyer, Judge.

Good lord, my father said.

I'll tell you something else, the chief said. The boy didn't do it. I don't think he knows who did do it. He does know the girl. They have been on dates, the movies, that sort of thing. Now you're going to ask me his name and I'm not going to give it.

We have pretty much established that this boy was nowhere near school at the time of the attack. My chief of detectives is working that angle. The boy is very upset but has been cooperative. His father has been cooperative. And that's the end of it.

There was another long silence as the men in the room shifted in their chairs.

I'm sorry I pressed you, Chief.

You should be, the chief said.

People did not talk to my father in that tone of voice, and certainly no city employee would think of doing so. I imagined my father's face reddening as he struggled to control himself. It was evident also that the chief of police was furious that he had been led in a direction he did not want to go, bullied first by my father and then by the mayor. But they were the ones who ran things in New Jesper. Chief Grosza was an unusual choice to head the police department, a decorated airborne officer in the war who, at the end, led an interrogation unit in Berlin. He was rumored to have had a difficult war, a survivor of the D-day landing and, later, the Bulge. The chief was tightly wound, slender of build, fit, unsmiling most of the time. He had married a New Jesper girl and when he was discharged he came home to her and applied for the chief's job, then vacant. He was hired, not without misgivings, and grumbling began at once that he ran the police force like an army unit, perhaps too spit-and-polish for a small town police force where years would go by without an officer discharging his weapon or even unholstering one. Still, any chief had to be aware of the various personalities important to the town's welfare, meaning who was related to whom and so forth. Tact was an asset. It took Chief Grosza time to understand the subtleties of law enforcement in New Jesper. The mayor had to explain to him that when a patrolman arrested the son of the bank president for speeding and discovered liquor on his breath he did not arrest the boy for drunken driving. The boy was driven home for parental discipline. The same courtesy was extended to the bank president himself, although in that instance discipline was more or less waived. Chief Grosza understood very well what he was told and did not appreciate it but like any good soldier he saluted and obeyed. My father insisted that the chief was efficient and hard-working and honest in his dealings with the mayor and the city council and his own patrolmen. Still, his personality was unfortunate. He was a difficult man.

Apologize to the judge, the mayor said.

Go to hell, said the chief.

Just a damn minute, my father said.

Hold on, the bank president said. He was hard of hearing and spoke in a voice that could have been heard in the street. Back off right now, Chief. We're working uncharted territory here. We're feeling our way. All we're trying to do is get to the bottom of this awful crime. Find the son of a bitch who did it and put him away. It's not personal, Chief. We all admire your service in the war and the job you've done here. So give us some room. We're all on the same team.

For what it's worth, I agree with the chief. This was the principal of the high school, his reedy voice in unfortunate contrast to the banker's baritone. He had been principal for thirty years, due for retirement. He said, The boy in question is not at all the sort of boy to be involved. In something like this.

My father cleared his throat yet again. He said, So the long and the short of it is that we do not have a suspect.

Correct, the chief said.

And we are unlikely to have one unless and until the girl speaks.

Yes, the chief said.

So the question is, my father went on, what do we do right now? What are the steps we must take? I believe we must take account of our community. The effect of this. The shock of it, frankly.

My father went on in that vein for a minute or more and then the others joined in, everyone except Chief Grosza, the principal, and Walter Bing. I was thinking about the boy being questioned, Joel Dexter. It was surely him. His father was a trial lawyer and he and Magda sat next to each other in math class, often passing notes back and forth. Joel was as hopeless as she was with numbers. That he could have attacked her was preposterous, if only for the reason that he was half her size and a weakling. Also, he was the class clown and had been since the second grade. Magda was the one who laughed loudest at his lame jokes. I remembered reading somewhere that given the proper circumstances anyone is capable of anything. But Joel Dexter was not capable of rape, never in a hundred years.

I agree with the judge, the mayor said.

I second the motion, the merchant said.

Something like this happened many years ago in my village in Bohemia, Walter Bing said. He had not spoken before. His voice was deep and heavily accented and carried old-world authority. Naturally he commanded respect as something of a local celebrity and successful businessman, inventor of the Bing tennis racket. He said, This was before the Great War. The Austrians ran things. There were many rivalries in our village, clans opposed to each other, ethnic and religious rivalries. Vendettas were common. A girl of one clan was raped by boys of another clan. They left her for dead. But she had just enough life in her to commit suicide by hanging. You can imagine the uproar. Our town was remote. We did not have newspapers. News traveled by word of mouth, gathering details as it went. We had courts but they were not—I should say they were not equipped for a matter of this kind. The boys were never brought to justice. There was no trial. But before the year was out two of the boys were dead. There was a death and two injuries in the girl's family also. The vendetta went on for years. I imagine it is still going on into the second or third generation. The rape of that girl was a terrible thing for our village and the surrounding countryside. Matters of pride and insult were always dealt with personally. That has not changed to this day. We had long memories in our community. Nothing forgiven, nothing forgotten. As I said, we were in a remote district. Nothing much happened there. I have wondered often if our memories were long because the future was always in doubt. We looked to the past because we could not see the future. And so my wife and I and our sons and a few of the most skilled workers in my shop came to America, not to make zithers but to make tennis rackets. We were all happy to leave but we have mixed feelings about the place we left behind. He hesitated, and gave a dry chuckle. The communists have it now. Maybe they can stop it. Shoot someone. Jail the others. Brainwash the remainder.

For a moment no one said anything. I imagine my father and the others were puzzled as to the exact point Walter Bing was trying to make. It was hard to see the connection between a village in remote Bohemia and New Jesper in northern Illinois. Vendettas were not a feature of life in America. At last, as the silence lengthened, my father said, How long have you been here, Walter?

Almost thirty years, he said.

So, the mayor said, where do we go from here?

You had no newspapers in your village, my father said.

No newspapers, Walter Bing said.

We have them here, my father said with a laugh.

We surely do, the mayor said.

Perhaps Alfred could speak to that point, my father said.

ALFRED SWAN was a third-generation publisher of the *World,* with his son, Alfred IV, waiting in the wings. My father disapproved of Alfred because, as he said, Alfred Swan believed that the First Amendment superseded all the other amendments, including the right to a fair trial. The motto of the *World,* placed in a little box to the left of the nameplate on page one, was *With Neither Fear Nor Favor.* To which my father replied, with some asperity, His favor, our fear. Alfred and my father got along politically because the publisher was a devoted supporter of the Republican Party and a perennial delegate to the Republican National Convention; all the men in my father's study that evening were Republicans, except for the mayor and Chief Grosza. Not that politics was involved in the discussion at hand. The rape of a high school girl had nothing to do with politics. But on the subject of the First Amendment Alfred Swan was immovable, aggressive to the point of angry hostility. Every few months he wrote an editorial on the subject and ran the editorial on page one. Alfred Swan was unbalanced, according to my father, who disliked zealots generally. He believed them unreliable.

What do you mean? Alfred asked.

For God's sake, Alfred, the mayor said.

We have a bad situation, my father said.

We certainly do, Alfred said.

Requires tact, my father said.

Alfred Swan did not reply to that, and the statement hung there.

I'm thinking of our community, my father said, and I thought of his words as an army advancing one foot at a time, the objective unclear but surely somewhere over the next hill or the hill after that.

What are you talking about? Alfred said, an edge to his voice.

I would like to know how you will handle this news, the mayor said.

Without fear or favor, the publisher said. The way the *World* normally handles, as you call it, news.

It's so ugly, the mayor said in a voice that indicated he was speaking to the room at large, everyone in it. The facts are terrible. They are obscene. Awful for that little girl and her family and surely we must be mindful of them. Even if she is not named, as I assume she will not be, her identity will become known. Her life will be ruined.

The life of this town will never be the same, my father said.

The story isn't fit to print, the banker said, his voice booming in the study. Who benefits if this story is spread over the front pages of your newspaper? My God, Alfred, the *Tribune* will be up here, and the *Daily News*. The Hearst people, the photographers, the radio. Who knows what riffraff, all of them asking impertinent questions, the girl's name dragged through the mud. The town, too.

The people of our town will be coarsened, my father said. We'll all be touched by it. It's black as sin, this event. It's the worst thing that's ever happened here. We have no idea who committed this crime. I'm prepared to take the chief at his word that the student being questioned is innocent. If that is how it turns out after investigation. In that event we have a crime without a suspect.

My father's voice was soft but his words were ragged with anguish. I think he wanted to believe in the essential virtue of New Jesper, and by virtue he would mean a fundamental innocence that, once violated, would vanish forever. It was true that the town was in the fist of more powerful interests, unconcerned with the general welfare of the citizens or their government. But that did not mean New Jesper did not have its own sense of self despite the fist. My father was suggesting, in his roundabout way, a quarantine against a terrible and mysterious virus of unknown origin. The men in the room, worldly men, had a duty to the community and the community was not at all worldly. Against this virus the town had no resources except its stubborn pride. As the banker said, the story of Magda Serra was not fit to print. To print would be a provocation.

I'm sure you agree, Alfred, my father said, to which the publisher replied with a smile.

It's just a hell of a thing, the mayor said.

I think I'll have that drink, if you don't mind, Judge, Alfred said.

Walter Bing said he would have one too, and the banker and the merchant followed suit. Chief Grosza and the principal declined. No one said anything during the preparation of the drinks, the rattle of ice and the clink of my father's whiskey decanter against glass. At last the company was settled and waiting for Alfred Swan to speak.

There are eight people in this room, Alfred said. We all know the details of this crime, or most of the details. I'm sure the chief has withheld the worst of them. When this meeting is over some of us will go home and tell our wives, of course swearing them to silence. And as surely as the day will dawn, this story will be all over town by close of business tomorrow. The first question will be: Who's the victim? The second will be: Who's the suspect? And the third will be: Why haven't I read about it in Alfred Swan's newspaper? What's the *World* covering up? That bastard Swan, you can never trust him. Swan only prints what suits him. Fuck him, they'll say. Fuck Alfred Swan and his newspaper. I'm canceling my subscription.

I remembered how startled I was. I had never heard that word used in our house. Occasionally my father allowed himself a "goddamn" and, in extremis, "shit," and never within my mother's hearing. Ungentlemanly behavior, my father said. The language of truck drivers.

That's not true, Alfred, the mayor said.

You fellows think that if the tree crashes in the forest and there's no one nearby to hear it, why then it didn't crash. But it did. And someone is always nearby. In a small town someone always has his ear to the keyhole. Alfred Swan is not the solution to your bad situation. The solution is to arrest the son of a bitch who did this, bring him to trial, and condemn him to death. There's an electric chair in Joliet specially for that purpose. Bought and paid for by the good people of the state of Illinois. They'll want to see it used. And they'll want to read about it in their newspaper, beginning, middle, and end.

Jesus, Alfred, the mayor said.

Jee-sus, Al-fred, the publisher mimicked and gave a short laugh.

That's enough of that, my father said.

Tell him, Chief, the mayor said.

I'd rather not, the chief said mildly but with an edge of malice. I wouldn't want to shock Mr. Swan. The others.

Tell him, the mayor said again. Tell him all of it.

The chief sighed, a long, drawn-out whistle. We got the call from the school janitor, the chief said. He was not coherent but eventually we got to the gist of things. We ordered up an ambulance and met the janitor in the gym. He was so upset he could barely speak. He pointed at the equipment room door, still ajar. The girl was in a corner, curled up. Her legs were covered with blood and there was blood on the floor. I was reminded of the war except this wasn't Omaha Beach or Bastogne, this was a high school gymnasium in America. It was only when we went closer that we saw she had a wooden ruler in her . . . Chief Grosza paused then, seeking an alternative to the barracks word, a clinical word or any word that would not offend the judge and his Republican friends. But the chief failed, and after the pause continued in his dry voice. The ruler must have reached her stomach because there was only an inch of it showing. And that was not all, gentlemen. There was much more. The ruler was the least of what was done to that girl.

And just then I heard a noise outside my bedroom door and moved quickly away from the open window to my desk, where the math book was lying open. If my father suspected for one minute that I was listening to him and his friends talking downstairs, that would be the end for me. So I sat at my desk pretending to do my homework. My bedroom walls were decorated with college pennants and a team photograph of the 1945 Chicago Cubs and a movie poster my mother had given me, *Casablanca*. My thoughts were with Magda but my eyes patrolled the room, the bookshelves crowded with boys' books, *Ivanhoe* and *The Last of the Mohicans* and two of Kenneth Roberts's novels and C. S. Forester and *Treasure Island* and a dozen others and a pile of magazines, *Collier's* and the *Saturday Evening Post*. I was not aware of any irony. In my father's house irony was subversive, a perverse answer to the tragic or inexplicable. It was insincere, the language of agnostics. In any case I was not thinking of the pennants on the wall or the contents of my bookshelves but of the conversation downstairs, wondering all the while what the chief meant when he spoke of "the least of what was done to that girl." It was obvious to me that the men in the room were appalled at what they were hearing from their chief of police and were baffled as to how to proceed. I cautiously moved away from my desk to the window once again, standing now as if idly looking into the street while I worked out my math problem.

. . . and that's about it, the chief said.

Jesus, the banker said. Jesus Christ.

Someone rose to fill his glass, again the clink of the decanter.

I've never heard of anything like that, the merchant said. Never in my life.

We appreciate what you're doing, Chief, Walter Bing said.

Thank you, Chief Grosza said.

We wish you luck, he said.

We'll need some, the chief said. We'll also need time.

So, Alfred, the mayor said.

Give me a minute, the publisher said, his voice thick and much subdued.

We have photographs if anyone wants to see them.

No one wants to see your photographs, Chief.

As you wish, Judge.

I'd like to, Bing said.

And me, Swan said.

After a moment my father said, So here we are.

Decision time, said the mayor.

Do you have a guess, Chief? my father asked. Who you're looking for?

No, the chief said. He's someone physically strong. An adult, I would say. Obviously a mental case. Of course we're checking the asylum downstate to see if anyone's absent without leave. No word from them yet. There appear to be no witnesses, and no evidence at the scene, except for the ruler, an ordinary school ruler with Magda's name on it. What we have so far is a clean crime.

Unless the girl speaks, the mayor said.

The doctor is doubtful, the chief said. At least in the near future. He described the girl's state as unresponsive. The word he used was catatonic.

And no wonder, my father said. Let's make certain she has everything she needs, medically speaking. Any treatment, any hospital. Whatever it costs.

I'll set up an account in her name tomorrow, the banker said. Let her mother know. She is not to worry about expenses.

How is the mother? the banker asked.

About as you might expect, the chief said.

Has she been interviewed?

I had a few minutes with her. She is suspicious. I mean, she is suspicious of me and the government in general. I think she is afraid. It's common enough among immigrants. Men in uniforms. Also, her English is not good. For what it's worth she has no record with us. She's just someone trying to get by, as best I can judge. When I asked her about her husband, she said he was in Puerto Rico. She heard he was dead, and if he was it served him right. The truth of the matter is, Mrs. Serra is terrified. She is not coherent. So I'll try tomorrow with an interpreter present. Right now, she's my focus.

Is there anything else we can do? Should do?

No one answered that question. The room was silent.

Are we missing something obvious here? my father asked. First the tramp, now this. Can he be the same man?

The thought had occurred to us, the chief said.

I don't know what's worse. One maniac or two.

But I think not, the chief said. I cannot imagine a common tramp in the vicinity of the high school without someone noticing. Such a man is conspicuous. He'd stick out. He would be seen and commented upon. We are questioning everyone at the school, students, teachers, maintenance men. No exceptions.

And you are careful how you go about it?

Of course, the chief said. We've only had a few hours.

This thing is out of control, my father said.

Not yet, the banker said.

You wait, my father said. Tomorrow our town's crawling with newspaper reporters. Imagine the disruption. The chief won't be able to do his work. We'll have a circus.

So, Alfred, the mayor said once again. What do you intend to do?

I intend to publish a story, Alfred Swan said. I will write it myself. Look for it tomorrow. That's the best I can do.

You are making a mistake, my father said.

You run your courtroom, Erwin. I'll run my newspaper.

And with that the meeting broke up. The men were out the door in minutes and I watched them congregate around the mayor's blue Buick. They stood with their hands in their pockets, heads bowed as if at graveside, all but Chief Grosza and Alfred Swan, who had driven away at once. My father returned to his study alone and I heard the clink of the decanter. I saw his shadow at the window and then his head as he leaned into the darkness. From the ear-to-the-ground cast of his head I knew my father was listening to the sounds he had known since childhood, crickets and the intermittent soft thud of a chestnut on the sidewalk. Across New Jesper Avenue all the houses were dark and the sidewalks empty. Then I heard the downbeat of Bechet's "Petite Fleur." My father was waiting for it because he turned his eyes upward as if the music were coming from the heavens, my old man's choir of angels with names like Jimmy Yancey and Fats Waller and the dissolute Jelly Roll Morton along with Bechet. He had a mystical feeling about them, as he had for the long-vanished Indians of our region, except he was kinder about the jazzmen. We listened for a few moments, he from his study and me from my bedroom, and then the music stopped abruptly and the street was silent once again. This was my father's regimen in September, early to bed, things in place as they always had been, except for the bad situation. His shoulders seemed to sag, his head downcast. I think he was hearing Sidney Bechet's music in his head, because he began to move his arms to a dirge beat as if he were conducting an orchestra. Then I heard him moan, a sound from deep within. My heart went out to him.

My father told me once that all you needed to know in life you could learn from American blues, mostly forbearance but other things too, like tolerance and compassion. I think he meant that two ways. They were serious people, the jazzmen. They had gravity. There was not a mill on earth they had not been through time and again. That was the source of their music and while you wouldn't wish the mills on anyone, something good came of it, this original American art form imitated everywhere but never duplicated because it rose from a specific condition. That was sometimes the way of things, not as often as you would like. My father was not entirely satisfied with that thought because he turned gruff, mixed another cocktail, and demanded to know if I'd done my homework and if not why not. Even the greatest musicians practiced their scales, even Bechet.

Now my father leaned far out over the windowsill, his head bowed, and remained there, deep inside himself, most troubled.

*

THE ARTICLE IN THE *World* the following afternoon was anodyne. It carried no byline and the tone was ex cathedra. There had been an incident at the high school and the police were investigating and expected an arrest within the week. That was the gist of it, elaborated over five paragraphs on page fourteen, nestled between two advertisements and an account of a recent zoning board meeting. That was the last word on the subject of the bad situation to appear in the *World* or anywhere else. The *Tribune* and the *Daily News* never picked up the story, as they had no means of reading between the lines. Magda Serra's attacker was never identified and in due course the girl and her mother left town for parts unknown; the rumor was that they had returned to Serbia. Magda never spoke of her ordeal and so far as anyone knew never regained consciousness. In fact, while she was in St. Vincent's Hospital and later on in a private facility she barely moved and never uttered one word. Of course there were rumors in town and in the corridors at school, but the rumors were guarded, side-of-the-mouth conversations, and in the absence of fresh information they died away, though a profound uneasiness remained, the uneasiness of the uncompleted thought. Most everyone assumed that the tramp's killer or killers had gone away to another part of the country but no one knew that for certain, either. In time both matters were forgotten or hidden away in an attic region of the mind, except by my father and the others who had gathered that night at our house; and they did not speak of it. It was true also that Mayor Bannermann was defeated at the next election, his twenty years in office cut unexpectedly short. Chief Grosza resigned and took a security job in Florida. The principal of the high school retired, as planned. And New Jesper began its long decline.

The atmosphere at home changed. My mother no longer sang as she went about her household chores. She was as incensed by the attack on Magda Serra as she had been by the tramp's death a month earlier. If the high school was not safe, what was?

New Jesper was not the place she thought it was and she no longer felt safe in her own house; now the doors were locked day and night. She worried about my safety. She wanted to return to Champaign where she grew up and where her parents still lived but she knew that was impossible. A judgeship was not transferable. My father insisted that the tramp's death and the attack on Magda were isolated events—appalling, certainly, but isolated. They could have happened anywhere. In Chicago murder was virtually a civic sport, public entertainment. Given enough time, he said, New Jesper would return to its normal self. The argument between my mother and my father continued each evening after dinner. From my bedroom I could hear the rise and fall of their voices and in my mother's tone a new insistence, an unfamiliar hard edge. For the first time in my hearing, my father was on the defensive, querulous and irresolute. My mother believed she had seen the face of evil and wanted to leave New Jesper for one of the North Shore towns.

We don't belong there, my father said. All they care about is their country club and the commuter train. Bedroom towns.

Safe towns, my mother said.

My father thought it unseemly, the probate court judge living out of town.

Your cases come from all over the county, my mother said. What's the difference which town you live in?

The courthouse is here, my father said.

You have a car, my mother replied.

I like walking to work, my father said. Gives me a chance to think, stretch my legs. I notice things. Someone is building a tree house for his kid. Someone else has bought a new car. Dry Goods has a sale. I'll say hello to half a dozen people and I'll visit for a while, learn what's going on. And there's a lot more than you might think, quite a lot more. People have troubles and they tell me their troubles. Sometimes I can help. I know we have a placid surface here but that's all it is, a surface. What we read in the

World is what Alfred Swan wants us to read, and that's all right. Alfred does his job as he sees fit. But there's a whole other life here, a civilization that's layered. And that's what I hear about on my walk to work and later in the courthouse. These things matter to me. They matter more than I can say. I was born here, grew up here, went to school here, practiced law here. Our friends are here. We've had a nice life here, you and I. Maybe the idea would be to get a new house, larger, with a better view of the lake. I've never lived anywhere else and never wanted to live anywhere else and that's why this is so damned hard for me, dear.

I'm not suggesting we move to California, my mother said. I'm proposing we move a few miles south. You'll still have your friends. You'll still know what's going on in New Jesper. They just won't live next door. Anyhow, maybe it's time to make new friends. The North Shore is—lovely.

We're too old to make new friends, my father said, an observation to which my mother did not reply.

You forget, Melody. I'm twenty years older than you are.

That's one of the things I'm thinking about. It's time for you to back off a little. Not work so hard. Take some time off.

It's giving up, my father said. You're throwing in the towel. You're surrendering to the barbarians.

They've won, my mother said.

I hate to believe that. I won't believe it.

Believe it, my mother said.

I see things from a different point of view, my father said. It's another way of life, being on the inside of things, and I feel responsible. I have a responsibility to New Jesper. I'm not sure you've ever understood that or appreciated it.

I understand more than you think, my mother said.

What I try to do is protect the reputation of the town, my father said. We're more than just the place where Walter Bing makes tennis rackets and it's sometimes seemed to me that everyone is trying to define us according to their own prejudices—big joke,

Oh, you come from New Jesper, where they make the tennis rackets, ha-ha. My aim is that we define ourselves. No one does that for us. We have a fine town here. It's a—moral town. I think that all things considered we handled the bad situations pretty well. Things could have gotten out of hand. We avoided publicity. Speculation was at a minimum. You hardly hear anyone talk about it, or if they do talk about it, they talk about it in private. It's out of mind, as it should be. It's old news. We—my friends and I—felt responsible, not for the situation but the response to the situation. How the matter was handled. We had a murder and an assault of the most appalling nature. We were on new ground, trying to deal with it. Do you see? I know the girl, especially, was a shock to you. Everyone was affected, like a death in the family. Thank God Alfred Swan decided to do the proper thing. My father paused then and I imagined my mother listening carefully and, this time, keeping her thoughts to herself. At any event she did not reply, and at last my father said, And what about Lee? His school.

This conversation took place on a Saturday afternoon in late October, a crisp autumn masterpiece of color, Cézanne's palette. My mother had made a pot of tea and she and my father were inside trying to bring their discussion to some worthy conclusion. I was outside on the porch, stretched full length on the glider, reading a story in the *Saturday Evening Post*. This was the story about the seaman home from the war who could not bear civilian life. He believed he was two people and neither of them fit in. Wherever he went he was an alien, unable to recognize himself in his civilian situation. I was well into the story but distracted by the brilliant surround and the conversation inside, fully audible through the open windows. Somewhere in the vicinity I heard a radio broadcast of one of the Big Ten games. My mother and father had forgotten I was there and I had the idea I had achieved a kind of invisibility. I heard my mother pour tea and then I heard her answer my father's question.

There are other schools, she said.

He's doing so well here, my father said, always on the honor roll. They think the world of him. Good athlete too.

He'll be on the honor roll wherever he goes, my mother said. His teacher told me he ought to skip a grade. He's way ahead of his class.

Skip a grade?

That's what she said.

He's old for his age, it's true.

My mother said nothing to that.

What about his friends?

He can find new friends too. Probably he needs new friends just like we do.

Have you asked him?

My mother laughed. Your son Lee can adapt to any situation. Don't worry about Lee. He's Mr. Adaptability.

I sat up at that. I had never thought of myself as adaptable. I was as reluctant to leave New Jesper as my father, though I had no bias against Chicago and its suburbs, unknown and therefore alluring. I even liked the Chicago newspapers and their remorseless quest for the novel and the scandalous.

He's growing up, my mother said. He doesn't go down below the hill anymore.

He doesn't?

No. Why would he? What's there for him?

I'll be damned, my father said. I told him not to, but I assumed he and Dougie Henderson would sneak down there anyhow, one more thumb in the old man's eye.

Down below the hill was just a boy thing, she said.

My father was silent and I heard the clink of a china teacup. He said, You're asking a lot of us.

I'm asking what's necessary for our family, my mother said, her voice rising. And in the dead air that followed I could hear the tide subtly turn, my father's presence receding. When he spoke it was with an unfamiliar wistfulness. He said, It's like giving up your own name. Throwing away your name and taking an alias, like a criminal.

My mother named three friends who had already left New Jesper and a fourth who was planning to, all of them moving to the North Shore. Lake Bluff, Highland Park. They had children too, and long family ties to New Jesper. This move is not unique to us, she said. No one wants to live in New Jesper anymore. It's dangerous. There's no future here. New Jesper is washed up.

If everyone leaves, it surely will be.

I don't have your loyalties, my mother said. Sorry.

Goodells have been here for four generations, my father said. That's a long time in this part of the country. It's like coming over on the *Mayflower,* something like that anyway. When my grandfather arrived from Pennsylvania as a teenager, the Sac and the Fox were part of the population. George Goodell was said to have gotten into a gunfight with one of them, shot him dead. That's the story I heard from my father, who didn't believe it but told the story anyway. My father gave a short laugh and said, I don't know. I honestly don't know. Maybe you're right. Maybe it's time, he said and his voice trailed away. He said no more, but I knew what he was thinking. He would no longer be the chairman of the Committee, or even on the Committee, with the mayor, the corporation counsel, the owner of New Jesper Dry Goods, the president of the bank, Walter Bing, and Alfred Swan. They would move along without him, ask someone else to take his place, probably another judge. The new chairman would be the president of the bank; and then I wondered if the Committee itself would dissolve without my father at its head. In any case he would no longer have a voice in the affairs of the town, the bond issues, the politics and personalities, the controversies large and small, and any bad situations that cropped up. These were civic undertakings with no reward except the satisfaction of helping the community. Keeping the lid on, as the mayor liked to say; beneath the lid was a multitude of bad situations. The satisfaction was richer because it was private, unacknowledged except in the *World*'s obituary when the time came. Living in a North Shore suburb my father would be merely another judge, nothing more. His influence would be restricted to that sphere. And one fine day he would awaken to discover a new streetlight across the way, and no one had asked his advice on its size or shape or its placement. He would be merely another taxpayer grumbling about the runaway cost of government. Bad situations would come and go without his counsel or even his knowledge. He would subscribe to the *World* and be unable to read between the lines and when he asked someone What's this about, anyway? the reply would be hesitant and off the point, Oh, it's nothing much, just another misunderstanding. It's been taken care of, Judge. Don't worry about it.

At the end of a long silence, my father exhaled as if he were rising from underwater. He said, Well, I hate the idea. Leaving the battlefield and shooting the wounded is the way I think about it, but maybe you're right. I suppose you are. You've always had charge of the house and I've never had cause to object. You've been a wonderful wife, Melody. Maybe it's time for a change of venue. But it's going to be a mighty big change for me, and for Lee too. And you.

I'll call a real estate agent tomorrow, my mother said. What's our budget?

My father must have been lost in thought because he did not answer.

The budget, dear, my mother said.

My father named a figure and that was that.

THAT SUMMER we moved south to the North Shore, my father supervising the move with his usual aplomb. He was making the best of it. My mother had found a gray shingled house with a wide front porch on a cul-de-sac a few blocks from the lake, causing my father to lament that he had lived his entire life within sight of Lake Michigan, its storms and its calms, its ice in winter and sailboats on the horizon in summer. The lake had always been a comfortable presence, a constant as he went about his business; the lake and the railroad anchored his life. Now to see the lake he had to climb to the attic, and what he saw there was the thinnest sliver of blue. It might as well have been a pond, six feet deep and a hundred yards wide.

But he adapted, we all did. The neighborhood was filled with brokers, lawyers, and advertising executives. On meeting them, their first comment was how long they had lived there, twelve years, fifteen years; they seemed to be saying, That's how long I've been rich. They were eager to specify where their children were enrolled at boarding school or college and these institutions were usually on the East Coast. My father took all this more or less in stride, making the best of things. His first North Shore act was to join a country club and revive his golf game, and in a few years he was a member of the board of governors and a few years after that he was chairman. As he knew he would, my father lost touch with the daily life of New Jesper and he fretted some about that, not knowing what was happening there. No one asked his opinion on civic matters, and when he himself inquired the answers were evasive, and so as time went on he arrived home at ever earlier hours, the better to squeeze in an afternoon golf game. New Jesper ceased to be part of his conversation, and if he ever thought about the death of the tramp and the assault on Magda Serra he gave no sign. Both matters slipped into the shadows, unresolved.

My mother took to the North Shore at once. She volunteered at the public library and in the course of her duties there she met many women whose advice she solicited regarding boys' schools in the vicinity. She made a list and we went calling, one school after another on the North Shore and beyond. By July our living room coffee table was piled high with brochures, all promising excellence of one sort or another, excellence of supervision, excellence of ends, excellence of means, with acceptance at a fine university as the payoff. Then commenced what my mother called "the winnowing," with three finalists. At my father's suggestion, she left the choice to me. So that September after we moved I left public education for good and enrolled as a sophomore at a private boarding school, the Ogden Hall School for Boys.

THE MARVELOUS APPROACH to Ogden Hall had not changed in thirty years, the long, winding drive past the railroad trestle through flat fields and the stand of firs to the great mansion house itself, most welcoming in its Georgian symmetry. On a bright autumn day the visitor almost expected to see women in long skirts carrying parasols and top-hatted men in spats, a tableau vivant; surely this could not be a boys' school. The solemn look of the house and its surroundings was reassuring, a coherent world well distant from the disorder and menace of the Cold War and the petty tyrannies and corruption of the Truman administration, not to mention the sordid depredations of the Chicago machine. Time enough for a boy to become acquainted with all that, adult responsibilities in the nuclear age and the mess in Washington; that time was not now. Meanwhile, the beautiful house and its grounds, the outbuildings and playing fields, offered a wholesome parenthesis in the rush and bother of events. All in all the placid yet fertile Illinois countryside was the ideal location for a school. So few distractions.

The headmaster, in his exploratory talks with parents, stressed the values of an earlier time. His favorite word was "straightforward." Ogden Hall proposed a straightforward approach to studies and sports, a straightforward approach to life itself, courtesy, honesty, and self-reliance, always giving one hundred percent. We allow our boys a certain latitude, the headmaster said. Ogden Hall is not a monastery. We have boys here who have seen quite a lot of life already, the consequence of irregular family arrangements, residence abroad, a broken home. Some of our boys have had difficulties in previous schools. Our aim is not to break their spirit but to channel it, working patiently to bring discipline from anarchy. Other boys have led sheltered lives of hearth-bound introspection, perhaps too hearth-bound and circumspect for the noisy modern world. Our object with them is to open things up, in the classroom and on the playing field. We at Ogden Hall believe in varieties of experience. One size does not fit all. Discipline in our school is straightforward: Keep faith with us and we will keep faith with you. We will never abandon a boy.

This talk, well honed over years of experience, was by turns inspirational and contradictory, high-minded and obscure. Its thrust was not to every parent's taste, and indeed more than a few of them departed the campus before the obligatory walk-around to inspect the dormitories, athletic buildings, classrooms, and scientific laboratories, always commencing in the formidable library with its leather-bound volumes of Balzac, Stevenson, and Dickens, a room that served also as an introduction to the school's benefactor, Mr. Tommy Ogden, not himself a scholar but a sportsman, civic-minded, now a gentleman of great age, an occasional visitor, always arriving incognito. Mr. Ogden never sought to cause a fuss. He never interfered with the school's operations except from time to time to make funds available for this project or that. The group's attention was then directed to an alcove on the west wall next to the fireplace, a bust of a lovely young girl whose deep-set eyes suggested turbulent emotions or high amusement, depending on the acuity of the viewer. She was Mr. Ogden's late beloved wife, Marie. The sculptor was the great Auguste Rodin, the bust carved from life at the atelier in Paris. It was said to be the last bust from Rodin's hand, as he died not long after. Marie had braved the howling winds of the U-boat-infested North Atlantic to present herself at the master's bench in the winter of the second year of the wretched war. Legend had it that it was Marie who insisted on the establishment of Ogden Hall. Let no expense be spared.

Alas, none of that was true. Marie did not journey to France until much later, and by then Rodin had passed on. The bust was of the Chicago girl who had gone with her sister and her mother to Rodin's atelier years earlier. In 1919 the girl died in the influenza epidemic and her heartbroken parents put the bust in a closet. They could not bear to look upon it. They thought it cruel and somehow contemptible to sell the piece and yet they did not want to conceal it in a closet, either. Herr Mackel learned of the family's dilemma and mentioned it to Tommy Ogden. Perhaps, Herr Mackel said—perhaps if you offered a donation to the Art Institute they would give it to you. Do it, Tommy said, do it at once, and he offered a price much less than he could afford but suitable enough. The Art Institute was delighted and some time later the bust appeared in the little alcove on the west wall of the library at Ogden Hall. Tommy was entranced by it, a superb example of the sculptor's art; the girl was even more alluring in marble than she had been in life. Absent any reliable information the legend had grown, accumulating details over the years. Tommy Ogden did nothing to disturb it, electing to regard the false story as his revenge on Marie. Besides, boys liked legends.

This discourse to parents and the tour that followed was made convincing by the presence of Headmaster Augustus Allprice, forty years old, six feet two inches tall with an athlete's build and an actor's self-assurance. In fact he had been an actor in his youth, playing summer stock on Cape Cod. The headmaster was also an accomplished yachtsman who had drifted into teaching by accident, a stint at Bennington followed by five years at a nearby prep school, where he had become a popular dean of students. A hitch in the navy early in the war was cut short by an inner-ear infection that affected his balance, a condition that recurred throughout his life. Augustus Allprice's one caveat on accepting the headmaster's post was that he be allowed to continue teaching his seminar on the novels of Herman Melville. Melville was essential to the moral and spiritual health of boys. Melville understood the world, its heartbreak and fatefulness, its obsessions, its fundamental enigma. Melville had seen a good part of it himself as a seaman. The headmaster's lecture on *Omoo* was open to any student who wished to attend, and at the conclusion he was always given a raucous ovation and the affectionate chant *Gus Gus Gus*. Augustus Allprice was careful to mention this lecture to parents, helpfully explaining—in case one or two of them had forgotten the text—that *Omoo* was the story of the aged vessel *Julia,* whose life below decks was reminiscent of a rowdy boys' school, practical jokes, high jinks, erratic behavior, tall tales, bad language, frustration. The *Julia* was bound from the Marquesas southwest to the vicinity of Tahiti—no one knew the precise destination because the navigator kept his reckonings to himself. He was suspicious of the crew; the crew was suspicious of him. The feckless captain is incapacitated by a mysterious fever, a mutiny ensues . . .

The headmaster's exegesis of *Omoo*—the word means "wanderer" in Tahitian—did not appeal to every parent. What had *Omoo* to say about the spiritual and moral health of boys? Some parents found a celebration of anarchy and a subversive political undertow, one tainted by a collectivist mentality. The captain of the vessel was a fool and a coward. The navigator was secretive and sly. Was this Melville a Red? The headmaster seemed condescending when he denied that Herman Melville was in any way a Red. Instead, he was a novelist, one of the greatest of the nineteenth century, one of the glories of American literature. He was a humanist. He was endlessly curious, something of an amateur botanist, a student of language, a close observer of art and architecture, an even closer observer of human nature in all its forms, a sensualist in his own way. The entire Pacific Ocean was not sufficient to quench his thirst for experience and the knowledge that came with it. There was always something fresh beyond the horizon line and a vessel at sea was a world unto itself.

Questioned on the suitability, indeed the relevance, of Melville's sea stories for teenage boys, the headmaster admitted he ran a risk. He could as easily read them *Treasure Island* or *Great Expectations,* great novels surely, but not on the same shelf as *Omoo. Omoo* mixed fact and fiction, memoir and history, and everything in between. He believed he had to take chances, roll the dice, because he felt it necessary to cut Ogden Hall from the common herd of midwestern boys' schools, not to mention the unspeakable citadels of New England—snobbish and cramped by tradition. We cannot compete on their terms because we are the skunk at the garden party. We are the nouveau riche among the aristocrats. Therefore we must set our own terms. We must wear our own hat, the headmaster said. He believed it essential to set Ogden Hall apart, assert an ambiance of adventure and risk-taking, something beyond the routine. An ambiance of tolerance together with an engagement with the world as it existed with the world that could be. Tomorrow will not be identical to today, at least I hope not.

Yes, the director of admissions allowed. Of course I see your point. Try to see mine. Our parents like the world they know as opposed to the world they don't know. The world they know has been good to them. They want affirmation, Gus. They want a positive pitch on things. Life for them is good, don't you see? And it will be good for their children as long as it *stays the same.* Our parents do not respond well to threatening atmospheres. You're driving them away, Gus. You're driving them pell-mell into the arms of the opposition. Your message isn't selling.

The tide may be turning, the headmaster said.

It's not turning, Gus. It's at flood. Why, we're about to get

President Dewey, for crissakes. And that's why your message isn't selling.

The boys like *Omoo*.

Some do. Most don't. Most boys don't understand your *Omoo*, Gus. They don't see the point of a life lived below decks. Why would anyone want to live in steerage? They're topside boys, don't you see? They're in the wheelhouse. They're the ones wearing the blazer with a crest on the pocket and the little billed cap.

It's good for them, the headmaster said.

We're beggars, Gus. Beggars can't be choosers.

This was Augustus Allprice's fourth year as headmaster, and each year had caused erosion of his idealism, a word he himself never used. He preferred "sanity." There were moments when he thought he was losing his mind, poised as he was between his dual roles of jailer and prisoner. He lived in a rose-colored cottage that had been the gardener's. The wages were good. He was vested in the pension plan. *Omoo* never lost its allure and each year he found a fresh facet of the book to stress and stress again. But he found the boys disconcerting, each year more arrogant and adolescent; they did not grow, they regressed. They seemed to want to emulate their fathers. They listened to the same music and went to the same films. They played golf. They dressed the way their fathers dressed. If they were allowed to vote, they would vote Republican. That was one more reason why Melville's life and work had meaning. The sea was life itself, both blessing and curse, never tamed. Gus wondered about Herman Melville's politics. There was every indication that he was a socialist. Certainly his sympathies lay with the crew; and yet Ahab, more obsessed even than Lenin, was his greatest creation. And Ahab had brought the *Pequod* to great grief. What would Melville do if he were master of Ogden Hall? Probably he would shoot himself in the head with a gun.

Gus thought often of Herman Melville, especially his last days in the customs house. He did not die a happy man. At the end of the working day Augustus Allprice retreated to his cottage and poured a glass of gin for himself and Anjelica and cursed the day he thought of schoolmaster as a profession. One glass led to another, and more often than not he and Anjelica would tumble into bed, rising only to prepare a late dinner or answer an insistent telephone call, one of the boys misbehaving, a fire in Marks dormitory or elsewhere on the campus. The Winston brat had beaten up a freshman. A girl had been discovered in a closet adjacent to the library. Would Anjelica have a word with her? Anjelica would not. Girl counseling was not in Anjelica's job description, and in fact her presence on campus was something of a scandal, though everyone agreed to look the other way. Augustus was feeling the wanderlust yet again and thought that this would be his last year at Ogden Hall. He wished to visit Patagonia and Anjelica was willing, indeed eager—anything to be quits with the school.

Augustus thought of Patagonia while formulating an answer to his director of admissions, a man much too old for his job. He, along with so many staff and faculty, had been recruited from an eastern school. Ted Weddle wished he were back there. He missed the village green and the movies on Saturday night and the Sunday matinee of the Boston Pops. His married children lived nearby. He missed the golden New England autumn. His wife hated the Illinois prairie, featureless and sullen, baking in summer and frigid in winter, not a hill for five hundred miles. Most of the faculty agreed. The students wished they were back east too, at Andover or Deerfield or one of the others. St. Paul's. In the East there were girls' schools nearby, Ethel Walker and Westover. Miss Porter's in Connecticut. They all thought they were too good for Ogden Hall and their parents agreed. Jesper, Illinois, for God's sake, to the back of beyond. But when a boy had been expelled from Choate, Groton, St. Mark's, and Middlesex the options were limited. Word got around, yet however far it reached it never quite got to Ogden Hall, the port in the storm. Many of the late-coming boys were from Chicago or the North Shore and their parents felt it was salutary that their sons be nearby, closely supervised by master mechanics. Refitted, the boy-vessel would be safely on its way, launched to a more acceptable climate, New Haven, for example, or Princeton. But first the boy had to graduate well. That was the reason for the investment in Ogden Hall—which, while not choosy, was not cheap, either. It did seem to Gus that everyone at the school wished he were somewhere else, New England or Europe or, as in his own case, Patagonia. A shame, really, because all these discontents resulted in a school that was nervously broken down.

Ted Weddle waited patiently for the headmaster to collect himself. He was often silent for minutes at a time, distracted by Herman Melville or the flamboyant Anjelica or his own anxiety. He was not a suitable headmaster, that was the truth of it. Gus Allprice's education was sporadic, some public high school in Maine followed by New York University and a transfer to Rutgers. He had published nothing. If he had a theory of education no one at Ogden Hall had ever heard it. He looked the part and that was that, six feet two and eyes of blue. One fact not generally known was that he was an orphan, a foundling. He had mentioned that one night when he was drunk. Ted believed that was the source of the headmaster's contempt for the parents he dealt with. Gus Allprice wished he had a father or mother who snapped fingers for him, making other people dance. No wonder he looked to Patagonia, one of the world's last frontiers.

He said at last, Perhaps not, Ted. Many do not buy what I'm selling. For the most part they don't care what I'm selling. They're buying a diploma and with the diploma matriculation into the Ivy League.

But Gus. Everyone's buying *something*—

The headmaster shook his head, observing that the boys were spoiled, negligent, and self-possessed even by the standards of upper-class adolescents. Their folly has been without consequence. They have never been denied satisfaction of any whim that came to them, the more outrageous the better. Their daddies are rich and wish only that their sons graduate well so that they can enter the family firm, the idea all along. Strange thing is, many of the boys are highly intelligent. Intelligent enough to see behind our out-of-date second-rate façade. I'm afraid we have contributed to their cynicism and in that one sense, and that one sense only, their cynicism could be said to be earned. Still, they're awful little shits, most of them. They've never done a day's work in their sorry lives. Parental inheritance. The parents are worse because the parents should know better. And that's why I read them *Omoo.*

This is not productive, Ted Weddle said. We're behind recruitment this year by thirty boys, that's a record at this time of the year. We need the little shits more than they need us, that's the truth of it. All of us here depend on Ogden Hall, Gus. Ogden Hall puts food on the table. In many ways we have a sweet deal here. Class size is what? Six, seven boys a class. Individual instruction, that's what we tell the parents. It would be a hell of a thing if we went broke.

We can't go broke, Ted. The Ogden millions.

We'll go broke if we don't have students.

No one will notice, the headmaster said, barking a laugh.

It's on your head, then.

Why did you come to Ogden Hall, Ted?

Oh, well, it's a long story—

I have time, the headmaster said.

I was old. My school, the one I had taught at for thirty-five years, wanted me out as director of admissions. They wanted a younger man who could relate to the students. The prospective students and the parents also. They used a word I had never heard before, at least in that context. They said I had the wrong image.

What did they mean by that?

Who knows? Wrong clothes, though my clothes were like everyone else's clothes, tweed jackets and flannel trousers. Striped tie. I think it was because I was old. I was sixty. Bald, as you can see. The students were young enough to be my grandchildren and that presented the wrong—image. Not the image of the school that they wanted, youth and vigor. They wanted something postwar.

Jesus, Gus said.

And I was careless. I had debts, not large in the scheme of things but more than I could handle. Millie had health problems, as you know. I didn't want retirement with debt on my mind. I needed to regroup so I came here, answered the ad in the *Bulletin*. That was three years ago and I'm no further ahead now than I was then. So this job means a lot to me, Gus.

Half our faculty has a similar story, the headmaster said. Had a falling-out with the administration. An incident with a student. An incident with a parent. Denied tenure, asked to move on with the promise of a glowing letter of recommendation to make things a little easier. They wanted to come to a new place, begin again. Everyone knows that Ogden Hall is flush with cash. So they arrive here with a bad attitude. It's not their first choice anyhow. Often it's not their second choice. They're like the ballplayer who's been sent to the minors; they believed it was only a question of time before they'd climb back to the Bigs. They'd be chairman of the English department at Exeter with an office of their own and a sabbatical every six years and the opportunity to pal around with a senator's kid. But they don't believe that anymore. Ogden Hall is the end of the line for them. We live in an atmosphere of disappointment and frustration. Resentment too, because everyone knows they've been dealt bad cards. Bad cards, bad luck, bad choices. The deck is stacked. *So* unfair.

Are you thinking about your message, Gus?

Not really, the headmaster said.

I wish you would.

Trouble is, we have no distinguished graduates. Not one we can point to and say, This is the face of Ogden Hall.

Give them time, Ted said. They're young. Too young to be chairmen.

You mean too young to appear on the cover of *Time* as the savior of American capitalism.

That's harsh, Gus.

Don't we have a ballplayer?

Young Flatley. Played a year with the Bears, got hurt.

Army general? Admiral? What about an actor?

None I know of. See, Gus. That's the advantage of the eastern schools, been around forever. At Andover when all else fails—the senators, the scientists, the ambassadors, the bankers and the writers and the Nobel Prize–winning economists—they haul out Humphrey Bogart. Who was expelled, by the way. And the school sent his parents a very friendly and consoling letter indicating that the young man, though perhaps not quite suitable for Andover, would do just fine in life.

I met him once, Gus said.

Bogart?

He's a brawler, the headmaster said.

That's not the point, Gus.

It would help if we had a gangster. Not Dillinger. Clyde Barrow, maybe.

What we have, Gus, is Tommy Ogden.

We're a young school, it's true.

Will you give your message some thought? It's a problem for me, Gus, because I'm the one catching the flak.

They were sitting in the headmaster's office, the former master bedroom the size of a squash court. Now Augustus Allprice stood and stepped to the window. The afternoon was dark, threatening rain. Clouds were boiling up in the west. Far in the distance he could see the railroad trestle. He stood in the window jiggling the coins in his pocket. He said nothing for a full minute, trying to imagine the Patagonian tundra as seen from a sailboat offshore, a springy thirty-eight-footer. Probably Herman Melville had visited Patagonia. He had been everywhere else, why not there? Gus thought he was probably miscast as a headmaster, as Melville was miscast as a customs inspector. Still, Melville did fine work in the later years of his life, living in New York and working at the customs house. And lost his audience because the later work was ambitious, complex and demanding. Gus watched a bright red Ford convertible motor up the drive, a pretty girl at the wheel. She stopped abruptly in a shower of gravel, tossed her head, alighted, and marched up the steps. She was someone's stepmother, what was the kid's name? Berry? Merry? He was one of the slugs with an IQ of 140 and an ambition of zero. A foul mouth and a bully in the bargain. The headmaster sighed, turning again to his director of admissions, waiting patiently.

The problem is Ogden Hall, Ted. The situation. The ambiance. The look of the place. The mansion, the gardens, the classrooms that look like bedrooms with their chandeliers and dressing rooms. After all these years you can still smell ladies' perfume. Ogden Hall doesn't look like a school. It never has. It looks like what it is, a huge country house converted to another use. It's a ship in dry dock. It has neither the look nor the feel of discipline or scholarship. Even the athletic fields look bogus. Parents and students come here for their first look and think that if they wait around long enough they'll hear a jazz band and a waiter will arrive with a tray of cocktails and a debutante will dance in from the wings. Listen hard enough and you can hear the thud of tennis balls on the clay court even though it's the middle of January, a foot of snow on the ground. God knows what thoughts the bedroom-classrooms inspire. We're shabby in these surroundings, faculty and students both, but mostly faculty because the students at least are wearing decent shoes. Things are out of place here and they always will be. Ogden Hall is misbegotten and that's the truth of it.

That's harsh, Gus.

My view, the headmaster said.

We have a beautiful facility. We're unique. All the parents admire Ogden Hall. The older ones even remember Tommy Ogden in his middle age. Tommy and Marie, a pair of scamps. Ogden Hall reminds them of their youth. You should hear the stories they tell, dinner dances in the garden, eight people at table. A full orchestra to entertain them, including the singer.

A tap on the door announced the headmaster's secretary, who looked in to say that Mrs. Berry was waiting. An urgent matter that requires your immediate attention, Gus.

Tell her ten minutes, the headmaster said.

She seems impatient—

Ten minutes, he repeated.

One last thing, Ted Weddle said. Anjelica was in the library yesterday looking for some book—

Balzac, the headmaster said.

She was wearing shorts again, Ted said.

It was warm yesterday. She often wears shorts.

And—what do you call those things?

Halter tops, the headmaster said.

Halter top, Ted said. Out of nowhere the library was suddenly crowded with boys. The little shits, all of them leering. It's not good, Gus. It just simply sends the wrong message. Anjelica is a very attractive young woman.

No kidding, the headmaster said.

The director of admissions flung up his hands in defeat. Can we continue this tomorrow? Same time?

The headmaster nodded in the direction of the portrait over the fireplace, Tommy Ogden in full hunting fig, camouflage forage cap pushed back on his head, canvas jacket, lace-up boots, a shotgun cradled in his arms. His face was tanned, his hair the color and texture of straw. An antlered stag lay at his feet, its pink tongue lolling and limp as an old sock. The headmaster said, They tell me that Tommy Ogden was an awful son of a bitch. Is, I suppose, since he's still alive somewhere. And I wonder all this time whether his live spirit haunts this school. Whether he floats from room to room, a kind of evil miasma whispering to the boys that it's perfectly all right to screw off your entire life. That life is better screwing off. That screwing off is as productive and rewarding an activity as any other. Screwing off, you need never take a backward glance and wonder what life's all about. Screwing off is its own reward. No one will care, and if they do care you can give them the finger.

Patagonia, the headmaster concluded, but by then the director of admissions was already easing himself out the door, promising to return the next afternoon. When he heard Gus murmur "Patagonia," Ted smiled gamely. Patagonia would not be the headmaster's solution. Patagonia was no one's solution, merely another wasteland at the nether end of a far continent, as pointless as an orchestra for eight people at table.

And one moment later Mrs. George V. Berry—given name Lucille, but Georgette to her friends—was in the room, offering a brisk handshake, settling onto the couch, arranging her legs, beginning to speak even as she settled. We have a problem with William, Augustus, or do you prefer Gus? William's father and I are not at all satisfied with his progress at Ogden Hall, or should I say lack of progress. Ogden Hall promises straightforwardness and individual attention but so far his father and I have received excuses and William one critical report after another, several of them incoherent. His grades are not as they should be and this is not the result we expect for our fifteen hundred dollars a year. The result we expect, and the result we will have, is an invitation for our son to join Yale's freshman class next year. Yale is the school my husband attended. It is his father's school as well,

and that would make William the third generation. Matriculation at Yale is my husband's wish. It is my wish. And it should
be your wish, Augustus. But we are not confident that anyone in
your school is looking out for William, who is very, very bright,
as we know from the Stanford-Binet. He is one of the brightest
boys in your school and yet his grade average is miserable. And
what I want to know is, what do you intend to do about it? Is
there a plan? I have spoken to his instructors one by one and I
must tell you I am not satisfied. His father is not satisfied. They
do not seem to us to be committed teachers. I see no zeal in your
faculty. I do not find a thirst to educate. As it happens, the boy's
father and I have identified the problem. William is bored. He is
bored because the work he is being asked to do is far, far below
his level. The boys in his class are dull. They have routine minds.
That's my husband's judgment and I agree with it. You have put
a racehorse into a stable of mules. That's the crux of it.

The headmaster's telephone rang then and he raised his hand
as he answered, spoke a few words, and replaced the receiver.

You were saying, Mrs. Berry.

We are wasting time, she said.

I would say so, yes.

So, if I may ask, now that you've been made aware of the situation. The mess you've made of things. What are your plans?

Georgette Berry had run out of gas. She had said everything
her husband asked her to say. She had hit every note. But this
headmaster had not responded, had not moved so much as an
eyelid. She could not tell if he had been listening carefully. He
was an attractive man but his blue eyes did have a faraway look,
as if they were not closely focused. He was well tailored in the
academic manner, wearing a blue button-down shirt and a soft
tweed jacket, patches on the elbows. The quality was good. He
had the bearing of a man who had been around. Someone had
told her he had worked as a seaman and she could believe it. He
had huge hands. The headmaster was rumored to have a woman

living with him in his house on campus, a cause for concern surely, though she herself preferred to be broad-minded, unlike so many of the midwestern hausfraus she knew. Georgette had grown up in the West, Los Angeles, and had run with the movie crowd. Love life among the movie crowd was never a cause for concern unless the story made the tabloids, an unlikely event because the industry employed an army of press agents who could make almost any story go away. They had a different view of things in the Midwest, even her husband. They were strait-laced on the North Shore. Her husband was always talking about some friend who had zipper trouble. She had to ask him what that meant, and when he told her, she laughed, apparently not the thing to do because he was angry with her and said it wasn't a laughing matter, there were children involved, not to mention reputations. Also, he had the view that Los Angeles was a kind of Gomorrah, even though that was where they met, George advising an actor friend of hers on a real estate investment. At first he seemed to fit right in with his good looks, his charm. He was rich. He was ardent. He had a beautiful golf game. When he proposed she accepted at once, although it meant that she had to move to Illinois. George was a different man in Illinois, his clergy-gray three-piece suits and wingtip shoes, garters on his socks, a fedora hat. George was a provincial, that was the truth of it. Illinois lacked vivacity.

Her thoughts were drifting now and she hauled them back in order to concentrate on the important matter at hand. The headmaster had not responded as she believed he should. He seemed to be waiting for something more from her, a fresh demand or insight. The silence lengthened and at last he smiled, but slightly. She did not find it an encouraging smile, this ambiguous twist of his mouth, as much frown as smile. He really did have the most startling pale blue eyes. Georgette wondered if she should invite him to dinner, him and the girlfriend. The girlfriend was said to be quite pretty. Something small and informal, ten at table, drinks and dinner on the terrace if weather permitted. In an informal setting her husband could press his case, make this Gus understand the stakes. The headmaster remained silent so Georgette repeated herself, something she hated doing because it meant she had not been listened to.

What are your plans, Mr. Allprice?

Plans?

Yes, plans. To resolve the situation.

Patagonia, the headmaster said.

I beg your pardon?

You asked me what my plans were. I am going to Patagonia.

For good?

I imagine not. For a while.

You are abandoning your post?

I cannot run a school from Patagonia.

No, of course not.

And I will be living aboard ship.

In Patagonia?

Offshore, the headmaster said.

Have you listened to anything I've said?

Of course.

But then—what about William?

I don't know. I have no idea.

I've never heard such a thing, Georgette said. She did not know how to proceed. Talking to Augustus Allprice was like talking to a statue. There was something—she sought the proper word—*militant* about him, and yet his manner was correct, his twisted smile conveying a kind of sympathy. George should have come himself. She was not cut out for confrontations with schoolteachers. She agreed to it only because she wanted young William out of the house and in faraway New Haven.

Someone will take my place, the headmaster said. You can talk to him.

I am talking to you, she said.

You must excuse me now, Mrs. Berry. I have a meeting with the faculty.

She looked at him as he stood, towering above her.

My husband will be furious, she said.

Is he often furious?

When he feels thwarted he is furious.

Will he take out his fury on you?

He might, she said. He is unpredictable. He is a lawyer.

I see, the headmaster said.

I knew we made a mistake with Ogden Hall.

There are other schools, the headmaster said.

Georgette found herself unaccountably on the edge of tears. This simple mission had turned into a debacle. Her husband had told her that the headmaster would fold when made aware of the facts. It was his job to accommodate himself to reality, to give help when help was required. Lay it out for him, George had said. He'll get it, believe me. Now she found herself adrift. But William is a *senior,* she said. There's no time to find another place for him.

The headmaster handed her the box of tissues that was always on his desk. When the telephone rang he turned his back to her and spoke for a minute or more, a problem in the chemistry lab. Someone had broken a vial and fumes were everywhere. The instructor had evacuated the room but the fumes remained and they were dangerous. Not life-threatening but nausea-causing, and it might be a good idea to get a doctor in to examine the boys. Yes, the headmaster said, and do it at once.

When he hung up the telephone he stood quietly looking at the portrait of Tommy Ogden, wondering if it was a faithful likeness. If it was, then Tommy Ogden had a bull's face, a long nose and heavy ears. Everything about him was bull-like except for the straw-colored hair. Gus wondered what provoked the sportsman into founding a school for boys and pouring millions into it. He never visited. He never inquired into its affairs. Gus had never met him and didn't expect to. He decided that Tommy Ogden was misbegotten. He stood looking at the portrait another minute, having utterly forgotten Georgette Berry. When he remembered he turned abruptly and saw to his regret that she was no longer in the room. The room was not in focus. Gus felt the inevitable headache gathering at the base of his skull. He put his fingers on the desk and lowered himself into the chair and sat quietly, his eyes closed. This was his first attack in months, the inner ear's revenge. The answer to it was simple. Patagonia.

BEFORE THE ADVENT of Augustus Allprice, Ogden Hall had suffered reversals, three headmasters in the first five years of its existence, four in the next fifteen. None of them were suitable. Two were alcoholic, one was a thief, another had falsified his CV. Two others had severe psychological problems, manic depression in one case, paranoia in the other. Bert Marks began to wonder if there was something pathological about schoolmasters, some gene that went haywire the moment a man assumed the title or aspired to one. They seemed perfectly reasonable men during the interview, in command of themselves and the material. Bert Marks looked on them as witnesses. Could they convince a jury? Did they make a good appearance generally, meaning well-spoken and well-groomed, decently tailored? Most important, did they go beyond their brief? Bert felt he had a musician's ear for the discordant statement, the one not entirely justified by the facts at hand. After the first two headmasters crashed and burned, Bert began to doubt his abilities. He had been hoodwinked as he had never been in his career as an attorney-at-law. He was not a trial lawyer but was often hired to be present at jury selection, so shrewd were his readings of character. These men seemed beyond reproach, solid citizens, men of achievement and integrity, yet they were charlatans. He had never hired a consultant in his life, and when a friend suggested he do so at once, Bert laughed in his face, it was ludicrous—and then he reconsidered. The first consultant turned out to be as addled as the candidate they were interviewing, a faux Englishman who claimed a background at Harrow and Cambridge and distant connections with the royal family. Easily checked, easily dismissed, along with the consultant, whose own credentials were not quite in order. Bert began to think he was dealing with a criminal subculture, nothing to do with the mafia but something altogether more sinister because it was so unexpected. He was interviewing schoolmasters, not second-story men or kneecap artists.

At last, admitting defeat, Bert Marks turned Ogden Hall over to his son and law partner, Bert Jr., with instructions to solve the headmaster problem once and for all. The need was urgent, for the school was on probation vis-à-vis its accreditation. Morale was low. Its reputation among other schools was rock bottom, a joke; the word Bert Jr. used was contamination. The North Shore boys set the tone—studied indifference, frequent references to the plebes among them, a mocking, supercilious attitude that spoke a kind of class warfare from the top down. Supercilious it certainly was, as Bert Jr. explained to his father, but also alluring. These boys were the canaries in the mineshaft of the modern world, the one that has brought Taft-Hartley and will bring Dewey. The North Shore and Chicago boys seemed much older in their three-button sports jackets and loafers—never was a shoe better named!—and a Lucky Strike in their mouths; the red and white bull's-eye logo had some mysterious erotic significance. Bert Jr. had the idea that the North Shore was a matriarchy, hence the boys' obsession with clothing—the shabbier the better during the day, but at night, out and about at roadhouses, they paid meticulous attention to what was on their backs. J. Press trumped Brooks Brothers and Tripp trumped both. They had strange relations with their parents, intimate with their mothers and distant from their fathers—unhealthy, Bert Jr. thought, a situation resembling some nineteenth-century Scandinavian melodrama. On weekends the boys drove to Chicago to listen to jazz music and drink cocktails, the fake draft cards certifying legal age supplied by an English instructor at fifty dollars a card.

That's one thing I've discovered, Bert Jr. said. And the other is that many of the instructors give private tutoring at seven dollars an hour. A boy isn't doing well because he's not completing his homework or is failing his examinations, usually both, and so he's tutored to bring himself up to snuff, and guess what, his mark at the end of the year is a respectable B-plus. Do you see the conflict of interest here? It's outrageous. I've stopped the fees. Not the tutoring. But do you know what? The instructors aren't tutoring anymore and this has caused hysteria among the parents because they are determined that their offspring receive any advantage on offer. Any conceivable advantage inside the rules or outside them. They'll force any issue. It's what they're brought up to do. Otherwise, what's the point of being rich? Ogden Hall is a bordello.

Bert Sr. was only dimly aware of class divisions. Class divisions were of no interest to him. He did wish his boy were a bit more worldly. All in all, Harvard was a mistake for any young man who wanted to make a living in Chicago. You had a client, and you served the client, and each case had its own ambiguities. No wonder they called law a practice. Bert Sr. did not think Bert Jr. an astute judge of human nature. If he was cut out for the law, it was as a judge, preferably on a supreme court somewhere, Illinois for example. You could tell in the wink of an eye how determined a client was. You could tell by his voice and his manner how far he was willing to go, and that, in turn, affected your advice to him. Class divisions didn't have anything to do with anything. It was idle chatter. He knew lawyers who lived on the North Shore and some were able and some were not. Very few of the North Shore lawyers were Jewish because of the wretched restrictive covenants concerning real estate, but that had nothing to do with class except in the broadest sense. It had to do with tribe. Fear was at the heart of prejudice, and fear was pri-

mal and not easily swept aside. It was hard for Bert Sr. to get his
mind around the customs of the North Shore. Why would anyone want to live on the North Shore when you could live on the
Near North Side? One train in the morning and another in the
evening, a bored wife and arrogant children, golf scores.

Bert was in his empty LaSalle Street office, his feet up, the time
late afternoon, Saturday. He often spent Saturdays at the office, a
quiet time to think and plan the week ahead. That meant worry-
ing about Ogden Hall, which was slipping slowly out of control.
Once or twice a week Bert had cause to wonder how different
his life would have been had Tommy Ogden not stepped into it.
An unlikely alliance surely, Bert an orphan boy deposited on the
steps of Hull House when he was five years old, a note pinned to
his jacket pocket written in Polish: *This is a Jewish child. Take
care of him.* In due course Bert was placed in a home with other
Jewish children and began to make his way in the world, finding
himself at twenty a law clerk in a small West Side firm. At thirty
he was managing partner. LaSalle Street was years away.

Of his origins Bert had no clue. He had the orphan's natural interest in the identity of his parents but was unable to learn
anything about them. His past was a blank slate, even his name
a gift from one of the jokers at Hull House: Marks, as in Karl.
He never knew where the "Bert" came from. His life began at
Hull House and when he thought of those who could trace their
families back three generations and more, he was amused. He
believed himself lucky to be alive, luckier still to have been able
to read law and become a lawyer. In those days you didn't need
a degree. Bert considered himself self-made, but even so he was
happy to make a substantial contribution to Hull House each
Thanksgiving Day.

He would never have met Tommy Ogden had he not gone
to a smoker at a West Side athletic club on a Friday evening
in June 1903. Two middleweights from the neighborhood, a
bare-knuckle affair, no referee. One of the middleweights was

a friend from high school who, Bert knew from experience, had a glass jaw and so he wagered twenty dollars with confidence. The smokers were raucous and there were always a few sports from the Gold Coast who showed up, drinking heavily and gambling recklessly. The sports lost money which was why they were welcomed, supplied with a white-aproned personal waiter, offered places at ringside. Bert collected his winnings and turned to the big man standing next to him, saying something sarcastic. The line, whatever it was, must have been funny, for the big man laughed and laughed, and he did not give the appearance of one who laughed often. They met again at the next smoker and the smoker after that, finding some weird, inexplicable affinity. They had nothing whatever in common, and whether for that reason or some other reason found each other companionable, one might almost say trustworthy. Soon enough, Tommy Ogden gave Bert legal business, mostly real estate transactions, adding to his spread at Jesper, a town Bert had never heard of. One night after listening to another shooting adventure and how content Tommy was at Ogden Hall, living alone without encumbrance, Bert mentioned a place he knew about, a place Tommy might find agreeable on those nights when living alone was itself an encumbrance. Villa Siracusa. Bert wrote the address and a name on his business card and a week after that he found himself on retainer and discovered that Tommy Ogden was not an ordinary Gold Coast swell but rich, with interests all over Illinois and the Midwest. He also discovered that these interests bored Tommy, who had a lust only for shooting and, it had to be supposed, the girls at Villa Siracusa. He needed someone to look after the interests and that was a full-time job, better exercised on LaSalle Street rather than in the corner office above a hardware store on Milwaukee Avenue.

Bert moved his family from an apartment way out Division Street to a maisonette on Pearson. He never mistook his arrangement with Tommy as anything but business, so in the evenings when he was invited to dinner at Ogden Hall he went alone, explaining to his wife, Minna, that he had a business meeting. She was happy not to be included. Minna was religious, and devoted to their son and two daughters. Every other weekend she visited her parents in Indiana, a faithful daughter. Tommy's language would have appalled her. She would not have understood his devotion to firearms. And later, when Marie came along, she would not have understood Marie. Bert's Saturday ruminations never came to a satisfactory conclusion. He never knew whether he had beaten the system or whether the system had beaten him. The conundrum was not cause for anxiety since the world was as it was. Instead, Bert Marks was amused. It did pain him to realize how much time had gone into Tommy Ogden's interests, among them his fantasy school, the endless recruitment of boys and men to teach them. His life would have been much, much different had he not spent so much of it on Tommy Ogden. But how different, in which way different, he was unable to say.

So four years ago Bert had told his son, Do something about Ogden Hall. And the something turned out to be Augustus Allprice, and he had worked out well. He was an adult, he listened to advice, and he worked hard. Ogden Hall regained full accreditation. The enrollment slowly grew to the point where there were even a few boarders from out of state and one forlorn lad from Canada. The faculty was still not sound but it was improving. Morale seemed on an upswing. The draft-card-supplying English instructor was denounced by a colleague, confronted, and forced to resign. This was a moment of high peril but Gus Allprice managed it all without a single line of publicity, a miracle in the circumstances, because the word had gotten out. Publicity would have killed the school—and Bert was obliged to reflect again on his ambiguous situation. The school dead, he would be a free man. But that was not the way he was raised or taught and so he took a deep breath and soldiered on, things on an even keel at last.

Then Allprice announced his resignation and Bert was besieged by parents, including that arrogant shyster George Berry, who, sensing vulnerability, was threatening a lawsuit. Bert had never heard of such a thing, litigation because your indolent offspring refused to do his lessons. Refused to open a schoolbook. Routinely missed examinations. Was abusive to his instructors, a sarcastic little bastard with a sneer to match. A meeting with lawyer Berry in Berry's office proved to be unproductive, and in due course the suit was filed and within weeks was dismissed, summary judgment. Plaintiff to pay all costs.

BERT MOTORED TO Ogden Hall for a final effort to salvage Gus Allprice, disappointed that Bert Jr. had failed to solve the problem and now had washed his hands of anything to do with Ogden Hall. Bert and Allprice had always gotten on, two adults trying to make the best of things, and the offer was most generous—an increase in salary, a four-figure bonus, an enhanced pension, reduced responsibilities. And it went nowhere. The headmaster was interested only in his forthcoming voyage to Patagonia.

He did have a few words to say concerning divisions among the student body. In the future it would be wise not to have quite so many boys who had so conspicuously and spectacularly failed elsewhere and looked on Ogden Hall as a seaman might look on Singapore or Papeete, whores and rum, agreeable shore leave following a punishing voyage, something they were entitled to, a reward for mischief. I'm afraid many of these boys are brighter than our instructors. But they are ignorant. They are undisciplined. They are agents provocateurs. They are bad influences on the school because their every action implies that the world is their oyster and proles will always be on hand to do the shucking. But some of them are worth saving, Mr. Marks. Worth trying to turn around because a few of them might actually amount to something beyond the possession of an English sports car and a willing debutante. They are of the ancien régime, yet we will have to bear with them for a time. The headmaster paused there, considering what he had said. He wasn't sure that Bert Marks was listening carefully, although that was what lawyers were trained to do. He said, These boys are resistant to learning. The unknown frightens them. They believe they are men of the world in training, but they are as sheltered as nuns. They have not learned or even thought about the thin line that divides pleasure from pain. They don't know it yet but they are standing on a beach that is eroding beneath their feet. Not soon enough in my view.

Bert Marks nodded thoughtfully. He had no idea what the headmaster was driving at. But he did know that it was often helpful to remain silent, as if he understood the situation, each nuance. However, not in this case.

Bert said, What?

The rich are always with us, the headmaster said.

Yes, but so what? They are what we have. They are what we have been given and so we must do what we can. We've undertaken a charge. We take their money, we agree to educate them. That's the contract, and while we know, you and I, that some of these boys are foolish and arrogant and therefore unteachable—we must try. Why can't you shape them up?

We are not taken seriously, the headmaster said.

It is your job to be taken seriously.

The headmaster smiled broadly. Yes, it is. And it is in that connection that I often think of Mr. Ogden.

That's not the point, Bert said.

So there we are, the headmaster said.

So it's a failure, Bert said.

Many of our instructors are old. They are disappointed with life. They have not aged gracefully.

That's not convincing, Bert said.

Nevertheless, the headmaster said.

You are not old. From my perspective you are in the prime of life.

It is time for me to move on.

But the job's not finished. You undertook to do a job. Signed a contract. And you have not finished the job.

The headmaster laughed. That's why, Mr. Marks.

All right. Listening to you now, I'm inclined to agree.

You should come teach here for a semester, Mr. Marks. Introduction to the Common Law, something like that. That would be an enlightening course, the rule of law as the foundation of a society. All citizens equal before the law. The headmaster watched the lawyer stir uncomfortably in his chair, his eyes fixed on the ceiling. You are well placed to conduct such a course, experienced, a man of the world. Our students would interest you. They have seen nothing of life. It is hard for many of them to see beyond the boundaries of this region. Your Middle West is a closed place. No visible horizon. I am not sure they understand the meaning of the law. The headmaster paused once more, trying to formulate one last thought. Also, this house and the grounds surrounding it are not suitable for a school. The aura's unfortunate.

Nonsense, Bert Marks said.

Live here a while, the headmaster said. You'll see.

I spent many hours in this house, Bert said, many, many strange hours. He remembered Marie Ogden's laugh, a kind of shriek. Tommy at the opposite end of the table pouring whiskey as the candles guttered. The servants, Francesca and the other one, parked along the walls as the conversation droned on. More monologue than conversation, now that he thought about it. Still, the evenings did have their moments. He remembered very well the night the Great War began, Tommy Ogden holding his information until the party broke up. Late summer 1914. They said the war was the beginning of the modern world. The nineteenth century died that summer. Not that it made much difference in Chicago, boom times once again, until the casualty reports came in from Belleau Wood and Second Marne . . . Bert looked up when Gus Allprice cleared his throat.

The headmaster had one last thought, this one concerning Herman Melville, his seamanship, his endless curiosity, his sympathy, his mastery of the English language, his profound understanding of the black heart, his exemplary life with its inevitable disappointments at the end. More than anything, the great writer was drawn to the unknown. The unknown was never to be feared or despised but embraced. The unknown was life itself. The unknown made men of boys. A noble soul, Gus Allprice concluded.

Bert quickly made his farewells, wishing the headmaster good luck in Patagonia and wherever else life took him. These sentiments were sincerely meant, but the lawyer was not certain the headmaster was all there. He had a dreamy look in his eyes, the sort of look Bert had long identified as anarchic. It was the look of a man who did not understand the world as it was. For God's sake, if what the boys and their parents wanted out of life was Yale, then get them into Yale. As for the rule of law, all men equal before the bar and so forth and so on, apparently this Allprice believed in a child's history of the world. Herman Melville might well have been a noble soul aboard his sailing vessel but this was Chicago, nobility measured in the length and width of a dollar bill.

In his car once again, returning to his LaSalle Street office, Bert had the idea that if worst came to worst the whole shooting match—as Tommy Ogden would put it—could be sold to the University of Illinois or Northwestern as a faculty conference center or secondary campus or retreat of some kind. Perhaps the State of Illinois would consider Ogden Hall an appropriate venue for a minimum-security prison or a mental hospital—and he would be rid of it. He knew whom to talk to and what to say and how much to promise and what would be returned to him, and at the end of the discussion the state would have a fine facility. He was too old to be chairman of the board of trustees of a damned school. Bert Marks believed he was a modern Sisyphus and Ogden Hall his stone. He had no understanding of schools or the people who ran them, Gus Allprice a case in point. Allprice was the man for the job until suddenly he wasn't, dreaming of a season in Patagonia. What was the point of it? What came after Patagonia? The man was a loon, and from the sound of him a left-wing loon, a crank. All his life Bert had sought clarity, and there was no clarity at Ogden Hall, merely an academic fog. Of course Tommy Ogden couldn't be bothered, Tommy away again shooting animals in East Africa, a cable the other day announcing that he had shot a bull elephant that his hunter had identified as a man-killer, nearly eighty years old, twelve-foot tusks. Tommy was living in a tent in the bush but from his description of the amenities it had more in common with the Ritz in Paris. He was eternally out of touch. Not that he would care if he were in touch. Tommy supplied the cash, someone else picked up the pieces.

Bert wondered if the headmaster had a point about Ogden Hall's "aura," if there was some malign spirit that had worked its way into the very fabric of the place. Perhaps Ogden Hall's history was too vivid to overcome or reconcile. Its books did not balance. That was what happened to the criminal financiers Insull and Yerkes. They overreached and were careless with their books. It happened all the time in America, creative destruction. There was hell to pay when books were out of balance, and not only in America. The French had never reconciled their revolution. Too many ghosts, a history too laden with contradiction and emotional violence.

His thoughts turned again to the inconclusive conversation he had had with Augustus Allprice. The only thing certain was that he would begin the search for a new headmaster at once, and that gave him a headache. Bert thought about that as he crossed the county line into Chicago, home at last, the familiar streets, the racket, the city's mighty industrial groan. Farther on, pausing at a stoplight, City Hall loomed large. The building was one of the least distinguished of the Loop, a coal bucket of a building, but appearances were deceiving because the coal bucket concealed the Hope Diamond—a political apparatus so costly, so exquisite, so multifaceted, so blinding in its flash of fire, that it had secured tenure for scores of Illinois political scientists over the years. And still they had not driven a stake into the heart of things. What they did not know about the politics of the city would fill Wrigley Field. Of course no one knew it all; in its dash and complexity it resembled the Dark Continent. God knows there were ghosts aplenty in Chicago but the city was beautifully reconciled, its books immaculate. You walked into City Hall and you knew exactly what had to be done, where the payments went and to whom and what was expected in return. That was the beauty of the city, its clarity—and balance. The ghosts were part of the balance. Everyone knew they were there but did not speak of them. Chicago was a place where a man could go about his business in safety and comfort knowing precisely what was what, unlike the anarchy and fatigue that defined Ogden Hall. Bert considered again the French Revolution, its aspiration, its zeal and its tumult, its long reach. The French Revolution was in some fundamental way unreconciled. Probably its meaning would never be reconciled, and with that thought Bert Marks stared once more at City Hall, a kind of Versailles. Versailles married to the stockyards, except in Chicago you knew where you stood. He decided that Ogden Hall's Robespierre was Marie Ogden.

AUGUSTUS ALLPRICE'S last day on the job came on a Thursday, mid-June. The campus had emptied for the summer holidays, except for those faculty members who could not afford to go away; and they were planning the annual end-of-term party. Gus was packing away his photographs and personal files, the memorabilia that littered his desk—two pieces of scrimshaw, a mariner's shackle, a brass compass, the business end of a harpoon which acted as a paperweight, a two-pen desk set given him by Anjelica, a miniature ivory death's-head purchased in an open-air market in Baltimore. He was whistling to himself, keeping tune with *La Bohème* on the portable phonograph, wondering what he had to show for his four years at Ogden Hall. He had probably saved the school from desuetude, no small thing. Of course he was as miscast as a headmaster as Ogden Hall was miscast as a school for boys. He had known that from the beginning and yet had stayed on. He had nowhere else to go until Anjelica had suggested Patagonia, and he knew at once Patagonia was the place.

When he heard a soft tap at the door the headmaster called out, Come in! But he did not turn around at once because he was deciding what to do with his Bert Marks file, six inches thick. He considered leaving it for his successor, marked with a note, Open Only in Case of Emergency, but decided against it. He threw the file into the already overloaded wastepaper basket.

Sir?

Yes, he said and turned around.

Lee Goodell, sir.

Of course, Lee. What can I do for you? Not much, I'm afraid. Your captain is leaving the bridge. He smiled at the boy, one of his favorites. Inquisitive, one of the North Shore crowd but something of a loner. Lee Goodell was old for his age, meaning he would not be out of place in a university. He was an excellent student, one of the boys who had no idea what he would do with his life but was patient about it. He kept his eyes open. He had never been in the headmaster's office and now he stood openly staring at Tommy Ogden's portrait.

Is that him, sir?

Yes. Mr. Tommy Ogden. Our founder.

There are stories about him. They say he comes here and looks around, never says anything. Goes away.

That's about the size of it, the headmaster said, craning his neck to look at the portrait. I've never met him.

Never?

Not once, the headmaster said. What are the stories you hear?

That he's big. Kills wild animals for fun. And that he founded the school on a bet. The stories vary on whether he lost the bet or won it. Nobody knows. And that he leads a reclusive life. He's got some farm up near Quarterday but he isn't often there. They say he has one house in Idaho and another in East Africa, and most of the time he's in mourning for his wife, Marie. Are any of those stories true?

Some of them. I've heard the story about the bet but I don't believe it. Also, I think he keeps the mourning under wraps.

He's a sort of legend among the students. Everyone wants to be like Tommy Ogden because he always does as he pleases. And of course he's rich. Lee Goodell stopped there, perhaps fearing that he had already said too much, except that Headmaster All-price was smiling as he looked at the portrait of Tommy Ogden in hunting gear. Lee said, He's so rich no one can tell him what to do. He does what he feels like doing when he feels like doing it. He's invulnerable.

Everyone's hero, is that it?

I think so, the boy said.

Yours too?

Lee thought a moment. I'd have to meet him. See what he's like.

A sensible thought, the headmaster said. Sit down, Lee. What's on your mind besides Tommy Ogden?

We're sorry to see you go, sir.

Miss *Omoo,* will you?

It was a great performance, sir. We all looked forward to it. Are you really going to Patagonia?

Leaving next week, the headmaster said. Staying a year.

I looked it up in the atlas. It's a long way away.

Very long way, Lee. You can't go much farther.

Then what?

Who knows, Lee. Who knows.

Gosh, the boy said.

Now. What's on your mind?

I've come about the football team.

Yes. Distressing, wasn't it?

Very, sir. Eight straight losses this year. Eight straight losses last year. That's the league record, by the way. No team has ever lost sixteen games in a row. It's never happened before. The final home game we had five students in the stands, our loyal supporters. Even they were booing.

I remember, the headmaster said.

They booed even when we scored a touchdown. The only one we scored. The other team scored six and in the fourth quarter they put in their second-stringers, freshmen and sophomores. They would have used the water boy but he wasn't suited up.

Still, you never surrendered. The headmaster gave an encouraging smile, wondering all this time where young Lee Goodell was headed.

Oh, we did, sir. Actually we did. We gave up. Coach gave up. No one cared. We went through the motions, lined up, made the snap, ran the ball, threw the ball. But we were sleepwalking. This year is the worst year of my life.

I'm sorry, Lee.

You were always there, even the away games.

I missed one game, Lee.

Yes, you did. We all noticed.

Trustees meeting. The business with the chemistry lab.

We understood. You were in a jam.

Putting it mildly, the headmaster said.

We were outclassed.

It's not a good feeling, I agree.

And we threw in the towel.

The headmaster nodded.

That's what people do around here, throw in the towel. It's the expected thing.

I'm afraid so, the headmaster said.

But next year will not be like this year or last year.

I hope not, the headmaster said, sneaking a look at his watch.

We have a plan, sir. The whole team, or the part of it that's returning. We have a scheme. We've been working on it for the past month and most all the pieces are in place. Hopkins has a grandmother. And the grandmother owns a place up near Fish Creek in Wisconsin. Big place, not as big as Ogden Hall but big enough. She's never there in summer. The idea is to go to her place in August and train. Serious training, workouts all day long. Thing is, and this is the important part, she has a man to look after things when she's not there, a sort of caretaker. And he used to play for the Packers. He was a lineman, big as a house. And the point is, he's agreed to train us. And teach us how to play the game once we get in condition. He really knows what he's doing. Lee leaned forward in his chair, his hands cupped as if he were receiving the snap from center. He played five years for the *Green Bay Packers,* sir. Svenson is his name. Do you remember him?

The headmaster shook his head. He was never a fan of the professional game.

He's the real thing, sir.

Wonderful idea, Lee. I wish you godspeed.

There's a problem, sir.

Tell me the problem.

Some of the boys can't afford it. Two of our linemen are from Michigan. The quarterback is from downstate Illinois. There are a few others, live far away. I wonder if we could get some financial aid from the school, transportation costs, one thing and another.

I'll leave a note for the incoming head.

We know who it is, sir.

You do?

Hopkins's grandfather is on the board of trustees. It's Mr. Weddle.

Ted Weddle?

Yes. An interim appointment. One year.

I'll be damned, the headmaster said.

The trustees are out of touch, Lee said. They don't know anything about schools, particularly this one. Hopkins says his grandfather is gaga, thinks Dewey is president. Because they're out of touch they think Mr. Weddle is the solution, but Mr. Weddle doesn't care about the football team. To him the football team is an embarrassment and ought to be disbanded. Our football team damages the reputation of the school. He'd like to devote the sports resources to tennis and baseball. And tennis is a game for weenies, which this school has more than its fair share of, the boy said.

Now, Lee, the headmaster said.

Dewey, the boy said.

The headmaster smiled at that.

It isn't much money, Lee said. Five hundred dollars would do it, for transportation and so forth. And a fee for Mr. Svenson. We wondered if you could slip it into the budget, your last official act. We can't have another season like this one and the one before. I know we won't get any support from Mr. Weddle. I'm surprised you didn't know about his appointment. It happened yesterday.

I heard a rumor, the headmaster said. I chose not to believe it. I've been out of touch these past weeks.

Is it a hard job, being headmaster?

Not hard. It's not commercial fishing out of New Bedford or

Gloucester. It's inside work, no dirty hands. It's demanding in its own way.

Parents on your back all the time I suppose.

The headmaster smiled. I'll see what I can do about your money. Ted Weddle owes me a favor, though he may have forgotten.

Funny he didn't say anything to you.

Isn't it, the headmaster said.

The headmaster leaned back in his chair, his hands clasped behind his head. He looked at the boy and then out the window at the tennis courts, the sun so bright it hurt his eyes. A doubles match was in progress, the football coach and his wife, the French instructor and Anjelica, everyone crisp in tennis whites. The coach was serving to Anjelica, serving and leering at the same time while his wife gritted her teeth. Anjelica did little bunny hops as she awaited the serve and it was not surprising when the coach's serve went wide. He was an oaf who had come to Ogden Hall from some school in Ohio, an indifferent instructor in German and coach of the track and football teams. He and young Lee Goodell did not get along, the usual disputes about playing time and game plans. Lee was reckless, the coach said, always pushing the other boys. He was small for his age, five feet eight or so, with every possibility that he had reached full height. The coach believed that his size accounted for his recklessness. He was fast enough, and tough, but all the same you wanted to turn away when one of the larger linemen caught him up and threw him to the ground like a rag doll. But the boy had sand; he always got up and trotted away, saying something insolent over his shoulder. He was not good with instructions, always preferring to go his own way. The last game of the season Lee was thrown to the ground so often and so violently that the coach took him out of the game early in the fourth quarter, fearing that Lee would be injured and he himself be blamed, as coaches always were when things went the wrong way. In any case, the game was long lost. The headmaster arrived in the closing minutes and did not take a seat but stood to one side, watching the rout. He remembered Lee sitting apart from the others at the end of the bench, his chin in his hand. Gus had always believed that a man learned more from defeat than from victory because defeat usually came with a lesson. The boy did look inconsolable. If there was a reward it was not apparent that day. It was also true that boys paid too much attention to the metaphorical apparatus of sport. Sport was not life, except the lessons learned from defeat.

The headmaster turned his eyes from the tennis court just as Anjelica charged the net and wrong-footed the coach's wife, match concluded. She glanced up to his window to see Gus's thumbs-up.

I hate to trouble you with this, Lee said.

It's no trouble.

If you can find the money it would mean a lot to me and Hopkins and the other boys. Also, I should tell you we are not inviting the coach to Fish Creek. He's a terrible coach and no one likes him.

He does his best, the headmaster said loyally.

Yes, he certainly does, the boy said with a wisp of a smile.

Remind me again about Hopkins, the headmaster said.

He's been everywhere before he got here. Eastern schools, at least three of them. Is there a school called Groton?

It's pronounced Grah-ton, the headmaster said, not Growton.

Well, that was one of them. I can't keep them straight. Hopkins's family has plenty of money but he doesn't want to ask them. He and his father are on the outs. They barely speak because his father disapproves of his girlfriend, Willa. She's twenty. Hopkins says she wants him to marry her, but he doesn't think he will. A lot of boys are on the outs with their fathers.

But not you, the headmaster said.

We get along fine most of the time.

Are you planning to become a lawyer?

Never, the boy said. Sitting in an office all day long reading case law, it's not for me. My father is a judge and his father was a judge and that's enough law for one family, don't you think? Maybe you have an idea, sir. Everyone else does.

Sailing ships, the headmaster said.

I get seasick, the boy said.

You can get over seasickness, Lee. What's it you want to do?

The boy moved his head back and forth and didn't say anything for a moment. Sculpting, he said finally. I like to sculpt. I like abstract work. I'm working on a head now of Coach Birney. He doesn't know it's him. It doesn't look like him. But it's him.

I wish I'd had a chance to see it.

You can see it, sir. It's in the art room. Look through the big window, you can't miss it. The head's shaped like a football.

The headmaster laughed, rising to shake hands. It occurred to him that this was probably the last time he would meet with a student. Maybe this one would amount to something and become the face of Ogden Hall—Ogden Hall's Apollo or Bogart or Roosevelt or Bix Beiderbecke or Ahab. He said, Good luck, Lee. I'll see that you get your money.

Thank you, the boy said. He looked out the window and added, Isn't that Miss Anjelica?

Yes, it is. In person.

Everyone likes her, the boy said.

I'm glad to hear it, the headmaster said.

May I ask you a question?

Sure, the headmaster said.

Are you and Miss Anjelica married?

No, Lee. We are not. What made you ask?

Gosh, the boy said.

AFTER THE GAME had ended, after the cheering, after Hopkins had carried him around the field on his shoulders, after the stands had emptied and the team had retreated to the locker room, Lee Goodell stayed behind to savor what there was to savor in the emptiness and silence of the field of battle. The sun was low in the November sky. He needed a few moments alone to allow his emotions to settle, this final game and the glorious Wisconsin August and the opening game and the following six games, all victories, the first undefeated season in any sport in the school's history. There was even a photographer and reporter from the *Chicago Daily News* present to record the finale of the Cinderella Season. Mr. Svenson had driven down from Fish Creek and was given an honorary place on the bench, a courtesy the coach seemed to resent. After the game Mr. Svenson had shaken hands with the entire team and then slipped away for the long drive back to Fish Creek. The old man had tears in his eyes. Most everyone did. By then the mood was subdued, as if the players could not quite believe what was in front of their eyes. That, and the knowledge that the game was over. The season was history. Tomorrow was any ordinary Sunday.

Now Lee stood alone on the sidelines near the bench, replaying the game. Hopkins's two touchdown runs, his own plunge over right tackle, leaning left as Mr. Svenson had told him to do and at the last moment pivoting right, arms pulling at his legs and body, pulling at the ball, and at last the arms falling away and he was free between the goalposts, on his feet. He had looked up into the stands to see Willa, Hopkins's girlfriend, dressed in a bright yellow sweater under a short mink jacket, chain-smoking Lucky Strikes while she jumped and jumped again, her hair flying. Point after touchdown wide, but it didn't matter because they were two scores ahead with only a minute or so to play, and still Willa cheered and cheered. The other team lost heart as they themselves had lost heart the year before, glum faces and bickering between the line and the backfield. Their coach was infuriated. The other team became timid and you could almost smell the discouragement. Lee sat on the bench trying, and mostly succeeding, to remember every play in every series and the moment before the game when a messenger from Western Union knocked on the door of the locker room to deliver a yellow envelope addressed to Lee Goodell but meant for the whole team, a florid Melvillean exhortation ending with the last few words of *Omoo*—". . . and all before us was the wide Pacific"—and signed simply "Gus." Everyone cheered and then sent up a full-throated chant: *Gus Gus Gus*. That would stay with him, along with his own score and the cheering and mink-jacketed Willa, her hair flying as she jumped.

Lee knew he should join the others but was happy being alone in the chill of autumn, the season ended. He was filthy, his jersey caked with dirt. His elbows were skinned and his arms smeared here and there with blood. One of his shoes was missing a cleat and his feet hurt. But he felt clean and wondered how many times in his life he would set out to achieve an impossible thing and actually succeed. Probably not very many times. Maybe never again, the approximate probability of being struck twice by lightning. Everyone had a ration card with only so many stamps for impossible things. All the same, today proved you could do it at least once in your lifetime and once was never enough. He did like the idea of twenty-year-old mink-jacketed Willa in her seat on the home-team side of the field. He remembered reading somewhere that men went to war because the women were watching. He saw Hopkins look often into the stands and after each touchdown essay a little strut. But it would be a mistake to make too much of a football game, four downs to a series, four quarters of fifteen minutes each—iron-bound requirements, the opposite of life itself. If such a day ever happened again in his life it would not take the same form. That thought took the edge off. Lee felt his elation age as a tree ages, branches bare except for brittle leaves. He wondered if all shooting stars took the same form and decided they did not, except to the naked eye from earth.

He took a last look around, not thinking of anything much except the tree branches stark against the darkening sky. What, he wondered, would he remember of Ogden Hall in the years to come? Gus Allprice certainly, and *Omoo* and Hopkins and his Oldsmobile and the school nurse who smelled of disinfectant that the older boys insisted was whiskey, and indeed the nurse often laughed for no reason at all and was clumsy with the thermometer. He supposed that the memory that would stay with him forever was afternoon study hall in the vast library. He arrived early to take the same seat each time, the one in the front row opposite the alcove next to the fireplace, Marie Ogden as Maître Auguste Rodin saw her. Her hair was piled atop her head, luxurious, promiscuous, immodest. She wore a half smile and no matter how many times Lee sketched the smile he could not duplicate what was in front of his eyes. Her nose was slightly turned up, indisputably the turned-up nose of a young girl caught in a moment of intense reverie. Lee thought Rodin found an entire life in his bust of Marie Ogden, what had gone before, what was present now, and what would be in the future. She had a conscience, but it was her own conscience. Lee wondered what she would be like to know intimately. But he knew the answer to that. The figure changed as the days lengthened, the bust in deep shadow in the fall and winter, coming to light again in the spring and early summer. In the darkest days of January and February Marie Ogden looked almost matronly, but the years fell away again in April and May. Often the study hall proctor asked him what he was doing, so deep in thought, and Lee replied he was puzzling over a math problem, differential calculus, and since his grades were always honors the proctor did not press the point. Lee suspected that Marie Ogden would be with him for the rest of his days and in that supposition he was not wrong.

Lee noticed a long black car idling well back of the far goal-post, hard to see in the shadows of the trees. The old railroad trestle was in the distance. Lee had seen the car parked there before the game and then forgot about it, an open Cadillac of the sort that carried President Roosevelt on his political campaigns. The occupant of the rear seat was smoking a cigarette in an ivory holder as the late president did, his arm draped casually over the door. The Cadillac's headlights winked on as Lee looked at them. He picked up his helmet and walked the fifty yards downfield, kicking at the torn-up clods of earth as he went. He watched a chauffeur alight from the front seat and stroll to one of the nearby oaks and stand there as if on guard duty. The passenger in the rear seat was an enormous man with a leonine head, mostly bald. He was wrapped in a raccoon coat. He was bigger even than Mr. Svenson. His face was deeply lined, pink in the chill of late afternoon. Dusk was coming on fast. The passenger held a silver flask in his hand. The hand shook a little when he poured whiskey into a cup resting on the attaché case next to him. The old man paused a moment, then drank it off and smiled crookedly. His teeth were long and yellow from nicotine. The smile came and went in an instant, replaced by a grimace as if he felt sudden pain.

He said, Congratulations.

Lee said, Thank you.

What's your name?

Lee Goodell, sir.

You run well.

Thank you. I had good protection.

A team effort, is that it?

Yes, sir, it is. Lee heard belligerence in the man's voice, an undertone of casual menace. His voice was thick.

An unexpected season, wasn't it?

Yes, sir, yes it was.

The best kind, the man said.

It feels pretty good now, Lee said.

It'll feel even better tomorrow.

Do you think so?

Know so. This sort of thing ages well. Keep it to yourself, though. Don't tell the world. The world doesn't give a shit. He poured another shot of whiskey and drank half. Do you know who I am?

No, Lee said. He heard the belligerence again.

I used to live here.

Lee looked again, the ravaged face suddenly familiar. He had seen it before but could not recall where.

I'm Ogden.

Lee could only nod but his eyes were wide as if he had seen a ghost. Mr. Tommy Ogden had never been observed on campus, though it was known that he paid occasional visits. According to school lore he never spoke to anyone. He never called ahead. If he was displeased with anything, the condition of the library or the tennis courts or the formal garden, he made his displeasure known by letter, registered mail. Lee remembered the portrait in the headmaster's office, Tommy Ogden as a much younger man. Gus Allprice had pointed at it and said with deep sarcasm, Our founder.

I used to hunt these fields.

Hunt?

Shotguns, Tommy Ogden said. Before that an air rifle. Deer used to gather right here on your football field, a herd of fifteen, twenty deer, big ones. Ducks too. Mallards all over the place. Do you ever see deer?

Not very often, Lee said.

Place used to be filled with deer.

I think they've gone away, Lee said.

I suppose they have. The damned suburbs crowding everything out, even the animals. Where do you come from, Lee Goodell?

New Jesper, Lee said. But we live on the North Shore now.

Plenty of North Shore boys here, aren't there?

Yes, sir.

But I suppose none of them are on your football team.

Lee thought a moment. A few, he said.

Too bad, Ogden said. It's good early in life to experience success. It puts you on the right track for later on, when it counts. You don't learn a god damned thing from defeat. That's the wrong track and defeat stays with you and becomes the expected thing. It's a chain around your neck. Remember that.

Yes, sir, the boy said.

It's why I like shooting.

I can see that, the boy said, but the truth was he didn't know what Mr. Tommy Ogden was driving at. His voice was thick and his teeth clicked when he spoke. Rememberclick thatclick, as if he had something stuck in his throat. His eyes moved warily left and right as Lee imagined a gambler's would. Lee had never met anyone like Tommy Ogden, even the fathers of the rich boys at school, the ones who seemed so—preoccupied. Of course Mr. Ogden was much older and widely experienced in the world. He did not wear his years lightly. Apparently he had gone from success to success in his own life and the successes had marked him.

Lee took a step closer to the car and saw that the old man had a wool blanket around his waist and legs. The air grew colder as the light failed.

You see that, do you?

I'm trying, Lee said.

Do you shoot?

No, Lee said.

Learn. Learn at once.

I owned an air rifle, Lee said. I haven't used it in a long time.

It's a skill that lasts your whole life. Start with birds and work up to animals, deer and the like. I killed my first tiger when I was twenty-two. I have killed many since. Beautiful beasts.

That's dangerous, isn't it?

It can be. You can't lose your nerve.

My father gave it away, my air rifle.

Why would he do that?

He didn't want it around the house. I think that was the reason.

Ogden grunted. What does he do?

My father? He's a judge.

Ogden nodded, giving a long sigh. Apparently that explained the disappearance of the air rifle.

I didn't mind, the boy said.

You should have, Ogden said, moving his shoulders in irritation. After a moment he said, I paid for your training camp.

Lee smiled broadly. You did? We would never have had our undefeated season without the training camp and Mr. Svenson. Thank you. If you'd like to meet some of the guys I can get them out here. They'd be honored to meet you. It wouldn't take a minute—

No, Ogden said in a loud voice. With trembling fingers he unscrewed the cigarette from its holder and flipped it away. He tapped the holder on his attaché case, a steady tattoo. He looked up and said, You caused me trouble with your undefeated sea-

son. You brought me unwanted publicity. I am a private man
and have always been a private man going about my business in
my own way. I was interfered with. I read articles about myself
in all the papers, including the god damned *Daily News* and the
Tribune, because I founded this school and gave my name to it.
Reclusive Sportsman. Great White Hunter. Filthy-Rich Man of
Mystery. They had photographers at the front gate of my house.
They telephoned me at all hours with impertinent questions to
which they expected answers. They tried to approach me here
in my car this very day but my driver Edgar backed them off.
Tommy Ogden barked another laugh. Edgar frightens people.
Edgar was a professional boxer at one time. I was a prisoner in
my own house until I threatened to sue them and keep them in
court for the rest of their miserable lives, bankrupt them if need
be. Publicity brings grief to people, reporters poking around in
your private affairs and all the time citing the people's right to
know. But it has nothing to do with the people, it has to do with
them, selling their god damned papers. You'll learn this someday—it's a scourge. Tommy Ogden settled back in his seat and
muttered something, moving his legs and sighing. That's what
your undefeated season did for me. Finally I said to hell with it
and went out west to shoot elk. Got back yesterday. The cigarette holder continued its monotonous *tap tap tap.*

Lee had no answer to that.

Swine, Ogden said.

Gosh, Lee said.

So you can think about that.

I'll try, Lee said.

Where are you going to college?

University of Chicago, Lee said.

There is no football team at the University of Chicago, Ogden
said. They abolished it. A distraction, according to the idiot
chancellor.

I'm too small for the college game, Lee said.

Never think that, Ogden said. That's defeatism.

But it's true, the boy said. He stood aside to make room for the chauffeur Edgar, returned from his vigil.

Ogden shook his head, unconvinced.

I intend to study the Great Books, Lee said.

Waste of time, Ogden said.

Not a waste of time, Mr. Ogden. I've read Stevenson and Balzac in your library. I've learned about Rubempré and Cousin Bette and Old Goriot and the others. *Goriot*'s pages were uncut, so I am the first student to read the book. The first anybody, for that matter. I cut the pages myself with my penknife. I have also been reading James Joyce, but I don't understand a word of *Ulysses* and neither does my instructor, but he won't admit it. I prefer the short stories. My other interest is not a waste of time, either. Sculpting. Sculpting in granite and marble. The boy realized he had spoken sharply, something he had rarely done to an adult and something he would not have done before today. He felt entitled to do it. He didn't see why the old man's contemptuous statement should rest unchallenged. Probably Mr. Tommy Ogden had not been challenged enough in his life. Lee believed he had an obligation to put down a marker. If Ogden didn't like it, let him say so.

But the old man seemed not to have heard.

He said, They'll take everything if you let them.

Lee said, I beg your pardon?

The newspaper swine. They take your photograph as if your face is their property and therefore public property and it's not— it's your property. You own it. Don't forget that.

Lee nodded as if he understood. He wondered if Ogden was drunk, because he poured another cup of whiskey and drank it off. He wondered if the old man was dissatisfied with his own face or somehow ashamed of it. You offered your face to the world every time you walked down a city street. Your face wasn't private like a diary or the contents of your wallet, except that to

Tommy Ogden apparently it was. Lee was about to make a retort but remembered that Mr. Ogden was the cause of the undefeated season. Lee would never have known but for this chance encounter. The old man deserved respect.

I approve of your sculpting, he said suddenly.

You do?

Are you going to keep on with it?

I expect to, the boy said.

Call me when you have something to show. Better yet, call this number and use my name. He produced his wallet and extracted a card and handed it to Lee. Mackel Fine Arts, with a Chicago address and a telephone number. He said mildly, I believe you will find the South Side an especially lively place.

I will?

Well, Ogden said, looking him up and down, giving a short bark of a laugh. Well, perhaps not, at least not yet.

I want to say one thing to you, Mr. Ogden. The words came blunt-edged and Tommy Ogden cocked his head, his eyes wary. Lee said, I believe Rodin's bust of your late wife is a wonderful work of art. It's a great thing to have in the library. It's an inspiration. It's been an inspiration to me.

Ogden nodded and appeared to suppress a smile. He said nothing for a minute or more.

It's meant a lot to me, Lee said.

Marie, Ogden said.

Yes, sir, Lee said.

It isn't Marie, said Ogden. It's some god damned Chicago debutante. I've forgotten her name. Get that straight. Get Marie out of your mind.

Yes, sir. But—

And keep this news to yourself. It's no one else's business.

But everyone thinks it's Marie.

Yes, they do. Idiots. It serves them right.

But she's a legend at the school!

Do you know what a legend is? Something unauthenticated. In other words, a god damned fairy tale.

With that, the chauffeur Edgar put the car in gear and backed away. Tommy Ogden raised an arm in dubious farewell and the car motored off in the direction of the road and the trestle beyond, leaving Lee standing alone in the darkness. He watched the open Cadillac until it disappeared around a curve and at that moment Lee's memory stirred. He recalled late-autumn evenings down below the hill in New Jesper. The Cadillac's red taillights reminded him of the lanterns hanging from the caboose railings of freight trains as they lumbered north to Milwaukee and beyond, vanishing in the darkness. The terrain down below the hill was wild and Ogden Hall's was cultivated but the vegetation was the same. The smell of it was identical. In a rush he recalled the disconsolate tramps beside their campfires. He recalled Earl Minning's sneer and the news of the murdered tramp and, weeks later, the rape of his schoolmate Magda and the Committee meeting in his father's study, Sidney Bechet later and all the rest. His father's anguish and his mother's apprehension. He had no idea what had become of Magda and her mother. They were living elsewhere, parts unknown. The Committee sought to suppress news of violence as Tommy Ogden sought to suppress news of himself, including photographs. Both sought to exalt the private sphere of life. Lee was surprised how often these memories returned to him, always at unexpected times and places, triggered by something as routine as the vanishing headlights of an automobile. Lee no longer read the *New Jesper World* but he remembered the inch-wide, inch-deep notices of the arrests of men discovered drunk, down, and out in the city park downtown or in an alley somewhere. There were two or three notices each day, the facts always in order, the name, the age, the time of the arrest, the name of the arresting officer, and any illuminating or lively circumstance: "the subject was barefoot." The date of the arraignment was always pending and so the story had everything except the story: How had he come to this place, a park bench at two in the morning? No shoes, an empty wallet, bad memories. None of these questions were Alfred Swan's concern. Alfred Swan's concern was the notice itself, the march of immaculate facts signaling the vigilance of the police and the scrupulous accounting of New Jesper's criminal justice system. The story of the man's life remained unknown and unknowable and in a certain sense irrelevant, and after three days in jail the miscreant was released and driven to the county line, pushed from the squad car, and told to keep walking north. That was Lee's father's estimate of the situation, disclosed one night after two brimming old-fashioneds, drinks that released the judge's subversive side.

Night came in a rush. Lee heard his name, Hopkins calling from far away. He stepped further into the shadows. God, he was tired. He stank of stale sweat and dirt and for the moment was enjoying his solitude. He could not stop smiling at the encounter with Tommy Ogden. He wondered what the old man's wife Marie was like, her personality, the fictitious inspiration for Ogden Hall School for Boys. More to the point, who was the Chicago debutante? She would be about as old as the century, a middle-aged woman—and how did her bust arrive at Tommy Ogden's library? Mysteries all. Tommy Ogden was a man who liked to lay false trails, and perhaps that was Lee's introduction to the modern world. He tapped his helmet against his knee and thought that he had seen and heard quite a lot for a boy barely eighteen years old. He had not seen or heard as much as Monsieur Balzac at the same age, or Herman Melville, either. But Balzac had Paris and Melville had the seven seas and what Lee had was the prairie and Chicago. The Illinois prairie was a sea of sorts but not of the sort that caused a boy to dream except a dream of escape, perhaps to live among the cannibals as Melville had done. Probably at eighteen Melville had some distant intimation of Ahab. What Lee had was an undefeated season and he would make of it what he could. He had the idea that he was one of those fortunates whose life would take surprising turns, experiences unimaginable at that moment. He knew for certain that Ogden Hall was behind him. Half a year remained but his heart was already set on the South Side of Chicago, Tommy Ogden's especially lively place, whose liveliness apparently did not include the Great Books. Lee wondered if the South Side was congenial to abstract sculpture, heavy pieces in marble or bronze. No use asking Mr. Tommy Ogden. Lee doubted that the founder of Ogden Hall knew anything of value to anyone but himself. He would be one of those who went through life collecting experiences as a numismatist collected coins, with no idea whose coins the hands had touched and no interest in finding out.

In the years to come Lee had occasion to tell the story of the afternoon rendezvous with Tommy Ogden, Filthy-Rich Reclusive Sportsman. Lee had a good memory and found no need to embellish the details, the surly chauffeur, the open Cadillac, the silver flask, Ogden's cigarette holder beating a tattoo on the attaché case, the cryptic remark about the South Side, and the offer to help with an art gallery when Lee needed one. The newspaper swine and the need to keep your face to yourself. Of course Lee never mentioned the mysterious Chicago debutante as Rodin saw her and no need, either, to mention Marie. Lee wondered what there was about Tommy Ogden's life that he was so eager to conceal. Lee doubted he would ever know, and come to think about it, he had no claim. The old man would take that news to his grave.

THE NEXT EVENING, the team gathered for a farewell meal in the dining hall. The occasion was subdued, as if all the energy and elation of game day had been no more than a distant illusion, not quite credible. The game was alive only in their memories, and the memories were wound down like an old clock, details fading in slow motion. Headmaster Weddle gave a listless speech. Hopkins was awarded the game ball. Lee was chosen by his teammates to give a response. He was tempted to describe the encounter with Tommy Ogden and his words of wisdom concerning the uselessness of defeat and the necessity of keeping any pleasure from victory to yourself because the world didn't give a shit. But in the end he said nothing of Ogden and gave the usual thanks to the usual people, specifically including Gus Allprice and the Packer Svenson. That night they organized a beer party at the gazebo well away from the Hall and the dormitories. Everyone got blind drunk and Hopkins had to be carried back to his room after he drove his Oldsmobile into a tree. The housemasters knew all about it but did not intervene. The beer party marked the definitive end of the undefeated season, and soon Christmas break arrived and the distant illusion became a very distant, very satisfying memory, one without any suggestion of regret or ambiguity. Lee knew without being told that there were few such experiences in life, at least in Illinois.

The day before Christmas robin's-egg-blue boxes arrived by special messenger at the homes of the twenty-two members of the Ogden Hall football team. They were from Tiffany's, New York. Each box contained a three-ounce silver cup with the boy's name and jersey number and the year engraved on the inside rim. The mothers noticed the stamp on the bottom that indicated sterling silver and said in astonishment, Well! My goodness! There was no note with the box or any indication of who sent it, befuddling the mothers who insisted that their sons write a thank-you note at once; but there was no one to send it to. Lee Goodell knew, but he believed that Tommy Ogden was owed his anonymity, if that was what he wanted. He certainly did not want the old man to be inconvenienced, forced to read twenty-two notes of appreciation, all composed by hand in schoolboy script. The benefactor thus remained unknown. Lee was delighted by the gesture and wherever he went thereafter he took the silver cup with him in his shaving kit, wrapped in its yellow chamois sleeve. Whenever he had something to celebrate he filled the cup with whiskey or cognac and gave the old man a salute before he drank it off; the vessel was identical to Tommy Ogden's. At such times he remembered the final game, Hopkins's two touchdowns and his one, the missed point-after, the cheering all afternoon, long-haired Willa jumping, Mr. Svenson's tears, and Tommy Ogden's open Cadillac idling beyond the far goalpost. A beautiful day, a beautiful season, and a secret to wrap things up. Yet it was also true that the day was never anything more than itself. If there was a metaphor present Lee never discovered what it was. The lesson seemed to be that it was a handsome thing to have someone's grandmother own a house up near Fish Creek with a caretaker who had anchored the defensive line of the Green Bay Packers for five years and was willing to teach what he knew.

FOR LEE, that was the last of Tommy Ogden. Lee never saw him again and within the year the old man was dead of natural causes, though the precise nature of the causes was not identified. Privacy even unto death, Lee thought. Tommy Ogden had controlled much in his life but he could not control the obituaries. All the Chicago papers carried obits in which "reclusive" and "rich" and "sportsman" and "eccentric" figured. The notice in the evening paper was particularly arch, sarcastic from start to finish. The composition of it caught Lee's attention. The piece seemed to Lee to reverse the principles of Alfred Swan's inch-wide, inch-deep notices. The facts were few, the suppositions plentiful, and the writing most vivid. Tommy Ogden's long life made quite a story, the more alluring for being utterly without verification. How much was true? About half, Lee guessed. And the difficulty was, no reader could know which half, and few of them would care.

Lee thought often about the encounter with Tommy Ogden and concluded that the founder of Ogden Hall was an enigma. Everyone wears a false face from time to time and motives are always a mystery but Tommy Ogden was sui generis. He seemed to be one of those men who lived entirely inside himself, the world at large of no special account except as a playground, his for the taking. In that one sense Tommy Ogden could be said to be thoughtless—except for the blue boxes that arrived one month after the final game of the undefeated season, the day before Christmas, a beau geste, and the more beau for being anonymous. Similarly the business card he so casually handed to Lee that afternoon, the name of a gallery that might be of use someday. Lee wondered who was left to mourn Mr. Ogden when he died. His wife was long dead. Everyone who knew him well was dead except for the lawyer Bert Marks. Surely there would be friends somewhere, shooting friends, drinking companions. Lee himself would have gone to the funeral but by the time the obituaries appeared the funeral had already been held, in a chapel north of Boise, burial private, no eulogies. Lee had many odd encounters in his long and productive life and savored them all but in its strangeness and incompletion none ever matched Tommy Ogden in his Cadillac. Lee decided at last that the old man's life resembled the leather-bound edition of *Old Goriot,* the one in the library of the Hall on a shelf near Rodin's superb bust, its pages uncut. No one would ever know the whole truth of him. Of course it was also possible that there was much, much less to Tommy Ogden than met the eye.

Part Three

TWO YEARS INTO his studies at the University of Chicago Lee found a basement room a six-block walk from his apartment. It was in a dangerous neighborhood but the room was perfect, solidly built, spacious, not soundproof but close enough. His neighbors were night people and rowdy at all hours and would not notice whatever noise he made. They made enough of their own. The basement's windows were curtained so that no one could see in. Lee finished classes in the late afternoon, went home for a makeshift dinner and two hours of study, and when that chore was done walked to the basement room to work on marble. He bought two floodlights so that the stone could be seen in its smallest detail. Lee carved blocks of marble twenty inches high, ten wide, severe in their verticalness, heavy. He had an idea that the dimensions of the marble, and an unexpected irregularity, perhaps more than one, would give a hint as to its interior, what spirit resided within. One might almost say what the marble was thinking, except now it presented a blank face to the world. Lee worked deliberately with chisel and mallet and soon enough found himself in a kind of trance, fully focused until well into the early morning and beyond. It was not at all unusual for him to work through the night and be unsurprised when he looked at his watch to find the time nine A.M., his English seminar already in progress. He knew it was late because his arms and hands ached. His back ached from the constant bending. Sweat burned his eyes. But still Lee was unable to leave the basement apartment, now dense with cigarette smoke. He slumped on the bench between the floodlights and looked hard, assaying what he had done and how well he had done it. Where were the flaws? A block of marble, once carved, could never be restored.

Lee thought of his heavy objects as conscious, teeming with thoughts and emotions. For the moment they were inscrutable. Lee sat for many minutes looking at his work and attempting to see inside it. He believed that in time he would find a means to penetrate its skin like an x-ray. He knew he would make a beautiful object but it was as yet undefined, an enigmatic block of black marble. There was more to it, as there was more to a human face than its surface features. He knew he was on to something but was uncertain what the something was. He had somehow to scale his marble as a mountaineer scaled a rock face, searching for a hold no wider than a fingertip. He knew very well that he did not have forever. Time was short. Lee believed that the stone was losing consciousness, knowing this was absurd but knowing also that absurdity was no barrier to a thought felt strongly. Disharmony was the way in. The stone was dying and would expire unless he finished his carving on time. He had a deadline.

One morning round about six, Lee stepped through the basement door into a pale winter sunrise. His work had not gone well but he was sweating just the same, thinking that failure was as arduous as success, whether or not anything was learned. He stood a moment, breathing deeply the cold air, the sharp beery smell of the street in early morning. No one was about and he did not move, thinking of the marble that refused to take shape. He wondered if it ever would or if he was on a fool's errand. Desire alone was never enough. They said that inspiration came from desire but that hadn't worked so far. He was looking at a beautiful girl who would be forever out of reach, one step ahead. The bleakness of the street, broken glass and bits of paper in the gutter, a mongrel dog nearby, threw a shadow on his spirit.

He stepped up the stairwell to the sidewalk, felt movement behind him, and was suddenly on the pavement. Someone was rifling his pockets and someone else was removing his shoes. Lee swung his foot hard and got one of them in the knee, causing a howl of pain. Lee was stronger than they were and felt them hesitate, looking at each other. They didn't appear to be much older than twelve or thirteen. He heard a string of obscenities and next a hand was on his chest and he was looking at a knife's blade. He had the boy's wrist in his grip but a sudden thrust caught him below his right eye, going deep, the blade working lower to his chin as if it were slicing through rubber, blood everywhere, the boy grinning. Cold air and blood were in Lee's mouth. He heard his own voice cry out and knew his strength was ebbing. In one violent maneuver he managed to wrap his arm around the throat of the one with the knife, a slender boy, stronger than he looked, remorseless. He stank of stale beer. Lee reached for him but his hand fell away and his vision fractured. He put his arms over his face as one of them laughed, a high-pitched giggle. Then they were gone and he was lying shoeless on the basement steps, blood on his shirt, blood on his hands and pooling on the sidewalk. He had recognized the one with the knife, a soft-faced neighborhood boy habitually dressed in jeans and a black leather jacket. He never saw the face of the other one.

Lee brought his hand to his cheek and saw that the hand too was cut and bleeding. This was his right hand, his mallet hand. If they had ruined his hand he would kill them. He thought of the ways the killing might be done but his mind wandered, refusing to concentrate, the street in and out of focus. For a moment he did not know where he was. A crowd had gathered around him but when he tried to speak to them, to ask for help, his voice did not work. He opened and closed his mouth but no sound came and he thought of himself as a beached fish. He saw lights and heard a siren, and the crowd, six or seven old men and a young girl, moved out of his vision. Lee tried to stop the bleeding with his good hand but that was unsuccessful and he began to lose consciousness and only then did he feel the sharp pain in his face and everywhere else.

THE WOUND WAS CURVED like an archer's bow and was the color and width of a twopenny nail. No one missed it, eyes locking on and suddenly averted; even the nurses were alarmed. His father was the exception, looking hard and tracing the line of stitches from right eye to chin with his forefinger, sighing and saying it could have been worse. He could be dead. A half-inch north and he would have lost his eye. As it was, his father said, you have a mark but that's all. His mother could not bear to look at him and left the hospital room to stand by herself in the corridor, her eyes filled with tears. She did not believe her son to be a careless boy. His wound was a consequence of the place he was living, the South Side. The South Side, in its insecurity and disorder, was no better than New Jesper. She thought they were done with it, her family safe. But now she felt herself pressed on all sides, as if she herself were a fugitive. Her son was safe in the hospital and she wanted nothing more than to return to the quiet of the North Shore, its lawns and ordered streets and her work at the library. Melody peeked back through the door. The nurse was rebandaging Lee's wound and saying they would release him in a day or two and meanwhile he should take it easy, not return to class right away. Blood loss had left him weak, and of course there was the shock of it, and he could expect it to take weeks before he was himself again. Melody did not believe that. Her boy would never be the same. He was marked for life as surely as if someone had touched his flank with a branding iron. She slipped back into the room, feeling like an eavesdropper.

Speaking in a half whisper, his words slurred, Lee told his father that the police had been by to visit. He had identified the two boys, the one with the black leather jacket and the other one whose face he never saw but did notice a deformed thumb on his left hand. He was thirteen years old, that one. The police knew who they were. They had been in trouble before but nothing this serious. It was a mistake for him to put up a struggle; all they wanted was his wallet and shoes. The police promised quick arrests but nothing had turned up so far. Lee said, How do I look? His father peered closely, smiled, and said, Better than Frankenstein, but not by much. The nurse smiled at that, packed away her bandages, and left the room.

His parents went away and Lee lay back, exhausted. He was unable to forget the knife cutting his skin below the eye and moving to his chin and the geyser of blood. The boys had given him a souvenir all right, and then he remembered that *souvenir* in French meant "memory." Probably his whole life people would look at him and then look away, wondering at once what had happened and concluding, automobile accident. Flying glass from a windshield. He raised his heavily bandaged right hand to look at it, as if there were anything to see. The bastard had sliced tendons but they had been repaired, no permanent damage according to the doctors. In a month or so he would be able to use the mallet and meanwhile he must do nothing to aggravate the wound. Some physical therapy, not much, would come later. His hand distressed him more than the damage to his face because his marble was losing consciousness and he had to return to it as soon as possible or lose the work altogether. He could not use his left hand because it had no touch. In his left hand the mallet was as useless as a baseball bat or a hatchet. He wondered if accomplished sculptors used both hands. Painters didn't. He wondered if ambidextrous writers used both hands, one to write dialogue and the other to write description. The right hand would be the dialogue hand because it moved faster. But poets would be the only writers to compose in longhand. The others would have a typewriter. Probably Michelangelo was ambidextrous with mallet or brush, either one. Lee had asked the doctors if there were exercises he could use to strengthen his right hand, and they said there weren't and any such maneuver on his part could damage the hand for good. What difference does it make? one of them asked. Your work will still be there when your hand is healed. No, it won't, he said but did not explain about the marble's lost consciousness.

He heard a noise at the door and looked up to see his roommate, Charles, and Charles's girlfriend, Laura, hesitant to enter. Lee raised his hand in greeting and fell asleep at once.

ON AN OVERCAST DAY a month later, Lee made his return to the basement studio. The day was mild and he heard jazz music from one of the buildings opposite his own, a jam session at three in the afternoon. A block from the studio he was stopped by two of the old men who were always about, telling stories and looking after things generally. They said they were sorry for what happened. They used to have a fine peaceable neighborhood but in recent years it had gone to hell, too many youngsters with time on their hands and no police protection. How are you feeling? They were looking at his scar and shaking their heads. Lee said he was much better, thanks, but the scar was painful in cold weather. And your hand? Lee shrugged, the jury was still out on his hand.

They introduced themselves, Ellis and Howard. They were up the street on the corner when the attack took place but arrived too late to do anything. The boys had run away. They were no longer in the neighborhood and the rumor was that they had left Chicago and gone to relatives in the South. No-good boys, Howard said. Lee listened and made no comment. There was a lot of interest in you, Ellis said, working all hours in that basement there. No one knew what you were up to, university boy and all. We don't see people like you in the neighborhood. So there was discussion. That's where I work, Lee said. But he saw they were unconvinced so he added, I'm an artist. I carve things.

They were silent a moment, listening to the music from a second-floor room across the street. Howard said, The police were rough when they shook down the neighborhood after your accident. It wasn't an accident, Lee said. After you were hurt, Ellis said. They picked up some boys on suspicion, took them to the station house, just beat the hell out of them. So there's some resentment in the neighborhood as you can understand. I'm saying to you, be careful. Lee nodded and thanked them. We don't like to see folks hurt, Howard said. We aim for a peaceable neighborhood but lately things have gone out of control, you understand? We're glad you got everything attended to, your face and hand. That's a nasty cut. Most nasty. They shook hands with Lee and walked off. In a moment he heard them laughing, some private joke.

He was surprised to find his door unlocked. He'd no doubt failed to lock it before the boys jumped him. Lee eased open the door with his foot, despairing of what he would find inside. Unlocked doors did not go unnoticed in the neighborhood. He stepped inside, the room in darkness. When he switched on the floodlights he saw that everything was as it had been, his tools in their places, the block of marble on the table. The oversize photograph of Rodin's *Balzac* looked down at him from one wall. Nothing had been disturbed, and he found that hard to believe. Still, something was amiss. The room had undergone a subtle change but he could not see what it was, and wondered if the change was only the passage of time, the room unsettled and not as welcoming as it once was. But everything important was accounted for, so he did not worry. Lee closed the door firmly and locked it and began a slow transit around the marble, fearing it had lost consciousness. He watched it as he would watch a sleeping friend. He did believe, on this inspection, that it had a faint pulse of life.

The room was warm. He removed his jacket and sat on the big stool in front of the table. He kneaded his right hand with his left, flexing his fingers, noticing how stiff they were, the hands of a plumber. His right hand was weaker than it had been. Lee knew what he wanted to do but did not know how to go about it, meaning where to begin. With a chamois cloth he rubbed down the black marble so that he could see the veins and sat quietly looking at them, thinking they resembled rivers as seen from a distant mountaintop. He had a sudden idea that a pot of tea might move things along so he put the pot on to boil and waited. On the wall next to *Balzac* was a mirror and he fetched that and placed it at an angle to the marble. He sipped tea and tapped the chisel against the leg of the stool, looking at the reflection of the marble in the mirror. This put him at a remove from the material. Concentrating on the mirror's image he made a scratch on the stone, so slight it was barely visible. Lee squinted at it, worried that one hasty move would spoil everything that had gone before. Really, he was afraid to proceed because the marble seemed to be looking back at him and daring him to get on with it. He wondered if the mugging had made him fearful, loath to take the next step. He had always been able to hold his own but he had never been in a street fight and was uncertain whether for the rest of his life he would look over his shoulder expecting the worst; and the boys remained at large. Lee did not move, remembering something he had read to the effect that if you were a writer the most dispiriting sight in the world was a blank sheet of paper.

He looked again into the mirror, concentrating hard. He and the marble were side by side in the glass. He placed the chisel at midpoint on the marble and in a series of mallet blows brought it down. His right hand hurt but he did not pause, knowing that to hesitate was to lose the feel of it. He did not know how long he was at it, thirty minutes, perhaps longer. He knew at once when to stop, intuiting the moment when the form was complete. His arms and hands were covered with marble dust. He rose and stepped back from the high stool, looking at what he had done. He did not move for many minutes. When the piece was lit properly it would be stunning. The marble was open now and breathing. He moved his damaged hand over it as a seer might do with a crystal ball, so pleased with what he had done that he wanted to cry out. His eyes moved back and forth from the table to the mirror, his face and the marble side by side, a double portrait. Lee had made a slash in the marble, curved like an archer's bow, the color and width of a twopenny nail. What was it that Tommy Ogden had said to him? You don't learn a god damned thing from defeat. Tommy Ogden, wrong again. Bless him all the same. Lee stepped back and then, looking left, he saw what he had missed when he entered the dark room from outdoors. In brilliant red pencil someone had drawn a scar on the right cheek of Monsieur Balzac. A souvenir from the neighborhood. An obscenity was scrawled beside the scar.

LEE'S ROOMMATE was an Englishman whose parents had been killed in the Blitz. Charles Fford had been sent to Chicago to live with American friends and ended up at the university, having no desire to return to London. London was crowded with ghosts and still in the shadow of the war and its privations. His family was gone and he had come to like Chicago's clamor. He had a girlfriend who lived off-campus and most nights he spent with her until he found it convenient to move his things to her place, openly living with her as if it were the most natural thing in the world. Lee was scandalized, believing the girl's reputation would be ruined forever. He thought they were libertines, Charles and Laura—and then he remembered that Gus Allprice had precisely the same arrangement with Anjelica and he had not been scandalized but beguiled. That was something to think about. In any case, when Charles and Laura invited Lee to dinner along with other friends, he found the evenings unselfconscious and hilarious.

The other friends included a senior from New Delhi and two sisters from New York City, all of them uninhibited and well traveled. Lee had the idea that the two went together, along with the money to pay for them, the travel and the uninhibitedness. The Englishman and the senior from New Delhi argued all the time about British rule in India, a subject Lee had never contemplated. Colonialism was not one of his interests, though all the time he was in grade school the world maps were mostly colored red to indicate the holdings of the British Empire. Charles and the Indian had a mutual Irish friend who disliked Britain almost as much as the Indian did. They would have furious rows but always made up at the end of the evening after many rounds of drinks. Lee often found himself the peacemaker, having no stake whatever in either the British Raj or the Irish Question, although it did seem to him an error for one nation to occupy another. Hadn't the American colonists settled the issue? Not quite, Charles replied. Americans opened the issue but did not close it and so there is residue.

Late on these evenings the talk turned to sex and the evident necessity for Lee to find himself a girlfriend, someone who would fit in, either of the New York sisters or some other unattached female of their circle. Lee had had two girlfriends while he was at Ogden Hall but neither of them worked out; they were summer girlfriends and in the fall they returned to their schools in the East, and the romance, if that was what it was, continued by mail. These suburban girls were very different from his schoolmates at New Jesper High School, something prim about them, but they were worldly too, like Hopkins's Willa. Lee was not successful at figuring out the suburban scheme of things, where so much transpired around the swimming pool at the country club. Nothing happened around the pool of his father's club except towel-snapping and mothers discussing their golf scores. There was nothing prim about the girls at the university, many of them from small towns like himself and dedicated to schoolwork when they weren't investigating the big city—or so it seemed; Lee had little firsthand knowledge, since he spent his nights in his studio.

He was bemused listening to Charles and Laura and the others discuss his prospects as the various attributes of young women flew by: humorous, not humorous, game, not so game, blond, brunette, redhead, fast, slow, bohemian or bourgeois, self-assured or shy. "She doesn't drink but she smokes and she has a nice smile." His friends felt that Lee spent too much time in his basement studio trying to make something out of nothing, meaning the blank blocks of marble, and all he had to show for it was a five-inch scar and a hand that seized up in cold weather, and the solution to that was a willing girlfriend in whose pursuit Lee had to make an effort, however small, and deign to spend one night a week outside the studio. None of Lee's friends had seen his work because Lee was not prepared to allow them inside. Them or anybody. What if they hated his marbles? For the time being his work was for himself alone. He doubted whether anyone else would admire it or even understand it, and he had staked everything on it, this private dream. Vocation, obsession, in whose name he had neglected his studies and was falling behind. He liked the idea of a girlfriend, though, and decided not to spend every night in the studio and perhaps be a bit more forthcoming on what he was doing there. When he spoke about his sculpture he called it "my line of work," usually adding, from some region in his memory, "quite straightforward." To anyone who didn't know him he might have been a telegraph operator or a bond salesman or, given the livid scar on his cheek, a mob henchman.

Lee did not mind being pressed by his friends. He was fond of all of them, including the Englishman's girlfriend Laura, a dark-haired beauty born and bred on the South Side, a shy, often distracted girl who had the softest voice he had ever heard and for that reason, among other reasons, rarely participated in the nightly arguments. Laura did tell Lee that Charles had no vital stake in colonialism but felt that someone should stand up for the British Empire, and he was nominated owing to his nationality—just like you feel about that town you grew up in, what's its name, New Jesper, a sentimental attraction. She felt the same way about the South Side. Also, Laura said, Charles liked to argue in front of an audience, as if their apartment were the House of Commons at Question Time. She was sure that at some point Charles would stand for Parliament and that would mean returning to Britain, something she had no stomach for. What would she do there? Her life was the university community, the Midway, Hyde Park and Kenwood and the dangerous neighborhoods that surrounded it. Now and then junior faculty members came by their apartment, lending the evening an adult aura—though it had to be said that Charles was one of those Englishmen who seemed to be born old, a man much too elegant to be surprised by anything under the sun.

The junior faculty were often the last to leave, the worse for wear from drink and arguing who would take the babysitter home. They were rich with university gossip, who was on the way up and who on the way down in the various departments, chiefly the English department, which was eternally in a prerevolutionary condition. But they were mostly concerned with their own projects—the novel in the desk drawer or the grant that would allow them to visit the Left Bank or the Lake Country or if the cards fell right the Soviet Union, as inaccessible and perilous and exciting as the African Mountains of the Moon. How important it was to see things at first hand, refuse to swallow the propaganda. And you had to be awfully careful how you went about it; Joe McCarthy's people were everywhere in Chicago, aided and abetted by the reactionary press. Even the South Side was under

surveillance—well, Charles amended, *especially* the South Side.
Lee was enthralled by these conversations but had little of value
to add. He had never been political. One night when they were
discussing the Central Committee of the Supreme Soviet he did
think to mention the Committee in New Jesper but did not. Who
would care? Who cared about New Jesper?

Are you really going to the Soviet Union? Lee asked Charles
one night.

I expect so, Charles said. I may go into politics. Know thy
enemy.

What about Laura?

She'll come too. Won't you, luv?

Nix, Laura said.

Lee was startled at these plans. It never occurred to him to
visit the Left Bank or the Lake Country or the Soviet Union either but now these places and others were in his mind. All that
he required was a passport and money for boat passage and the
desire. He imagined a summer in Europe, beginning in a small
hotel in Montparnasse—or was that Montmartre? He had the
idea he would take a year off when he finished school, travel
the continent with no fixed itinerary but Paris and the atelier of
Maître Rodin would be at the top of the list. Perhaps there were
photographs of Rodin at work on the bust of the Chicago debutante. Come to think of it, he didn't have to finish school. He
could devote himself exclusively to his line of work, take it as far
as he could, and then embark on the voyage. The boat would be
filled with girls as eager for adventure as he was and interested
in sharing the room at the hotel in Montparnasse.

Suddenly Lee had another angle of vision as to what surprises
life might bring. He realized that he, like his father, had always
lived within sight of Lake Michigan. The vast horizons of the
Middle West did not bring the world closer; the world was out
of sight, somewhere back of the rolling prairie. He felt himself in
the world when he was in his studio in the dangerous neighbor-

hood well into the night and early morning, carving marble. In his infatuation with the South Side he had grown apart from his parents and their milieu, the long trek to the North Shore made less and less frequently. They were puzzled by him, disconcerted when he met them at the country club for Sunday lunch wearing a long red scarf and smoking a French cigarette, regaling them with stories of Charles and Laura, the prerevolutionary condition of the English department, and much else. The Goodells' friends had warned them of the socialist influence of the university, too many Great Books, too few fraternities, one more reason why Lee, who did seem to be such a nice boy, so well-mannered, so bright, so motivated, would be much, much better off at North-western. Of course his parents and their friends had no inkling of the sculpture studio, though the five-inch scar was an unhappy reminder that the South Side had its wild aspect. They wondered what else besides talk their son was up to in his new life among intellectuals. When Lee called it an introduction to the modern world his father was only too happy to agree, though without enthusiasm.

THE FINAL TWO MONTHS of the spring term Lee studied conscientiously and earned fine grades. That led to a summer internship in the law offices of Bert Marks & Son, a reward offered to especially promising Ogden Hall graduates. The job was worthwhile not only for the money but for the after-hours conversations with old Mr. Marks, whose knowledge of the municipal life of Chicago was encyclopedic. Lee had come to cherish the South Side and the university community, finding it an island of sanity and civic virtue inside Chicago's irrational rough-and-tumble.

Bert Marks looked at it the other way around. To him, the fastidiously beleaguered spirit of the South Side could exist only because of Chicago's rough-and-tumble, which was not, as a matter of strict fact, as irrational as Lee seemed to think. It was corrupt—another thing surely—and corrupt on a scale so lavish that it took your breath away even as you howled with laughter. The exquisite sensibility of the South Side could exist in no other city, not even New York. Look on our great metropolis as a laboratory, my boy. Watch the rats in their cages. Keep your eye on the head rat, the one who gets to the food first. The one who pushes the other rats aside. The one who gets the girl. The one who, push comes to shove, eats the other rats and any other animal within reach. Chicago's *alive*, you see. Chicago doesn't wait for permission. It takes what it wants when it wants it. South Side's alive also, Bert Marks concluded, but perhaps not so much. Fact is, the saint needs the devil more than he thinks he does. Without the devil, the saint's just another old fart standing on a soapbox talking to himself.

I've been meaning to ask you, Lee. Where did you get the scar?

Neighborhood boys, Lee replied.

I'd say you were in the wrong neighborhood. You crossed a boundary. It's important in Chicago never to go where you're not invited.

It was the wrong neighborhood then, Lee said. But it's my neighborhood now.

When the old lawyer looked at him doubtfully, Lee offered to tell him the story. The short version, he added, and the lawyer nodded. A month ago he had been in the neighborhood—Lee saw no reason to speak of his basement studio and what he did there—and was stopped by two of the old men who were always about, Ellis and Howard. They looked him over and observed that the scar seemed to have healed nicely, hardly noticeable—untrue but a considerate thing to say. They went on about this and that, the weather, the White Sox, the chances of Congressman Dawson winning his seat in the fall—that last accompanied by a smile since the congressman was accustomed to running unopposed. Ellis and Howard said the boys who cut him were back in the neighborhood. They did not care for the South where they had gone to stay with relatives. The boys had no interest in cotton farming. The girls were country. Everyone was poor. And here Ellis offered Lee a cigarette and took one himself, lit them both, and remarked on the fine June weather, not a cloud in the sky. Howard said, The boys aren't looking for trouble. In the way of things in such a large and turbulent city Lee's knifing, unfortunate as it had been, was largely forgotten. The newspapers had not paid much attention at the time and there was no follow-up beyond the innocent boys who were taken into custody and slapped around.

I believe we mentioned that to you, and the resentment in the neighborhood.

Yes, Lee said. You did.

Ellis said, There's so much work for policemen to do we believe they've just let your case go. It's on the books but they're not paying attention, do you see what I mean? And so we're wondering what you would do if you saw those boys back here in the neighborhood quietly minding their own business same's the rest of us getting along from day to day. Ellis and Howard stepped back, looking at the cloudless sky, listening to jazz music drifting down from a second-story window, a piece played adagio with just a bass, piano, traps, and alto sax. Lee thought a moment and said, I would shoot them. Howard said, Do you have a gun? Lee said, No.

That's a puzzlement, Howard said. I hardly know what to say to such a threat. Do you intend to get a gun?

Lee said, No.

Well then, Ellis said, that's a different story. Haven't we reached a meeting of minds? It's like Mr. Dawson's election, a peaceable affair, normal, without excitement. What I mean to say is, predictable. I suppose that's true, Lee said. You will not be bothered, Howard said. Those boys know they did the wrong thing and will not repeat it. They do not want to spend more time in the South. The neighborhood will see to it you are not disturbed so long as you keep things to yourself. We all mind our own business here and in that way we all get along.

Bert Marks listened to Lee's story without saying one word. And when Lee finished, the old lawyer nodded slowly and offered a crooked smile.

You've learned a valuable lesson, young man. Thing about Chicago is, it's generous. Live and let live. It's good you've found that out. Other cities, they tear themselves apart exacting revenge. Boston's like that, family rivalries, tribal rivalries. Boston's an old city. Why, at one time the Congregationalists and the Episcopalians were at each other's throats. Can you imagine it? I'm not saying that revenge is not a factor here too, but it's not dominant. It's recessive. We're a young city and we look ahead, not backward. We don't care about yesterday. Cities that care about yesterday are cities in decline. Boston's in decline. We work things out here, try to give everyone a slice of the pie. Even those boys. It's a small slice but still a slice and that's why the motto of our city is Can Do. And a new generation is on the rise. There's a man on the scene, an up-and-comer. You don't know his name. He's a behind-the-scenes man now but I suspect he'll run for mayor in a few years' time and he'll win because he's a fine Democrat and at the same time a realist. He loves the city, you see. And wants to make it prosper. And if you go along, you'll get along. Mr. Daley likes people who look forward. He understands the principle of the egg and the omelet and that's why we're entering a golden age in Chicago. I think you're mature beyond your years, Lee. I know about your meeting with my late friend Mr. Tommy Ogden. He spoke so highly of you. He asked me to do anything I could, and I'm doing that now. I've never asked your plans when you graduate from our great university. Have you ever thought of the practice of law?

OR LEE GOODELL the law would not do for a simple reason. It was not physical enough, the work done inside your own head during daylight hours in a drowsy office in a downtown building. Lee liked ground-floor space and a certain amount of disorder inside the space. He liked sweat, a reminder of football practice at Ogden Hall and his afternoon adventures down below the hill in New Jesper. He was not attracted to collaboration, a necessary feature of the legal life: associates, clients, judges, bailiffs, court reporters, juries. Its essence was a remorseless search for precedent, that which had gone before. What had gone before was the controlling conscience. If you were an artist, precedent was not the solution. Precedent was the problem. He thought of lawyers as an infantry surveying the battlefields of distant wars. He thought of them as buzzards picking over carrion and writing the results in a prose so opaque—well, it was double Dutch, the so-called brief, which was never brief but stretched like a wave in the open ocean, rising, collapsing, re-forming itself until it petered out on some foreign shore. He preferred the mallet and chisel and knowing that however hard he worked on the stone its interior would never reveal itself entirely. In that way it resembled an inspired musical figure and life itself.

Besides, law was his father's trade.

*

TO HIS SURPRISE, one year later Lee found himself something of a big man on the Chicago campus, someone to be looked up to and speculated about, the long scar on his face as distinctive as a black eyepatch or a top hat. He was often seen in the company of faculty, including the very senior, very eminent department chairmen who taught undergraduate classes, part of the Chicago tradition, "the deal." Evenings he was a regular at the long bar of the tavern on 57th Street drinking with junior faculty from the English and history departments, all of them engaged in animated discussions of the Great Books between drafts of German lager. Often they were drunk, their voices rising on the neap tide, the grand names sailing forth—Spinoza Wittgenstein Adorno Nietzsche and the Russian butterfly beavering away at Ithaca, Nabokov. Lee said little but listened hard, never more attentive than when the evening drew to a close with its ritual denunciation of the economics faculty, crypto-Republicans who would bring the American experiment to its knees unless steps were taken at once. Lee rarely stayed after ten o'clock.

Lee was an excellent student but did not look much like a student, roughly dressed, his books and papers carried in an old Boy Scout knapsack; his cigarette was a giveaway, however. He was understood to be a prep school boy—a graduate of that very peculiar institution near Jesper downstate, Ogden Hall, scandal-ridden but still surviving—but he didn't look like a preppie, with the long scar and an unruly mop of coal-black hair and a musclebound gait that suggested a rodeo rider or a middleweight wrestler, a young man who could take care of himself. It was known that most every night he went to his basement studio in the dangerous neighborhood away from the campus to sculpt—and here the rumors varied widely because no one had seen his work, not even Charles or Laura or the sisters from New York City or the foreign student from New Delhi. Sculpture was not an unusual avocation at Chicago, known for its eccentric student body—fencers, young communists, Arctic explorers, bridge fanatics, game theorists, astronomers, motorcycle enthusiasts, phrenologists, and here and there a scapegrace. Even so, it was remarkable that Lee was rumored to keep a loaded revolver in the studio. He was not a participant in campus life, not that the university was much celebrated for organized activities outside the classroom. There was a baseball team but games were sparsely attended, the bleachers a fine place to read a book on a fine spring afternoon, game or no game. Athletics in general were frowned upon as something more compatible with the wretched Big Ten, specifically Northwestern or the University of Illinois. In any case there were no cheerleaders in short skirts twirling batons, nor raucous homecoming weekends.

Lee did not know what to make of his notoriety except that he liked it. The university encouraged individuality. A refusal to conform was seen as virtuous, though there were objections that the near-religious pursuit of nonconformity was itself conventional, business as usual. Hegel was revered on the Midway: for every thesis, an antithesis. Lee was having the time of his life.

AT DAWN OR A LITTLE LATER Lee would venture from his studio with a mug of black coffee, leaning against the railing that led to the basement, and watch the neighborhood come alive, a few pedestrians going to work, a few more coming home, cars motoring slowly down the street. Cats and a few dogs prowled the neighborhood. The morning light was always pale and dusty and for a few moments it was as if time had ceased. Lee was deep into his thoughts of the marble and what it was yielding. He was leaning against the railing but his mind was still in the studio and remained there until he heard music from the storefront church across the street, voices foreground and a piano behind. He sipped coffee and listened to the music, which trailed off now and again into the purest blues. The lead voice was a soprano who belonged in Orchestra Hall but he doubted that Orchestra Hall was much in her thoughts just then. The rattle of a garbage truck obscured the music but when the truck turned the corner the soprano came back and the chorus joined in, everyone taking a closer walk with thee. Lee noticed ash in the air but when the ash touched his hand it disappeared, snow flurries from the lake. He wondered how it would be to start the day with hymns and readings from scripture. He had never been to a morning church service in his life. There was no religious study at Ogden Hall and his parents were secular people, not even church on Easter or Christmas.

Then the street was filled with children, some escorted by their mothers, others by their older brothers and sisters. Their reedy voices filled the street and Lee was reminded of his own schooldays in New Jesper, down Chestnut Street to Hawthorn and across Hawthorn to Oak. The school, a red brick pile, sullen in aspect, was on the corner. They were like fish, the girls in one pod and the boys in another. They always slowed a little before they got to school, thinking there might be a cancellation and they could go home. Those were the best times, when he and Dougie Henderson would spend the day down below the hill. Snow was the promise of a day off, a kind of gift. The advantage of a small town was that there was always one forbidden place and everyone knew where it was. Small town, small world. In cities there were many such places and no one person could know them all and some were truly dangerous. It had been years since he had visited New Jesper. Dougie had moved away and was living in Denver, selling cars. Lee wondered if the town had changed and if neighborhood boys still defied their parents to prowl along the railroad tracks. Of course they would—unless the memories of the murdered tramp and the assault on Magda Serra were still fresh, and that was doubtful. The children he saw now were hurrying to catch up, to get to school before the bell. The door of the church opened suddenly and parishioners spilled out. They were mostly middle-aged women in hats, bundled against the cold. Through the open door he could hear the piano, a recessional, and it too had the tone and timbre of the blues.

Lee lit a cigarette and finished his coffee, comfortable in the cold, his thoughts turning again to the mallet and chisel and the block of marble and what it would yield or if it would yield anything. Not today. He was finished for today. At times he felt the marble had a life and mind of its own but that was tomorrow's business. He wanted to speed things up but it seemed he worked to a slow-paced clock. Lee felt someone stir nearby and turned abruptly, dropping the cigarette, his fists up.

Ellis and Howard stepped back, alarmed.

You'll catch your death, Ellis said. It's cold. That cotton shirt's not enough.

I didn't notice, Lee said.

How have you been getting on? Howard asked. Everything all right?

Fine, Lee said.

No trouble?

No trouble, Lee said.

You're part of the neighborhood now, Howard said.

I guess that's right.

You understand, it's unusual. Except for the locksmith around the corner and the other one, we don't know his name, the fat one on the run, white people don't live here. And when one moves in, that excites curiosity. But you, you keep to yourself, don't ask questions, and that helps a little bit so far as curiosity's concerned.

I don't live here, Lee said. I work here.

Oh, yes, we know, Ellis said. He looked thoughtfully at the sky and sighed heavily. I believe we'll have real snow by the end of the day. Cold too, that wind from the lake. Comes all the way from Minnesota. Beyond Minnesota. Sometimes I wonder what made us settle here, my God it's a long train ride. But I know the answer to that. You should get a nice warm coat.

Lee said, What's the answer?

Jim Crow, Ellis said. You see, we're from Mississippi. That's where Jim lives. He's here too, but not quite so much.

What does that mean? Lee said. Jim Crow.

Ellis looked at Howard and they both smiled. Trouble, Ellis said. It means trouble. But you don't have to worry about it. So let's return to the matter at hand.

Lee blinked. He was unaware that there was a matter at hand.

Everyone wonders what you do here, Howard said.

I carve things, Lee said. I carve marble. I'm here because the basement's cheap, thirty-five dollars a month. The heat works.

That's good. It's good to be warm in the Windy City.

Steam heat, Lee said.

Even better, Howard said.

We want to ask you a question, Ellis said.

Go ahead, Lee said.

It's in the nature of a favor, Howard said. Ellis will explain.

We have some money from the city, Ellis said. As you know, there's an election just around the corner and City Hall thought they should make a contribution to the neighborhood so's to make certain that things go well at ballot time. And thanks to our fine congressman there'll be a little federal money because the election concerns them too, up there in that Washington. And a generous contribution from folks who work at the university. This is our plan. We intend to have a clinic on this street, next block over. Open nights and weekends so when people are sick they have a place to go. A place where injuries could be treated. Of course serious cases would be forwarded at once to County Hospital, where they have facilities, an emergency room and so forth and so on, x-ray machines, and the like. We wondered if you could help us out, Mr. Goodell.

Lee, he said.

We thought you could help us out, seeing as how you're part of the neighborhood.

I don't have any money, Lee said.

Howard smiled and shook his head, murmuring, No, no.

I don't know anything about medicine, Lee said.

You don't have to, Howard said. We have trained professionals. Doctors who volunteer their time and registered nurses and so forth and so on.

We have to have someone who can keep records, Ellis said. Log people in and log them out. Make sure the files are maintained. Take their insurance cards if they have insurance, which most of them won't. Our community distrusts insurance companies and doesn't have money for the premiums if they did trust them, so they'll need help with the forms. That's what we need.

Keeping records, Howard said. We thought you would be good at that.

Why? Lee said.

You're up there at the university. That's what they teach you, isn't it? Those professors we read about. And I'll bet you're a fine student, Lee. You must be, to spend so much time here in the neighborhood. We already have a volunteer for the weeknights. So we're only talking about two nights a week, Saturday and Sunday. I'll bet you'd have time for that.

I wouldn't be good at it, Lee said.

How do you know? You haven't tried!

Some things you know, Lee said. Instinct.

We were hoping you could help us out, Ellis said. He smiled, most friendly, most ingratiating, and not giving one inch. The street was mostly empty now, the children in their classrooms. A bus lumbered by, filled with women. A very old man emerged from the church, looked at the sky, and waved at Ellis and Howard. He shouted something unintelligible and Ellis and Howard both laughed. A private joke, Lee surmised. And a private language for the private joke. He lit a cigarette and watched the snow fly, imagining himself as a clerk at the clinic, logging people in and logging them out, keeping track of medical histories, making sense of private language, all-night affairs surely. He had no desire to clerk and no particular wish to devote his weekend evenings to sick people, none of them known to him. He supposed he lacked civic spirit. Something perverse about it, Lee thought. He drew a breath and saw the labyrinth in front of him and knew there was no escape. Ellis and Howard were clever men.

Come with us, have a look at our clinic, Howard said.

It's only up the street a little, said Ellis.

Five minutes, Howard said.

You'll have to forgive the looks of it, Ellis said.

The cleaners are due next week, said Howard.

Maybe you could answer a question for me, Lee said.

Certainly, Howard said.

The boy who cut me. What was his name?

Oh, Howard said, that's in the past. That's old news.

All the same, Lee said, I'd like to know.

That's information that could cause trouble, Ellis said.

No trouble, Lee said. I wouldn't tell anyone.

You would keep the name to yourself?

I would, Lee said.

The boy's name is Topper, Ellis said.

Last name? Lee said.

The name he goes by is Topper, Howard said.

Give me a minute, Lee said.

He went back inside, put a chamois cloth over the marble, picked up his coat, locked the basement door, and joined Ellis and Howard for the walk up the street. They were animated, describing plans for examining rooms and a small operating room for emergencies. Someone had given them a four-foot-high Mosler safe to store dangerous drugs. The women of the neighborhood were especially enthusiastic at the prospect of a place to go for aches and pains, arthritis and diabetes, problems with their bowels; and for the younger ones, prenatal examinations. They hoped the clinic would be friendly and comfortable, unlike the industrial medicine practiced at County Hospital downtown, in and out in fifteen minutes and they were not polite about it. You had to wait hours before being seen and the staff was always rushed. Somehow they were always at the end of the line.

Ellis, Howard, and Lee paused in front of the building, constructed of clapboard, two stories high, conspicuously vacant. Two of the front windows were broken and trash had accumulated on the stoop. Two cats fled at once. It had begun life as a two-bedroom house but Lee guessed it had had many lives. Ellis produced a key and they stepped inside a dark room, the broken windows so narrow they admitted little light. The prospective waiting room was the size and hexagonal shape of a country parlor, peeling wallpaper, a small chandelier fixed to the ceiling. The room could hold no more than ten or twelve people. In one corner was a plain wooden desk of the sort schoolteachers were issued. All the room lacked was a pencil sharpener and a blackboard.

In a dark corner was a pile of rags, including a threadbare blanket that moved as Lee looked at it. A bare foot showed itself, then an ankle, a languorous movement, and as quickly withdrew. Ellis stepped to the blanket and carefully pulled it back, revealing first an empty bottle of gin and a ragged pair of hands and at last a woman of indeterminate age sleeping soundly. Howard took a good long look and sighed. The woman's face was badly scratched, her hair a wiry thicket. Ellis pulled at the blanket again, then quickly put it back. She appeared to be bare above the waist. Ellis looked at Howard and shook his head, murmuring something unintelligible. Howard said, Poor soul. Ellis said, We'll let her sleep. He stepped to the closet door and looked inside. Then he opened the door to the corridor and looked up and down, no sign of life. The woman said something in her sleep, a kind of croon. Ellis moved the blanket again so that she could breathe more easily. They both stood quietly a moment. Lee said, Shouldn't we get help? It's hard to know where help would come from, Howard said. The police, Lee said. The police would not be helpful, Howard said. We'll think of something. Meanwhile, we have to get these windows repaired. Really, Lee said, shouldn't we call someone? But that question went unanswered. Howard stepped to the desk and rapped it twice with his knuckles.

That's your desk, he said.

We'll get you a good chair, Ellis said.

And a telephone and a typewriter, Howard said.

From the federal funds, Ellis said with a wink.

THAT AFTERNOON, enduring a lecture on *Leviathan*, Lee remembered the long-ago evening at his house in New Jesper eavesdropping on his father and the other important men of the town discussing the assault on Magda Serra, her injuries and the terrible aftermath, willing themselves not to listen to the details of the assault, as if hearing them would be itself a contamination, too toxic to bear. But in the end they listened, and Lee remembered the stricken silence and the throat-clearing as attention turned to Alfred Swan and his newspaper. Swan's mulishness. Swan's responsibilities. Within a few days the story was all over the school, spoken in whispers, including the appalling particulars; and many of those, Lee knew, were invented. No one wanted to plead ignorance so the stories grew wilder as the days passed and then, lacking fresh information, they died away. What remained was an uneasy void. Lee was unable to say whether the community was better off not knowing than knowing. His father believed that it was. He was convinced of it. The word he used was morale, as if New Jesper were an army in the field facing a dangerous enemy. The judge did not give the enemy a name but his German forebears would—*schrecklichkeit*. Frightfulness. Ellis and Howard were similarly interested in discretion but not for the same reason. Howard said the police would not be helpful. In that he was surely correct. They would take care of the destitute woman in their own way, and that way was none of Lee's business because he was not of the community. Lee believed that Ellis and Howard were—abashed. Embarrassed by what they found with Lee as a witness. Something of that was present in New Jesper too.

He wished he had pressed the point and angry that he hadn't: Call the police, call an ambulance. But Howard and Ellis were men three times his age and kindly in their own way. Lee was an outsider and in no position to insist on anything. Who was he to lecture anyone? Lecturing was not his métier, obsessed as he was with his hammer and chisel and the conscience of marble. He wondered if the remorseless pursuit of the frightful made you a better man. Maybe it only made you wised-up, another thing altogether. He wondered what Magda Serra would have to say in her own behalf. Her opinion was not known. She had gone away to another part of the country. Her mother had not been heard from. They were the ones directly concerned and certainly Magda would not have enjoyed seeing her name in the paper with all the relevant details, her reputation slandered. Yet her sense of outrage and, he supposed, violation would make a newspaper article beside the point. And if she were of a particular temperament she would want everything laid out, no detail too small or too intimate to be ignored. Do you want to know what happened? This is what happened. The public's right to know. Lee supposed that in New Jesper the story was a dead letter, forgotten along with the death of the anonymous tramp, and he had no idea how Magda would react to that. Perhaps not at all. Perhaps what New Jesper remembered or did not remember would be a matter of indifference to her. In that one sense the outrage committed upon her was strictly personal. Lee heard his name called and looked up to listen to a question about the ethics of Thomas Hobbes. He answered the question and went back to his recollections, to no good resolution. He wondered if events at the clinic would enlighten him. He suspected that his thoughts on the matter of Magda Serra were about to clarify. Lee realized that he had led a protected life growing up in the house on the hill, the vast lake beyond. When a tramp came to the door he was given an apple and sent on his way. The police protected the community and when there was a question, any question at all, the chief was summoned to discuss the way ahead with your father and his friends. A consensus was reached. The lid stayed on. Lee wondered if this protected life was the best preparation for Chicago's hard knuckles, but he knew the answer to that. There was no good preparation for Chicago.

Remember Hobbes, the professor said. Kind, timid, and tall. Believed in the submission of the people to the state, be it king or parliament. On permanent sentry duty for the Establishment, friend and retainer to dukes and earls. First-rate mind. Played a keen game of tennis to the very end of his long, long life. Wrote his autobiography in Latin verse. I believe he was more sociologist than philosopher.

But either way, he is very important.

Next week, Goodell will explain why.

THE FIRST FEW WEEKENDS at the clinic were slow and Lee was able to become acquainted with the staff, Dr. Petitbon and the nurses, Eloise and Pearl. They worked at Cook County General and Dr. Petitbon had a separate private practice in Kenwood. All three had signed on for six months, weekends only. They showed Lee the forms and taught him the routine, patient when he was slow to catch on. Pearl said, If they don't want to answer a specific question let it pass; just try to get the vital statistics. When Pearl asked him what he studied at the university and Lee replied Great Bookkeeping, she laughed and laughed.

Dr. Petitbon said that business was slow because the neighborhood was suspicious of the intent of the clinic. They were reluctant even to give their names, worried that medical histories or other personal data would be collected and fall into the wrong hands, perhaps shared with the police, who already had more information than they needed or was healthy for them to have. Lee himself was the object of particular suspicion until Ellis and Howard reminded everybody that Lee had a basement room up the street and had lived among them for almost a year. There were no complaints about the young student, always polite and friendly but not too friendly. Most important, he kept to himself and did not ask idle questions. Neither did he volunteer information about himself.

The fourth week was very busy and marked by a terrible incident. A fourteen-year-old boy was brought to the clinic by his mother. In the waiting room he suddenly dropped to the floor, unconscious. He was thin as a rail and seemed to fall slowly in pieces, bone by bone beginning with his ankles. He was a tall boy, well over six feet, with enormous eyes. Lee saw him fall and shouted for the doctor, who came at once but could do nothing. The boy was dead, no visible marks, no signs of illness. He was standing quietly with his mother when he closed his eyes and fell. The mother was too horrified to speak and when she did open her mouth the waiting room was filled with a high-pitched wail, a ululation. When the doctor put his arms around her, she shrugged him off. When Lee fetched a sheet from the examination room and attempted to cover the boy, the mother snatched it from his hands and threw it into a corner. She took her son's head in her arms and rocked to and fro, and still the primal wail, as if she had infinite breath and would wail as long as she lived. Dr. Petitbon called for an ambulance, and when the ambulance arrived two policemen arrived with it and entered the clinic first, guns drawn.

No, no, the doctor said, there's no need for that here.

Who are you? the sergeant asked.

I am the doctor in charge.

What did he die of?

I'm not sure. But there was no violence here. The boy walked into the clinic with his mother, fell unconscious, and died.

Can you get her to shut up? The sergeant pointed at the mother.

No, the doctor said.

I'll have to make a full report.

An autopsy will be performed. The coroner will be notified.

Are you the only witnesses?

As of right now, yes.

I'll need to take your statements.

Lee said, No crime was committed, Officer.

Who are you? the sergeant asked.

He is my assistant, Dr. Petitbon said.

He's a kid, the sergeant said.

A student at the university, yes.

The sergeant raised his eyebrows in mock respect. What's your name?

Lee Goodell, Officer.

The sergeant looked at him a long moment, his hand on his chin. That name's familiar. You ever been in trouble with the police?

Lee smiled winningly. No, sir.

When the police left at last they had interviewed each patient—there were only two of those, the others having departed when the boy was pronounced dead—along with the doctor, the two nurses, and Lee. They left with the ambulance containing the boy's body and the mother, the mother continuing to ululate. When the door closed behind them Dr. Petitbon left the room and came back with a bottle of scotch and four glasses. The nurses demurred but Lee nodded his head.

They sat drinking scotch a moment or two, no one speaking. I know that boy, the doctor said suddenly. His name is Ernest Tullis, and never was a boy better named. He rarely spoke, rarely changed expression. He knew what was in store, all right. I saw him a year ago or more when his mother brought him in for a checkup. She knew perfectly well that her son was not healthy. Her manner was guarded. The truth was, she was terrified. I made the usual tests and discovered that he has, had, what we call a hanging heart. It's congenital and very bad news and there's no real treatment for it. And this evening his heart gave out with no warning as it was bound to do sooner or later. A year ago I tried to explain that to Mrs. Tullis but she was not interested and I did not press the matter. I gave the boy a death sentence and what use to her were the details? There was nothing to be done, not then and not now.

Dr. Petitbon refilled Lee's glass and his own and said no more. The room was quiet. The nurses said good night. Lee set about tidying up the reception room and was still at it when Dr. Petitbon said good night and departed for his home in Kenwood. But in a moment he was back for a final word.

He said, You don't have to do this, you know.

I don't mind, Lee said. It'll take me five minutes.

I mean the job, Lee. You don't have to stay. I can get someone else.

Why would I quit? Lee said.

Suit yourself, Dr. Petitbon said and closed the door, this time for good.

Ten minutes later Lee let himself out and walked in the direction of his basement studio, thinking he could put in a few hours on his marbles. At the corner he heard a racket of conversation from a first-floor apartment. There was a piano also and the window curtains were drawn tight. Lee paused, listening to the piano and the laughter. It was an after-hours club, called in Chicago a blind pig, the phrase dating from Prohibition. The party would last until dawn, perhaps beyond. Lee continued across the street but then changed his mind. He was not in the mood for a hammer and chisel, and he could never remember not being in the mood. He turned toward the campus. The night was cold and no one was about. Here and there in apartment windows were Christmas lights and one with a white-bearded Santa Claus with a crimson cap but otherwise no sign of life. Lee hurried along, thinking of the boy with the enormous eyes and the hanging heart. One second he was there and the next second he wasn't. Lee could tell by the way he fell that he was dying, surely dead before his body struck the floor. The life went out of him in an instant and Lee tried to understand how he was so certain of that. He had never seen a dead person. But he knew at once and so did the doctor. The boy was as still as a block of marble and nothing moved within, either. He passed two more Christmas-lit windows before he entered Hyde Park and heard a commotion ahead, music and loud voices, another blind pig. Through the first floor window he saw an enormous Christmas tree, filled with lights and ornaments, a winged angel at the summit. The tree reminded him of the ones in the living room at New Jesper, piles of presents stacked under it. The tree in the window blocked any view of the inside but the laughter and the music were cheerful. He heard women's voices. Then Lee noticed the brass plaque beside the door, the size of a calling card.

CHEZ SIRACUSA
BY APPOINTMENT ONLY

The apartment was empty, Charles evidently spending the night at Laura's. Lee looked in the refrigerator and brought out a can of beer and went to the living room to drink it. The time was late, near two A.M. He sipped beer and looked at the clutter in the apartment, stacks of newspapers on the couch and laundry in the kitchen, dust balls in the corners of the room, empty beer cans in the wastebasket. A Christmas tree would improve things, give a sense of the holiday season, good will toward all men and so forth. Lee picked up *Leviathan,* read a page, and put it down, much too heavy a text for so heavy a mood, backbreaking in the circumstances. He sipped more beer and decided he was living the wrong kind of life, one divided between the classroom and his studio with the clinic on weekends. The clinic was threatening to overpower the other two. Ernest Tullis was not the last dead boy he would see—and then he understood why he knew the boy was dead. The giveaway was his eyes, a dull gray film had covered them, and looking at his eyes he knew the worst without being told. The boy's last image was Lee himself, a stranger. Something obscene about that.

He was acquiring experience, all right. He doubted Thomas Hobbes knew as much at his age, timid as he was. It seemed to Lee that he was witnessing things he had no right to witness. He had neither the right nor the desire. The truth was, he was an impostor. He would have to ask Charles when he came home: Have you ever seen a dead man? How did you know he was dead? Then he could say, I know. Do you want to hear? Probably if he stayed around the clinic long enough he would become a first-rate amateur diagnostician. He had already seen one broken leg and a burned left hand and a teenage girl with a temperature of 104. He had administered the thermometer himself and given the girl a gingersnap afterward but she did not appear to appreciate the gesture, snarling something about good-for-nothing white boys. Of course she was out of her head with fever. Pearl told her to shush but she didn't feel like shushing so she repeated what she said, adding, Why don't you go fuck yourself, white boy, but quietly enough so that Pearl did not hear.

Lee did thrive in his studio and tolerated the classroom but the clinic was another order of experience altogether, one of those wars of choice the tyrants of the Middle Ages were so eager to wage. Wasn't it Alexander who wept bitter tears because there were no more worlds to conquer? Yet when Dr. Petitbon had asked if he wanted to give it up, Lee refused without a second thought. He supposed it was pride. Lee yawned deeply. God, he was tired. He couldn't get the clinic out of his mind, the shabbiness, the smell of it, the fear in the eyes of the patients. It held a fascination. Fascination was the right word too. Fascination implied that the clinic was a kind of urban circus put on for his benefit, a grisly minstrel show for the white boy. Lee pulled another beer from the refrigerator and contemplated the idea of fun. Where in the Hyde Park scheme of things did fun come in? He wondered if Thomas Hobbes had ever written about that, and if not why not. *Leviathan* did not mention fun, at least the parts Lee had read. Of course Thomas Hobbes had his tennis. Often the idea of fun came with a girl. In order for real fun to happen a girl had to be involved. Lee fell asleep holding a half-empty beer can.

ON SATURDAY NIGHT a month later, near midnight, they were closing the clinic when the door flew open and three boys rushed in. Two of the boys were half carrying, half dragging a third, who was unconscious. The unconscious boy was covered with blood, his shirt soaked with it. Pearl and Eloise had gone home and Dr. Petitbon motioned at once for Lee to assist him. The moment they had him on the examining table the boy's eyelids opened and he struggled to sit upright. Lee pushed him down and ordered the two others to leave the room and wait outside. They loudly refused until the doctor barked at them, threatening an unspecified telephone call if they did not leave. Then he shut the door behind them.

Lee fetched bandages while the doctor used scissors to cut away the boy's shirt and trousers. He had wounds in his chest and both arms and his body was scraped raw from being dragged on pavement. The arm wounds were deep but not serious. The doctor applied a tourniquet to both arms and fixed bandages to the wounds, blood staining the bandages but not leaking through. Next he turned his attention to the chest wound and told Lee to call an ambulance, they had an emergency; and in the meantime they would do what they could. Hearing this, the boy began to struggle again until the doctor told him to stop it. For the first time Lee looked the boy full in the face and saw that he was the one who had cut him, who had taken such pleasure drawing the knife from his right eye to his chin. Lee smiled maliciously and saw the look of recognition. Lee tightened the tourniquet without being especially gentle about it and the boy sighed. He did not appear to have the strength to cry out. The doctor was bending over the boy's chest, examining the wound, and then he began to probe, not deeply but in an exploratory way. The boy did cry out then, weakly and without conviction. Terror was everywhere on his face and he no longer looked at Lee unless he was forced to. The overhead lamp was bright in his eyes.

Loosen that tourniquet, the doctor said.

Of course, Lee said.

I need another bandage, the doctor said and held out his hand until Lee put a bandage in it. Did the ambulance people give a time?

Soon, they said.

Have you ever given an injection?

Once, Lee said. Eloise showed me.

I'll do it then. Hold this bandage to his chest. Gently.

The doctor filled a syringe with something, then pushed it home into the boy's biceps, withdrawing it at once. This should help the pain, he said to the boy. And then he asked, What is your name?

Robert, the boy said.

Last name?

Jones, he said.

The doctor raised his eyes fractionally and grunted.

They call him Topper, Lee said.

You know him?

We met once, Lee said.

Last name Jones?

I don't know. I doubt it.

The doctor turned again to his patient. How did this happen?

Topper moved his shoulders and said something unintelligible. Meanwhile the doctor poured sulfa into the wound along with something else, unknown to Lee. He worked with skill, patiently without being slow about it. The expression on his face was bothered. All this time Lee was staring at Topper, thinking they were engaged in some unusual and perverse transaction. The boy's eyes kept shifting away and back again. His face had acquired a dull sheen in the brightness of the overhead light. He said in a slurred voice, Am I going to make it?

You have a deep wound in your chest. The angle of it is strange. There's very little blood. I don't know how deep it is or where it's gone. I don't have the facilities to treat it properly. The wound must be x-rayed and I don't have an x-ray. I was supposed to have one but I don't. I want you to stay quiet until the ambulance comes. I am going to look at one of my medical books. Dr. Petitbon turned to Lee and said quietly, Stay with him. Behave properly.

Topper watched the doctor move to his desk in the corner and take down a heavy book from the shelf above. Then he closed his eyes and his body seemed to relax though his breathing was heavy. Turn and turnabout, Lee thought. And then the boy's hand moved so that it touched Lee's. He thought this was involuntary but could not be sure. The boy's hand was clammy and soft to the touch. He looked peaceful in repose but still his hand did not move. Anyone looking at him would believe he was dying. Lee looked at the chest wound, an inch or so below the heart. He wished he knew more of anatomy, the exact placement of the heart and whatever organs were below it. The liver? Kidneys? The boy's breathing was louder now and irregular. Lee heard Dr. Petitbon mutter something and close the medical book. At the same time the boy's eyelids flickered open and with no sign of recognition. He moved his mouth as if to speak but no sound came. Lee thought to himself how quickly and completely the unfamiliar became familiar and the personal so profoundly impersonal. Lee had the idea that the boy would die on the table and he knew he did not want that to happen.

The doctor said, Lee, open the safe and get me morphine.

Lee did as he was told and the doctor stood quietly a moment, indecisive, the vial of morphine in his palm. He moved his hand up and down as if weighing the vial, testing it; and then he put it aside.

The doctor moved closer to the boy on the table and said, Are you in pain?

The boy shook his head, but that too could have been involuntary.

The doctor said to Lee, Hold his hand.

Lee took the boy's hand and squeezed it gently, with no response. He said, Can you hear me, Topper? When the boy stirred but slightly, Lee said in a voice not his own, I think we're losing him.

We're not losing him, the doctor said. Not yet. He bent again to look at the chest wound, raising the bandage to inspect the cut, the width of a knife's blade. There was very little blood and he supposed that was a good sign. Lee noticed Topper's fingernails were bitten to the quick and filthy. His knuckles were filthy. Lee wondered what had happened to him, a gang fight or a vendetta of some kind. Maybe Topper had simply been in the wrong place at the wrong time, a common circumstance in Chicago. Infantry officers called it a meeting engagement. Lee remembered his own pain when the knife's blade entered his skin below the right eye and the sting when it sliced through his cheek and the evident pleasure on the boy's face. But that pain was nothing compared to the pain that came later, when his adrenaline lapsed.

Where is the goddamned ambulance? the doctor said quietly, as if he were thinking out loud. He looked at his watch and sighed heavily. This boy belongs in a hospital and he belongs there now. I don't know what more to do.

Voices in the waiting room told them that the ambulance crew had arrived. Lee opened the door and they entered with a stretcher and an oxygen mask. Lee and the doctor moved Topper from the examining table to the stretcher, the doctor explaining the wounds and what he had done. The attendants listened without apparent interest. One of them put a stethoscope to the boy's chest and announced that the heartbeat was irregular but appeared to be strong enough. They put the oxygen mask over his mouth and nose, then muscled the stretcher through the waiting room and into the ambulance outside. Lee and the doctor stood on the sidewalk in the cold and watched them go, the bleat of the siren beginning at once. They waited until the ambulance turned the corner and the street was silent once again.

Dr. Petitbon said something Lee did not hear.

Lee said, Pardon?

Who was that boy? How do you know him?

He was the one who cut me, Lee said.

So you took some revenge, the doctor said.

Yes, I did. I'd do it again.

We don't do that here, the doctor said. That's not one of the rules of my clinic, taking revenge on the patients. What in God's name were you thinking?

Have you ever been cut?

That's beside the point, the doctor said.

Not to me. It hurts like hell.

I'm sure it does, the doctor said. And that's still not the point.

I gave the tourniquet an extra twist, that's all.

With the boy helpless on the table.

I didn't see him as helpless. I saw him as my enemy.

Do you still see him as your enemy?

Lee thought a moment, remembering fingernails bitten to the quick. No, he said finally. It's not personal anymore.

Well, the doctor said, that's a start.

I wanted him to know that I was there and that I remembered. But I did my best. I tried to help him.

My clinic is not *the street. The street* is something else. You have no conception of *the street* in this city. These boys grow up with nothing. They have nothing except the street where they go to meet other boys who have nothing. Dr. Petitbon turned away, shaking with rage. His voice had risen an octave. He was a short man with a small head covered tightly with oiled wavy hair. He was slight of build, soft-spoken, elusive of manner, dapper in his own way. But now he seemed undone, perspiring heavily. He seemed to want to say more but did not know how to go about it. Dr. Petitbon stood in the doorway looking at the ceiling, opening and closing his hands. He said, I'll let you know if he lives.

I hope he does, Lee said. It's over now.

All right, the doctor said. I'll clean up the examining room. You take care of reception. And we'll go home.

He turned to go back inside, his shoulders bent, his eyes now downcast. He looked defeated. Lee guessed the doctor was no more than thirty, thirty-five years old. He had never thought to ask. Dr. Petitbon always had a worried expression and spoke a musical southern idiom in such a way that his words were often lost. Pearl had said he was originally from Louisiana, the bayou country, come north to find opportunity. Of the doctor's personal life Lee knew nothing. He wore a wedding ring but never spoke of a wife or children. He went about his work with thoroughness and concern but did not appear to derive pleasure from it, medicine a chore like any other. Lee wondered if he was one of those men who had gotten into the wrong business and by the time he realized what he had done it was too late. The one thing Lee knew for certain was that the doctor liked a drink of scotch at the end of the day, sometimes two scotches. Money did not seem to interest him. His suits were well worn and he drove a black Chevrolet coupe, prewar.

Lee straightened the chairs and tables and the magazines on the tables, *National Geographic*s and the *Reader's Digest*s. The papers on top of his desk were scattered and he collected those and put them away. Something was missing but he did not know what it was. Then he remembered the two boys who had arrived with Topper. What had happened to them? They had left no trace of themselves in the reception room. Lee sat at his desk and lit a cigarette and thought about what Dr. Petitbon had said about *the street*. The way he spoke, *the street* sounded like a foreign country with its own laws and customs, a totalitarian regime of enforcers, and the clinic a refuge like Switzerland, except when the enforcers paid a call. The doctor had a right to be furious about the tourniquet. Of course his sympathy would lie with his patient. The fight wasn't fair. But it wasn't fair the first time, either. Lee decided then that he wasn't cut out for clinic work, too many frightened people in one room at the same time. They were frightened and suspicious of unfamiliar surroundings. The patients looked through Lee as if he were a pane of window glass. Even so, he vividly remembered his turn of mind when the personal became impersonal; maybe that was what people meant when they talked about professionalism. A professional was never shadowed by doubt and sought the comfort of the impersonal. But that was not Lee. The truth was, he had no future at the clinic, which he now saw as a claustrophobic zone with no resemblance whatever to Switzerland. True, he had seen a side of life he had never seen before—as if that would be a consolation to the patients. A round of applause, please. Lee put his cigarette in the ashtray and stood up. Time to go home. He looked into the examining room and saw Dr. Petitbon pouring a glass of scotch. The doctor said good night without looking up or offering a nightcap.

Then he said, I don't want you here anymore.

Lee said, All right.

The doctor said, I don't know how you got here in the first place.

Lee smiled. I was invited.

It was a mistake. You have no training.

That's true, Lee said.

Good night then, the doctor said. He gave Lee a long, troubled look and said finally, Good luck.

You too, Lee said.

Lee closed the door quietly and took a last glance around the reception room, the chairs and tables, the eye chart on one wall, the magazines, the ashtrays filled to overflowing. The space was not hospitable. No one could feel at ease there, or confident. Then Lee saw what was missing—the clinic's typewriter with its case, no doubt a final salute from Topper's friends.

WHEN CHARLES FFORD returned to England to join the Foreign Office, Lee took up with Laura, moving in with her his junior year. Laura's apartment, small, crowded with books and secondhand furniture, was a gift from her parents, a symbol of feminine independence. They wanted Laura on her own but also nearby. Her father was a much-admired economist at the university, her mother a lawyer at one of the downtown firms. The apartment was her mother's idea. Laura's family, both sides, had lived in Hyde Park since the 1880s, a point of some pride. They thought of themselves as old Chicago, keepers of the city's pioneer conscience—always assuming the city had a conscience, Harold Nieman always added, a matter of eternal dispute. Laura called her parents by their first names and always had, even as a little girl. For Lee, that took some getting used to.

Lee and Laura were serious from the beginning, serious enough so that Laura warned him that she would never, ever leave the South Side. That was non-negotiable. Her family was important to her, and her family had always lived on the South Side, in the Hyde Park house built by her grandfather. She thought Hyde Park, in its variety and tolerance, its civic spirit, was unique in America. Where else did the races exist so harmoniously? Certainly there was nothing remotely like it in the Midwest. Neither of the coasts held any attraction for her. She wouldn't mind visiting Europe but she could never settle there. So if Lee had any ideas about New York or Los Angeles or Paris or Rome he should tell her so that she could make other plans for herself. He was surprised at her vehemence, and charmed too. Her desire to remain where she was matched his desire to be someplace else, anywhere that was not New Jesper or the North Shore. Hyde Park was fine with him.

Each Sunday they went to her parents' house for lunch, riotous affairs that usually lasted until late afternoon, the table crowded with physicists, economists, writers, labor leaders, and the polymaths who constituted the Committee on Social Thought. Harold Nieman was a wine connoisseur and bottle after bottle appeared, was consumed, and replaced at once. Lee was a popular figure at table, often contributing stories from his boyhood in New Jesper and later at Ogden Hall. He was surprised that many of the guests were aware of Ogden Hall and its eccentric founder. Only once, filled up with wine, did Lee tell the story of the death of the tramp and the assault on Magda Serra. He stopped short of describing his father's role in the—he supposed the word was containment. He never spoke of his sculpture—he was still not prepared to explain himself—nor of his volunteer work at the clinic. He had no idea Laura's father knew anything about it until one Sunday afternoon when he said, Tell us about the clinic.

It's an ordinary clinic, Lee said. I don't work there anymore.

I didn't know you had any medical training, Harold said.

I don't. I logged them in and logged them out. A clerk, that's all. Except one time, Lee thought but did not say.

Every night?

Saturday and Sunday nights, a six-hour shift depending on the casualties.

Well, then, why did you quit?

The clinic was claustrophobic.

Harold Nieman frowned as he opened another bottle of wine and filled glasses at the table. Everyone was silent, listening to Lee.

You weren't mistreated?

No, no, Lee said. Dr. Petitbon was very decent. He drank more than was good for him but he was a decent man. A troubled man, I think.

He drank in the clinic? the writer James Ball put in.

Not on the job, Lee said. After work. Scotch mostly.

It's never a good idea, drinking at the office.

He thought it was, Lee said. The work was difficult. His equipment was substandard.

Tell them about the x-ray, Laura said.

We didn't have one, Lee said. The x-ray was always on order but it never arrived. Dr. Petitbon was flying blind most of the time and the clinic was always crowded. But it was better than nothing to the people who needed it.

You said claustrophobic, Harold said. What do you mean, Lee?

Airless, Lee said. I was out of place there.

It's understandable, Harold said. Sick people—

To sympathize is not always to understand, Lee said.

I beg your pardon? the writer Ball said.

Lee did not reply to that.

What kind of cases did you get? Harold asked.

All kinds. Pneumonia, the common cold, broken legs, hypertension, unwanted pregnancies, suspicious growths. One time a boy came in and died in front of us, a bad heart. There were cuttings also.

Saturday nights were the worst, I suppose, Harold said.

Usually, Lee said and changed the subject, to everyone's evident relief.

Walking home arm-in-arm that night, Laura asked Lee why he did not mention the boy Topper, and Lee said that he had yet to reconcile the matter. He hated the scar on his face. Laura said she didn't mind, she'd become used to it. The truth was, she sort of liked it. The scar gave character. It hurt like hell, Lee said. One minute he was standing in the doorway to his studio and the next he was on his back and the minute after that the damnedest pain he ever felt, except later when it was worse. At any event, Topper seemed to have survived his own wounds. They had both survived, so you could say that was the end of it, only it didn't seem like the end of it to Lee. Let it go, she said softly and squeezed his hand. You're right, he said. I'll try my best. She said, Try harder, and he had to laugh at that.

They were bound for Lee's studio. She often came with him at night, reading her philosophy books while he worked, looking up now and again when the *tap-tap* of his mallet reached a certain rhythm. That meant he had forgotten she was there and she could watch him without feeling self-conscious about it. In the studio she was surrounded by his black marbles, ten of them now. Three more and he would have enough for a proper show, if he could convince a gallery to give him one. Lee had told her he worked better when she was in the room, although much of the time he forgot she was there. That was all right. He felt her presence subconsciously. He never asked her opinion on works in progress, only the finished pieces. It took Laura a while to distinguish among them. They were variations on a theme, rounded forms with a slash high to low, the differences quite subtle. One thing about them, they were indisputably from the same hand. Each marble seemed to cause a different emotion in the viewer. All of them required a concentration that she did not always have and did not believe was normal; seeing beneath the skin of things was never simple. She would sit for many minutes looking at a piece before she ventured a thought. One or two of them were enigmatic in the extreme and she could make no coherent response except to say she was easy with enigma, though enigma was not a particular virtue in Hyde Park. On this night, looking up when the *tap-tap* ceased abruptly and Lee stepped back from his worktable, she rose from her chair to join him, her book still in her hand. I believe it's done, he said, what do you think? She stared at it hard for five minutes, then turned away and burst into tears, her face buried in her hands. Startled, he took her in his arms and they rocked back and forth a moment. Lee did not speak.

I have a scar too, she said at last.

He knew every millimeter of her body and the only scar he had seen was a little one on her thumb, a childhood mishap.

She said, I had an abortion when I was sixteen. The doctor hurt me. You can't see the scar, it's inside. I know it's there.

Laura, Laura, he said.

I was reminded of it, she said and offered a bleak smile. Number Ten reminded me.

Lee smiled back. His pieces were not named. After Number Ten would come Number Eleven.

Do you mind? she said.

Of course I mind, he said softly, and when her eyes filled with tears he went on, I don't like to see you hurt.

The abortion, she said.

I don't care about that, he said.

My father took me to the doctor. Mother couldn't bear it, she was so cross with me. Harold prides himself on being good in adversity. He was, too. She was silent a moment and then put her hand on Number Ten, patting it as if it were alive. She said, We went to him at ten o'clock at night. The doctor was a friend of my father's, not some Mister Buttonhook somewhere. He had a nurse who disapproved. He hadn't done many abortions and didn't like doing mine but agreed because Harold was a friend. It's quite painful, you know. Very painful.

Maybe it always is, Lee said.

Not always, Laura replied. According to reports.

I don't know anything about it, Lee said.

I hated the way the nurse looked at me. I was so ashamed. I still am.

No, he said. Please.

You're sure you don't mind? That it doesn't make a difference between us?

It makes no difference, he said.

My high school boyfriend, she said.

I don't care who it was, he said.

It wasn't Charles is what I want you to know, she said. We were in the back seat of a DeSoto. We had been to a dance and then parked at the planetarium, near the lake, a beautiful summer night. A million stars in the sky and the moon somewhere over Michigan, etcetera etcetera. Laura raised her arms and let them fall, a gesture of resignation. Things got out of hand. He never knew how far out of hand. What was the point? We broke up soon after, she said. He wanted to stay friends but I couldn't see the point to that, either. I wasn't thinking clearly. Maybe I wasn't thinking at all. Has that ever happened to you? Reaching a point where your mind's blank as slate, not a coherent thought in your head? Laura picked up the chamois cloth and began to polish the marble with brisk circular strokes, paying particular attention to the high-low scar. She stepped back from Number Ten, frowning. She said, Does it go high to low or low to high? I mean, upstroke or downstroke?

High to low, he said.

I guess it wouldn't make any difference.

Everything makes a difference in sculpture.

It does?

Yes. The smallest thing.

Okay, she said.

Everything has a reason, he said.

I understand, she said.

You didn't have to tell me about the DeSoto, front seat or back seat. The etceteras didn't add much.

I know. I'm sorry.

It's a closed book, he said.

Not entirely, she said.

To me, I mean.

Okay, she said. I never said anything about it to Charles or anyone else. Only you. Is that all right? What I mean is, something about your stone reminded me what happened when I was sixteen years old.

He moved her slowly in the direction of the couch.

Yes, she said. That's a good idea.

And then we can go home, he said.

Maybe I'd like to stay here for the night.

We can do that. We can do anything you'd like.

That's what I'd like.

Laura sat on the couch in her underwear and looked up at him. She said, I didn't know what you'd think. When we first met I thought you were strait-laced, a small-town boy in a big city. She smiled broadly. From Bethlehem to Gomorrah in the blink of an eye, she said. Don't give me that smile. I know it's true. Charles told me once that you thought we were libertines. Libertines! I laughed and laughed because, truth was, I was charmed. I was charmed that you would take me for a libertine. You know, sometimes around here we make a fetish of tolerance. That's Hyde Park for you. But sometimes we do laugh at ourselves. Not often enough. I liked you the first time I saw you, that stupid touch-football game you organized. I liked the way you ran. I liked the way you looked when you ran, a boy's abandon. I wondered then if there was a possibility of something between us. Charles was already thinking about going back to London and that would mean the end of us, Charles and me. Not that I ever thought we would be permanent. Charles wasn't ready to settle down and I've been ready since I was sixteen.

He watched her take one barrette out of her hair and then another, placing them carefully side by side on the table.

She said, I told you about the DeSoto because I didn't want there to be anything mysterious between us.

Even a DeSoto?

Especially a DeSoto, she said.

He didn't reply but couldn't help a smile because where he came from secrets were treasured. They were the coin of the realm. If it wasn't a secret it wasn't serious. Shared, a secret lost its magic. The definition of a secret was knowledge worth keeping to yourself and remembering, the privacy that held a community together. A neighborhood, a city, a whole nation even, and most of all a marriage. Secrets were both sweet and sour, and disclosed were devalued: gossip. Lee turned the idea this way and that and decided finally that it was another of his half-baked thoughts, subject to revision. Even so, it was hard to imagine a society without secrets, everything aboveboard and straightforward, a parking lot filled with DeSotos. Why, even the socialists said that was the problem with capitalism, too many secrets held by a banker cabal—yet that would seem to make Laura's case, wouldn't it?

Lee said, Promise to keep it to yourself now.

The cat's out of the bag, Laura said with a sly smile. Stay where you are.

Later, near dawn, they were walking to her apartment. Lee carried her philosophy book and an umbrella against the cold drizzle. No one was on the street and the street seemed to go on forever, bounded on either side by three-story houses with porches and lawns, no light in the eastern sky, the houses dark. They seemed to be at the limits of the known world. The moon was out of sight and he doubted it was anywhere near Michigan.

Laura laughed suddenly and said she had important news, she'd saved it. She had been offered a teaching fellowship in the philosophy department and she thought she would take it. The department chairman, Altschuler, told her she would make a fine philosopher, maybe a better philosopher than her father was an economist—that last said with a sly smile, the chairman and her father were great friends. Of course Chairman Altschuler had a caveat. She had to be prepared for resistance from her colleagues in the department, who believed that women's brains were wrongly wired for consecutive thought on, say, the nature of virtue or the essence of language or naturalness. Also, women's emotions were unfortunate, dominated as they were by blood and dark rhythms. Women were at a disadvantage. Could a woman have written the *Tractatus*? Altschuler laughed when Laura said she hoped to God not, the *Tractatus* being essentially a mind scrutinizing itself—a normal thing in the community, witness Descartes—but a futile enterprise surely, of scant practical value and a text so difficult it was said to be more obscure in the original German than in English translation and all that quite apart from the lurid speculation that Wittgenstein was insane. In any case, Laura went on, anyone who could write so obscurely and yet so brilliantly—here and there flashes of tremendous originality amid the darkness—is not a philosopher but a prophet, and deserves to be read as such. So, yes, she thought she could handle whatever her colleagues dished out so long as she didn't have to wash them—the dishes.

When Altschuler stopped laughing he said fine, it was settled, and informed her they wanted to publish the paper she had written, original work, he thought, and, ah, prophetic in its own way. However, it would be a very, very good idea if she brushed up on her German, as department colloquies were often conducted in that language. She had wanted to tell Lee before, but then she looked at Number Ten and was moved to tears and there was the matter of the DeSoto and the consecutive couch sex following the DeSoto and what with that and one thing and another she forgot about the fellowship and the paper they wanted to publish.

So, she said, what do you think?

Take it, he said. I've always thought it would be wonderful to have a philosopher for a wife—the loaded word arriving spontaneously, unbidden and unexpected, but in the circumstances most natural. Still, he was alarmed at it.

A what? she said.

Isn't that where this is leading?

I think it is, she said.

You're my darling, he said.

You too, she said. You very much too.

We can scrutinize ourselves, he said.

Every minute, she agreed.

They moved along through drizzle and gathering fog, the street as dark as he had ever seen it. Laura was full of plans, the wedding, the reception following the wedding—and should the honeymoon come now or later? She spoke so softly he had to dip his head in order to hear her, and he had the clear idea she had been thinking of these plans for some time. Lee was thinking of marathon sessions in his studio, finishing three new pieces to make his baker's dozen, and then he could arrange for a show. He had never thought much about money but he was thinking about it now, calculating what he and Laura would need to live decently. He hoped his parents would approve of her. They had met but once and the evening had been mostly successful until his father made a remark about Adlai Stevenson, causing Laura to color; the governor was Hyde Park's idea of a living God and worshiped accordingly. Laura's voice was softer than usual in reply. His father, grown hard of hearing, pretended to understand and smiled warmly. Of course he assumed Laura agreed with him. He was accustomed to agreement and Laura tactfully declined to set him straight. The meal ended lamely but Lee's mother did manage to take him aside after they left the restaurant to whisper, She's lovely.

A gray wash was visible in the eastern sky. Here and there lights winked on in the neighborhood. Lee and Laura paused at the corner, disconcerted by piano music and raucous laughter that drifted from an upstairs window of the brownstone opposite. A woman was singing "Ain't Misbehavin'" in a voice coarse as sandpaper. Lee remembered the place, remembered also the little brass plaque beside the door:

CHEZ SIRACUSA
BY APPOINTMENT ONLY

Lee turned to Laura. I've seen that house before, he said.

Oh, she said, that dreadful place. We've tried for years to shut it down. We've signed petitions. We've marched, sent delegations to the city council. No use. They have protection downtown.

Blind pig, he said.

Cathouse, she replied. It's been there for years and it'll be there forever. It's what we have in Hyde Park instead of Marshall Field's. It's disgusting.

The singer had swung into "Fine and Mellow," singing parlando, the music smothered for a moment by a burst of applause. Lee saw sinuous movement behind the open window on the first floor. He had never visited a cathouse, did not know how you went about it, making the appointment. There was said to be a cathouse in New Jesper, but it was only someone burning a red light in an attic window of a house in the colored part of town. As they listened to "Fine and Mellow" the door of the brownstone opened and an elderly gentleman moved slowly down each step. He was unsteady on his feet but not so unsteady that he couldn't turn his head and blow a kiss to the woman holding the door for him. Once on the sidewalk he adjusted his fedora and stood quietly in the rain. Presently a black sedan arrived and he eased himself into the rear seat. Then the sedan moved off at a stately pace, turned the corner, and was gone. Lee said nothing to Laura but he was all but certain that the gentleman in the fedora was Bert Marks. Of course that was impossible, inconceivable really. Bert Marks lived on the North Side. Why, Bert Marks was seventy-five years old at least.

Something in Lee's manner, the little involuntary whistle he gave, caused Laura to ask, Do you know that man?

Lee said, That is the chairman of the board of trustees of Ogden Hall, my old school.

She said, That is appalling.

Lee sighed. Yes. All but inconceivable.

MONTHS LATER Lee took the train up from the South Side to have lunch with his father at the Drake. The old man wanted to know about wedding plans and there was one other thing he wanted to discuss, something peculiar, and he said no more. Lee arrived an hour early because he liked to walk along Oak Street Beach, especially on calm days when the great lake was flat as a plate and the color of dishwater, the sun glowing dully in the Chicago haze. When he was a boy he liked to watch the pocket aircraft carriers maneuver on the horizon, plane after plane landing on the decks, pilots fresh from flight school learning to land on a platform about the length of a football field. Now and again a pilot would misjudge the wind or the speed of the carrier and make a poor approach and crash the plane or send it wheeling off the deck, where it would drop like a stone to the bottom of the lake, taking the pilot with it. They were only boys, many of them, some as young as seventeen, and when their training was done they were sent to the Pacific where the carriers were twice the size with names like *Enterprise* and *Hornet*. The accidents were never reported in the newspapers but his father always knew about them, the type of aircraft, the age of the pilot, and what went wrong. That was the closest the war came to Chicago but it was close enough. Lee had nightmares, the pilot trapped in the aircraft as it sank, quickly at first, then slowing and drifting in the underwater currents, the plane ghosting along like a silver manta ray, the water opaque, the bottom invisible. In Lee's version the plane drifted for an eternity, a kind of watery purgatory neither here nor there, the pilot alive and conscious owing to his

oxygen mask. Every effort he made to extract himself was useless. Lee woke in a cold sweat.

Now he looked up to see sailboats on the horizon, a promise of summer just one month away. Still, Lee shuddered at the
memory of his childhood nightmares and wondered whether aircraft remained at the bottom of Lake Michigan a mile or so offshore from the Outer Drive and all the way up the North Shore
and beyond. Then he thought, Enough of that; the day was fine.
He continued to stroll, the Near North Side another world altogether from bohemian Hyde Park, the men in suits and ties,
the women in stylish dresses and high heels, purposeful of gait.
Lee watched a flight of starlings wheel overhead, its formation
changing in the blink of an eye, giving the illusion of a helix,
then a hesitation and the starlings were gone, swarming north.
The date was the twentieth of May, not warm but comfortable
enough that people were sitting on benches, their faces upturned
to the pale sun. He stood with his back to the gray lake, scrutinizing the apartment buildings on Lake Shore Drive, great vertical fortresses of granite and concrete. From their summits you
could see almost as far north as New Jesper, and with the aid of a
telescope to Milwaukee and northeast to the steel mills of Gary.
At least that far, he thought, though he had never visited a penthouse apartment on Lake Shore Drive. Many of them were constructed in the 1920s, the golden age of lofty living in Chicago.
Fifteen Hundred was the address the girl had given him at the
party the night before. When he looked at her without comprehension she smiled and added, Lake Shore Drive. The girl was a
friend of Laura's. Her family were art collectors, always on the
lookout for fresh talent from Chicago.

Be nice to her, Laura said. You never know. Maybe you're the
talent they're looking for.

Fifteen Hundred was there before him now, five black limousines arrayed nose to tail under the porte-cochère. At some mysterious signal the doors flew open and chauffeurs alighted to stand

at attention as the entranceway filled with well-dressed women, all wearing furs and hats, waiting a moment in the spring sunlight before dispersing to the limousines. Lunch, Lee thought, and then the Art Institute or the opera or theater, one matinee or another. The limousines glided away, leaving the doorman in his silver-gray uniform standing as straight as a sentry, importantly shooting his cuffs, then clasping his hands behind his back and moving into the shade of the awning. A model for Degas, Lee imagined; or, if you wanted to be rough about it, George Grosz.

The girl's name was Jill White, a forceful girl who had matched him drink for drink at the party. Probably her mother was one of those in a fur and a hat bound for the Loop. He tried to imagine Jill in a cloche hat and a fox fur but could not, though Degas would. They had argued about the future of socialism in America, disagreeing but not unpleasantly. She insisted that the internal contradictions of capitalism would bring Wall Street to its knees, the revolution at hand at last, and he replied that there were internal contradictions to everything under the sun, even human beings, even God, and perhaps God most of all. The truth was, Wall Street was an abstraction to him and the capital markets were as unfamiliar as a Havana casino.

Jill White was lost in thought a moment, then asked him if he believed in God. Not yet, he said, and that brought a smile. You're not from Chicago, she said. The accent's wrong. Where are you from? Lee hesitated two beats and said, New Jesper. Jill laughed merrily and said she knew all about New Jesper. New Jesper was the town their maids came from, arriving each morning at eight via the North Shore trolley. Her family couldn't live without them, Tish and Lorraine, gems both. Tish was related in some obscure way to the singer, what was his name? Jill had forgotten the name but he was well known to anyone who listened to popular music. He was the one with the silky voice, often singing on *Your Hit Parade* and other radio programs. So I'm *au courant* with New Jesper, Jill said. Of course, Lee said quickly, I

can see that. It's well known that New Jesper was a supplier of
maids. If you wanted a steel worker you went to Gary and if you
wanted a brewmaster you went to Milwaukee but if you wanted
a maid, a professional, you went to New Jesper. In fact the city's
motto was "New Jesper, City of Maids," though to people who
lived there it looked like any other small Illinois town with the
usual internal contradictions, *au courant* in its own way. Naturally in New Jesper the maids were required to believe in God
whether they wanted to or not. Jill made a face and after a pause
said, Ouch.

Bitch, Lee said to Laura later. Who does she think she is?

She's a deb, Laura said. I was watching. I think you frightened
her.

Nothing will ever frighten that woman. Rosa Luxemburg
bomb-throwing from her penthouse at Fifteen Hundred.

Jill and her parents are on the outs, Laura said. That's the reason, if you're interested in reasons. Jill speaks her mind.

Maybe I worried her a little, Lee said. But not enough. Jill invited me—us—to the cocktail party her parents are giving, Saturday night.

Did you accept?

I did not.

Laura said, I didn't know you had such feeling for New Jesper.

Lee said, You never forget where you're from.

Well, Laura began doubtfully.

You certainly haven't.

True enough, she said.

And the price was right, Lee said.

What do you mean by that?

Bye-bye, White collection.

LEE LOOKED AT HIS WATCH and saw that he was due to
meet his father in ten minutes. Even so, he lingered a while longer,

appraising the fortress atmosphere of Fifteen Hundred. He had never been inside such a building; surely no apartment would have fewer than eight rooms, one set aside for a maid sleep-over in the event the dinner party ran late. He wondered what moves you would have to make to acquire an apartment on Lake Shore Drive, the hoops you would have to jump through; and then at a specific moment you would own the hoops and the apartment both. He watched the doorman greet a slope-shouldered middle-aged man in a white Panama hat and step smartly to the curb to blow his whistle. In seconds a taxi pulled up under the porte-cochère, the driver alighting at once to attend to his passenger as the doorman returned to sentry duty. Lee did not move, watching slope-shoulders remove his Panama hat before sliding into the taxi. The hat in his hand seemed as handsome an accessory as spats on a parrot. Lee decided then that apartments on Lake Shore Drive would surely exact a kind of revenge, something unexpected. A messiah complex or altitude sickness or a preoccupation with hats. No doubt you would walk a little taller when you lived there and be pleased with yourself at the envelopes you distributed at Christmastime, each banknote mint-fresh and crisp as parchment—and that was Lee's sudden intimation that he had left New Jesper for keeps. Home was Hyde Park, Laura's apartment and his studio on the perimeter of the university and the work he did there. Lee turned to give one last look at the flat gray lake, recalling once again the aircraft carriers far offshore and the trainer planes maneuvering into position, from that distance scarcely larger than insects, their pilots no older than boys. The routine took some getting used to. Approaching the carrier deck, the pilot would be laden with emotion, fear and exhilaration both, no margin for error. Just one wrong move, a misjudgment of speed or of wind, the position of the sun, the angle of descent, any distraction—

Adieu, Fifteen Hundred.

*

JUDGE ERWIN GOODELL was seated at a table for two in the middle of the busy dining room, the waiter setting down an old-fashioned as Lee approached. The old man was dapper in a gray summer-weight suit and bow tie, his expression content. Lee ordered a martini and apologized for being late. His father said that was all right, he had only arrived minutes before, traffic on Skokie Highway. Isn't this a nice room? I've always liked the Drake, locally owned, good food, good service. Then he commenced an inventory of his ailments, chronic indigestion, shortness of breath, and a bad knee. For the first time in his life he was playing golf from a motorized cart, the latest thing at the club. His game was sour because of the knee. He was having trouble sleeping and now, the latest indignity, he was seeing a podiatrist to have his toenails clipped. Arthritis in his fingers made toenail-clipping a chore. He took a sip of his old-fashioned and sighed. My memory isn't worth a damn, either. What's new with wedding plans?

It'll be a while, Lee said. We think July, after graduation next summer.

In Hyde Park, his father said.

Yes, indeed. And there's something else. Laura and her mother want you to officiate. In the university chapel. I like the idea too.

Well, he said, I'm touched. Thank you. Your mother will want to know every detail.

When we know them, Mom will have them. Lee thought now was not the time to mention the participation of the English professor James James, who had recently converted to Buddhism and intended to recite a sutra of his own devising. Professor James was an old family friend and Laura's godfather, and he would not be denied, especially since he promised to shave his head for the occasion.

Have you lost weight? his father asked. It looks to me like you've lost weight.

I don't think so, Lee said.

I've gained ten pounds this year. I don't mind. Your mother minds.

Lee said, Let me ask you a question. Have you ever been inside Fifteen Hundred?

Lake Shore Drive? Sure, years ago. Some judicial conference at the Blackstone and one of the federal judges gave a cocktail party. The apartment was enormous. There must have been a hundred guests, plenty of space left over in the living room and the dining room next to it, drinks, a buffet, fully catered. Beautiful view of our lake. Why do you ask?

Invited to a party. Declined.

You should go. You should broaden your horizons, Lee. Chicago's got a lot more to it than Hyde Park. There are fine people on the North Side, professional people, lawyers and such. Then the waiter was at the table, and after giving their orders the old man lost his train of thought. Instead, he began to speak of his days at law school, the excitement of the law, its challenge, its essential virtue. You put aside bias and followed the law until it was seen that the law itself was unjust and then you overturned it, like the Dred Scott matter, and then it was not a decision by an appellate court but by the people themselves in ratifying the Fourteenth Amendment to the Constitution of the United States. I suppose you've given no further thought to law school, he said.

Lee had never given any thought to law school but he did not say that. He said, I don't think so, Dad. I have another interest.

And what interest would that be?

Sculpture, Lee said. That's what I've been working on.

The waiter arrived with steak broiled rare and fresh drinks for Lee and his father, asked if anything else was wanted, was told no, and departed.

Did you say sculpture?

Yes, marble sculptures.

You probably don't know it but I was responsible for commissioning our statue of Lincoln and causing it to be put on the courthouse lawn. Carrara marble from Italy. That was twenty years ago. It's been judged one of the finest Lincoln statues in all of Illinois, and there are plenty of them. Is that the kind of sculpture you have in mind?

Not exactly, Lee said.

That seemed to put the conversation in a cul-de-sac.

His father said, I always hoped you'd go to law school, preferably the University of Illinois but any of the good ones would do. Michigan, even Chicago, if that's what you wanted. As you know, I worry about the politics of the University of Chicago, all those German émigrés. They come with baggage, long on theory, short on the practicalities. They have a collectivist mentality.

Well, Dad, not really.

But his father was not listening. He continued, Your grandfather was a lawyer and a judge and that's what I am and I hoped you'd be one too. The Goodell name means something in northern Illinois and I hoped you'd carry it on, and your son, if you're lucky enough to have one. I count myself lucky in that regard. You've never been a disappointment to me, son. The old man paused to cut his steak and Lee noticed that his fingers trembled. He was aware suddenly that his father was mortal, aging before his eyes. He realized once again that his father was nearly old enough to be his grandfather and that accounted for their friendship. So many of his friends had a rivalry with their fathers, and mutual wariness and always a struggle for dominance. Reconciliation, if it came, arrived on the deathbed. Lee hated to distress the old man and he knew to the syllable what was coming next. His father chewed thoughtfully and then he said, Have you sold any yet?

They're not for sale, Lee said.

Well, what does Laura think? The old man smiled brightly, a last roll of his dice. She's a sensible girl. I knew that the first time I set eyes on her. And now I understand she's going into the philosophy department to work alongside her father. He must be tremendously pleased. He must be delighted. You should talk seriously to Laura about this sculpture business. She has a good head. She's down to earth, a practical girl like your mother.

Laura agrees with me, Lee said. And her father's an economist.

Same church, different pew.

I'm sorry about the law, Lee said.

It's all right, son, his father said. That was my dream, not your dream.

Same thing'll happen to me, you know. I'll want my boy to go into the sculpture business and he'll say, Not on your life. I want to be a judge like my grandfather.

Wouldn't that be something, the old man said.

Count on it, Lee said, amused at the idea, pure fantasy. His sculpture was private and he had no interest in sharing it with anyone or making a legacy of it. But his father chortled at the idea. They sat for a moment in companionable silence.

Alfred Swan helped me out, his father said. The Lincoln statue. Alfred wrote an editorial a week for six months. Put their feet to the fire, the county board. Bullied them into it. They didn't want to spend the money even though it was well known that President Lincoln visited the courthouse once and slept the night in New Jesper. So there was a proud history, you see. Alfred was standup when you needed him. He had his faults but he was standup too.

The room began to empty, tables of well-dressed women side by side with tables of men in business suits, women looking into their purses and men consulting their wristwatches, an atmosphere of well-being, everyone mildly hilarious after such a fine lunch. A few of the men played dollar poker for the honor of picking up the check while the women meticulously counted out dollar bills and change, even-steven to the last penny. Lee thought there was a lesson to be found there somewhere. His father had introduced him to the dining room of the Drake when he was seven or eight years old, his birthday, dressed in short pants and a white shirt and jacket. Then as now his father had done most of the talking. The room had not changed over the years and his father had not changed either, except for deep lines in his face and the tremor in his fingers and his newfound enthusiasm for non sequiturs. The tables continued to empty and soon Lee and his father were alone but for two tables of men talking business, consulting documents, every few moments writing something in the margins. Their voices were inaudible and conspiratorial, though to anyone up from Hyde Park the North Side was conspiratorial as a matter of course. Hotel dining rooms were the Finland Stations of capitalist conspiracy. Lee watched this Kabuki with amusement until he heard his father clear his throat importantly.

That's what I wanted to talk to you about, his father said. This peculiar business I mentioned over the phone. Alfred Swan's part of it. He paused, evidently gathering his thoughts, and then he lowered his voice and said, Magda Serra's back in New Jesper. She arrived two weeks ago with her mother, apparently staying with friends. People have seen them here and there around town. One of the places they went to was the library, where they read old issues of the *World,* and you can guess which date they wanted. And when they found it they copied the article by hand. They were seen near the high school. They spoke to no one. Then, on Friday, Magda's mother called Alfred Swan and asked for an appointment. Alfred wasn't there—he and some friends had gone to Florida to play golf. The mother rung off without another word. And then she called me.

Lee had lit a cigarette and was listening hard.

Of course I told them to come over at once, my chambers. They wanted to know if there had been any progress on the case. I said I didn't think so, and if there had been I would have known. As you know, Chief Grosza died a few years ago. The high school principal moved to Decatur. Funny, it's not that long ago, really, but there's hardly anyone around from that time. Walter Bing, Alfred. The bank's been sold, you know, to a syndicate from Aurora. So there's a—I suppose you could say—loss of memory of that time.

Lee said, Who did the talking?

Mrs. Serra, the mother.

Not Magda?

A word here and there. But she was alert and certainly understood everything that was said. But she never smiled, not once, and sat quietly while her mother and I talked. Mrs. Serra was suspicious that Alfred was not in town. He seemed to have left the same time Mrs. Serra and her daughter arrived. I did assure her that Alfred was an avid golfer and was often away to play courses around the country. He spends more time on his golf game than he does his newspaper. His son's the publisher now, in name only. Alfred doesn't trust the boy. He thinks Alfred Jr. is unsound. He's right, too.

Did she believe you about the golf?

I don't know. I think so. It's the truth.

What else did Magda say?

I asked her if she remembered the events of that day, the—assault. The questioning by the police. The time she spent in the hospital. She took the longest time to answer, as if my questions were unfamiliar to her. I was sorry I brought the matter up. But she said finally that, no, she remembered nothing. She had amnesia for some time. And slowly she recovered her health and began to talk again and remembered her schooldays in New Jesper, the house she lived in, her friends. But of that day and the days following, nothing.

Lee was himself back in those days, a clear recollection of Magda and the classroom they shared, the various teachers. Lee said, Did Mrs. Serra say what she and Magda were doing in New Jesper?

I didn't want to pry, his father said. I didn't want it to appear as an interrogation. But it was the obvious question and when I asked it, Magda said her mother thought that if she returned to the scene of the assault she might remember something. She might remember who assaulted her and the circumstances, at least an idea of who it might have been. But the memory was locked away. Magda used an interesting phrase. She said her memory was asleep and would not awaken no matter what she did or what she saw or how hard she tried and she tried very, very hard. I remember you telling me she was a plump girl, always laughing, a mediocre student. But when I saw her she was slender. A pretty girl but she looked undernourished. She never smiled, and as they were leaving she said she had completed her studies and intended to become a teacher. She was working toward certification, grade school level.

Did she say where she was studying?

She did not.

Lee said, I remember those days as if they were yesterday. I remember the math teacher, Mr. Salmon, and the civics teacher, Mrs. Wool. The walls of the classroom were painted light green. Mrs. Wool had a world globe on her desk, lit from the inside. Magda sat next to me in Mrs. Wool's class. Always giggling, Magda.

You were listening to our meeting, weren't you?

Some of it. Most of it, I guess.

We were doing what we thought best for the town.

Yes, that was evident.

You shouldn't have eavesdropped.

Lee smiled and said, I'm afraid it was irresistible.

Listening to the grown-ups.

Being on the inside of things, Lee said.

I knew you were there, his father said. I could hear the floorboards creak, and as you'll discover one day, you always know when your own flesh and blood is nearby. It's almost a sixth sense.

I thought of raising hell with you and decided not to. What was the point? Your introduction to the real world, I suppose. His father shrugged and pushed his chair back from the table. The dining room was empty now, the time past three o'clock. The waiter was hovering with the check, and when he saw the old man's chair move he placed the check on the table and stepped back. The judge nodded but did not otherwise acknowledge the waiter.

The judge steepled his fingers and stared off into the vast silence of the dining room of the Drake Hotel. He did not speak for a full minute, his demeanor reminiscent of the courtroom. He said at last, I guess that's a fortunate thing, your good recall of those days. You've always had a good memory, Lee, and now you can put it to account. Magda wants to see you and my guess is that she wants to go over that ground, her school days in New Jesper. Magda remembers you in a fond way. She says you helped her in her studies, homework and the like. She says you were kind to her and not everyone was. Magda sends her best wishes and said she'd be in touch.

Part Four

THE WEDDING WAS POSTPONED indefinitely owing to June Nieman's pneumonia, a virulent strain that kept her in the hospital for a month with another two months at home in bed. She very nearly died. Laura was inconsolable for much of that time, spending part of every day at the hospital, though her mother was in quarantine and unable to see any visitors, even her family. Laura and her father played chess in the waiting room, suspending the game every half hour or so to appear at June's door to assure her they were there and looking after her. June was usually unconscious and motionless in her bed. Laura came home in the afternoon in tears, saying how small her mother looked in the bed, small and so thin she looked weightless. The lightest breeze could carry her away. Most evenings Laura would return to the hospital to sit in the waiting room and look in on her mother, believing that her mere presence would make some difference, of reassurance or confidence. As often as not her father would be there too, and they would resume their games of chess. Once she came across her father praying, his hands folded at his chin, his eyes closed. Laura had never seen him pray; they were not a religious family. The sight of her father at prayer unnerved her.

After her second week in the hospital June was awake but her fever was still high and she was hallucinating, one day conversing with circus acrobats, the next a much-loved aunt who had been dead for years. One afternoon June insisted Oliver Wendell Holmes Jr. was in the room, advising her on a case she had been researching before her illness. The doctors assured Laura and her father that hallucinations were a common side effect of pneumonia and its high fever but Laura was not convinced; she thought her mother was slipping into another world altogether, a world from which she might not be retrieved. When the hallucinations passed, June was apathetic, eating poorly, and barely able to muster a smile when Harold and Laura made their visits, Harold passing on amusing university gossip. One of the history instructors had taken up with a sophomore, and why not, since his specialty was the medieval papacy. One of the assistant deans had defected to Harvard, and it served him right. June took all this in listlessly. Her doctor said her morale was rock-bottom and no wonder. She had no defenses and seemed unable to imagine a future for herself and her family. This will take time, the doctor said. Have patience. Be of good cheer. Laura later told Lee that her mother's illness changed her outlook on life. The disease struck with no warning whatever, and would this always be the way of things? She was terrified during the worst of her mother's ordeal, never having been in the presence of serious illness. An arrested pregnancy was not an illness.

That time I visited you in the hospital, she said, your face wrapped in bandages. You had trouble speaking, remember? You were out of it, not yourself. I had never been in a hospital before, the antiseptic smell, the nurses so brusque. You had the pallor of a prison inmate. I hated it. That was the worst until now.

The Hyde Park community rallied round, bringing books, bringing meals, looking after the cat, cleaning the house. The Niemans and Lee were invited to dinner any time they wanted to come. Colleagues taught Harold's classes. Laura was given the semester off, her fellowship postponed until she felt able to take it up. Still, Laura believed things were out of control. She and her father had managed to survive the tempest but only barely, and who knew when it might return and carry them all away.

Laura was living in a steady state of uncertainty, even peril. For a time she visited one of the many Hyde Park psychoanalysts, this one trained by Herr Freud himself, but the psychoanalyst was mainly interested in her dreams whereas Laura was interested in her mother's dreams. Where in the world had the acrobats come from? And who summoned Mr. Justice Holmes? Nothing Laura had read in four years of inquiry into the work of philosophers had prepared her for the emotional turmoil caused by her mother's illness, not even the great Stoics. And, she added with something approaching contempt, especially the great Stoics. The truth was, no one knew anything of value. The philosophers, in their preoccupation with the mind, had neglected unruly emotions. Her life had been turned upside down and she had no idea when it would right itself, if it ever did. She had lived in a beautiful world and now that world was gone and replaced by something ugly, menacing, and negligent. The doctors were no more help than the philosophers.

In the last analysis, she said to Lee, you have only yourself and your family to rely on when you're waltzing with the unknown. You've been wonderful. I feel closer to you than I ever have. You have such patience. You're never rattled. Does that come from working with heavy stone? Maybe that's why you work with marble.

You bet, Lee said.

Only promise me one thing. You'll never get sick.

I promise.

You've got to mean it, she said.

I'll never get sick, Lee said.

I couldn't bear it, Laura said.

You could. But you won't have to.

How do you *know?* she demanded, suddenly near tears.

Goodells know, he said. It's a family trait like blue eyes or a clubfoot. We Goodells have second sight. Lee was smiling as he said this and when he was finished Laura was smiling too. That night she turned a corner. Soon after, her mother did also and by Christmas her health returned for good and life resumed its normal pace, more or less.

NEW JESPER AND OGDEN HALL were much with me at this time. I was conscious of having entered a wider world, Chicago and Hyde Park and the university together with my studio. There were many like me at the university, small-town boys good at studies, very good at examinations, not experienced in the world. The world was the classroom, its maps and histories, its novels and poems and plays, its sciences and religions, the facts written in chalk on a blackboard. Shakespeare, Copernicus, Hegel, Luther. Master Shakespeare and you mastered the world, at least the British part of it. Reading Shakespeare, you knew where you stood in the Elizabethan scheme of things, the specific identities of the rulers and the ruled. How difficult it was translating Shakespeare to New Jesper, where the rulers were identified only as "they."

I understand they're floating a new bond issue. Sewers, I hear.

Have you seen the new stoplight up New Jesper Street? When did they decide to do that?

They're not saying much about it but there was a bad situation at the high school the other day. Some poor girl assaulted. They're expecting an arrest any day now . . .

I was different in my view of the order of things, owing to my father's position in our town. To me, they were not "they" but something approaching "we." I was an accomplice of "we." I think at a very early age I understood the American system, the country so various, so large and unruly, poised to fly apart at any moment. The system was founded on compromise and reconciliation, an infinity of checks and balances but always the willingness to look the other way until the world forced close focus. The states passed a constitutional amendment. The nation went to war. The small towns of America played no role in this except to supply the votes and the armies. Really, the decisions were made elsewhere, by others who were better educated and better informed. They were authorities. They held the high cards. I thought of them as Homer thought of the Fates, entitled to make any decree they wished (and in due course a notice appeared in the *World*). Laura said to me once, You have such patience. You're never rattled. You—she laughed here—never give instructions. I suppose she was correct. I think I never wanted to make the choices my father was obliged to make—indeed was eager to make—to keep the lid on lest, lidless, the pot boiled over with unforeseen consequences. People had to be protected from themselves, and my father along with the publisher and the bank president and the others were the self-appointed protectors. They had tremendous confidence in themselves and a shared view of the world, its surfaces and undercurrents, its caprices. Someone had to decide. They decided, for the good of the community, its morale. Of course at the bottom of it, the foundation of it, lay the enigma of class in America. But of that they never spoke.

During the course of June Nieman's illness I spent nights in my studio, determined to finish the three pieces that would give me the hoped-for baker's dozen. When I had them, I would have a show. One gallery on the South Side and two downtown had expressed interest on no more faith than rumor generated by Laura's father, who was widely acquainted with Chicago's art world, then a small but lively place given to sudden and often inexplicable enthusiasms—the French expressionist Bernard Buffet, for example, who for a time was as ubiquitous in fashionable living rooms as the Social Register. Buffet was a North Side phenomenon. Hyde Park leaned more in the direction of the anguished German expressionists, Beckmann, Dix, and Kirchner, altogether more strenuous, more disturbing, than the Frenchman. However, the North Side was where the money was, and the North Side was always eager to support local talent. Harold Nieman said I could forget about the North Shore. Except for a very few very well-heeled and very cultivated merchant princes and their wives, the North Shore was a wasteland. Stay away from it, Harold said. Republicans lived there.

Graduation came and went. My father agreed to continue my allowance while I finished the three pieces, which I was working on simultaneously. I had never done that before and I have never done it since, but in those months I was filled with a fanatic's energy, sleeping no more than three or four hours a night, eating infrequently, slowly losing confidence that this work would amount to anything. Laura spent one or two nights a week at the studio and the other nights in our apartment or at her parents' house or, when her mother was in a bad way, in the waiting room of the hospital. By that time I had acquired a telephone and Laura called every night with a medical report on her mother and whatever other news she had gathered. She knew enough to let the telephone ring and ring before she hung up, knowing that I was so absorbed in my work that I often did not hear the ringing. I was always happy when she called, her voice so soft and seductive. We would often spend thirty minutes or more on the telephone. She was clever the way she went about the calls, the first few minutes a slow recitation of the mundane details of her day, aimless chitchat while she waited for me to arrive in her world from my own and turn my back on Number Eleven and, as she said, join the party—meaning, listen to her voice as opposed to the voices in my head. I thought of it as akin to the crafty opening of a novel, setting a false scent, lulling the reader, encouraging the reader to enter an unknown house; don't worry, everything's going to be fine.

I was happy too when she dropped in at the studio, though twice she quietly slipped through the door and went straight to the couch and to sleep before I even knew she was in the room.

When you are twenty-one years old your powers of concentration are formidable, and later the power of concentration can be translated to absent-mindedness. I would step back from Number Twelve and light a cigarette while staring a hole through the marble, determined to discover the nature of the interior, look left, and there she'd be, eyes closed, breathing softly. I thought there was something miraculous about it, as if she were delivered to the couch by some supernatural agency. How did she get inside without my noticing? I always worked better when she was in the room despite the temptation to join her on the couch; the temptation easy to yield to. At any event, I always yielded. I had an idea that if we were ever rich enough to afford a house we would buy one with a full basement, a large basement with room enough for my table and marbles and of course a couch big enough for two. Laura would have a spacious room upstairs for her own work, and that room too would have a couch beneath a big bay window, and beyond the window a street with serious high-crowned trees. Both the basement and Laura's study would have telephones, each phone with its own number so that we could call when the spirit moved.

One night she said, When will you be finished?

Soon, I said.

How soon?

Maybe next week, I said, gesturing around the room. Numbers One through Ten were arrayed on pallets along the wall, numbers Eleven, Twelve, and Thirteen on my long worktable. There was almost no free space except for the couch. The floor was thick with marble dust and I knew I would have to set aside some time for housecleaning, though not just yet.

That soon?

Maybe, I said.

You're holding something back, she said.

I've lost confidence, I said. That's what this is, a confidence game. You have to have an iron belief that what you're doing is good. Your best. The best you can do, and if you lose that belief it's chaos.

I don't believe that, she said.

It's true, I said. It's the worst feeling imaginable.

Listen to me, she said and embarked on a kind of soliloquy on the emotions of low moments and high, as difficult to decipher as the *Tractatus*. Think about it long enough and you'll be as crazy as Wittgenstein. She said, Think only of the work. Not your own relation to the work but the work itself as if it were being composed by someone else, a separate mind inside your own mind. Do you see? Step back. Concentrate only on the matter at hand. Keep your emotions focused on the matter. You keep thinking of it as a confidence game you'll lose and we cannot allow that to happen. Do you believe that?

Yes, I said. I like the use of the word "we."

We're together, she said. Go back to work now.

I believe I will, I said.

One last thing, she said. Harold has a friend he wants you to meet. His name's Alvarez. Alvarez and his wife own a gallery up on the North Side. They like new work and they want to see your marbles.

HAROLD NIEMAN was as good as his word. The gallery was located off Michigan Avenue not far from the Drake Hotel, a second floor space with dead-white walls, perfect for my black marbles. The owners were enthusiastic about my pieces but warned me at the same time not to get my hopes up. New work was difficult to sell and an unknown artist was a dubious, not to say reckless, quantity and a tremendous amount depended on luck, the right crowd, the right setting, the weather, what the headlines said that morning. News from Korea, news from Wall Street, news about the election. Mim Alvarez said, We want them in a good mood. We want them upbeat and confident. We want them to walk into the casino feeling lucky, as if they could successfully draw to an inside straight. We want them thinking that their lives won't be worth turds unless they have one of your marbles in the parlor. We want them thinking about peace, progress, and prosperity—especially prosperity in the form of lower taxes. All these things are beyond our control except for the drink and there'll be lots of that. And one more thing. They'll want to like you. They'll want to see an artist with a great future ahead. They'll want in on the ground floor. They'll be sizing you up, Lee. Put on a good face. Make nice to them.

We were sitting in their gallery, Laura and I, and Mim and her husband Jason. Jason was explaining how they began in the business. I inherited some money from my aunt, Mim put in. That started it, Jason said, but I was the one who got to know Herr Mackel just at the time he wanted to sell and return to the old country and a farmhouse he owned near Seebüll, almost at the Danish border. So we bought the gallery, Herr Mackel retaining a percentage—for his retirement, he said. He died last year and the percentage died with him. And here we are. Why are you shaking your head, Lee?

Did he handle an artist called Tommy Ogden?

He did. We have half a dozen of Ogden's pieces. Decent work. Hard-edged, quite original in composition. I think he had no formal training at all. He began with hunting sketches, then turned to brothel scenes in the manner of Toulouse-Lautrec, except with Ogden the scenes were more domestic than erotic. Herr Mackel was a friend of Ogden's and swore the brothel was somewhere in Chicago but he never found out where. I had the feeling he knew much more than he was saying. Strange thing is, Ogden's prices keep going up. Have done ever since his death. It's too much to call him a cult figure but he definitely has an audience. Do you want to see the ones we have?

We walked into the print room and Jason Alvarez pointed at the side wall, six sketches grouped around the sign TOMMY OGDEN. They were all of women—women painting their toenails, reading, knitting, washing their hair, resting, looking into a mirror. On careful inspection each drawing contained a jarring object, a small revolver on a nightstand, a porcelain tiger, a compass, a man's bow tie, binoculars, a rifle's telescopic sight. The composition was dense in the German manner, most carefully drawn. It was hard to imagine Tommy Ogden's heavy fingers executing such meticulous work. But there was no denying the emotion that went into it.

I think the brothel is called Chez Siracusa and it lives to this day, I said, and that was all I said.

Mim Alvarez handled the art and her husband dealt with the money. It was his idea to put a high price on my pieces and the same price for each, except for Number One, which was listed at fifteen hundred dollars. The others were set at one thousand even, a very high price in those days. If we are going to fail, Jason said, we might as well fail big. The gallery took fifty percent. They would expect a guest list from Laura and me and another list from Harold and June but the bulk of the guests would come from their own client list, proven buyers whose checks always cleared the bank. Jason Alvarez would romance the press, meaning the five daily newspapers and the two or three radio stations that might mention the opening. Posters would be prepared and distributed widely but mainly in Hyde Park and the Near North Side. The piece Mim chose for the poster was, naturally, Number One, with a smallish photograph of me, lower left, in profile, which seemed to emphasize the scar that ran from eyeball to chin. The photograph of Number One was shot in such a way that a careful observer would notice the perpendicular cut in the marble and associate the two. Laura was skeptical of this project, believing it an unfortunate "signature," as she called it. She compared it, not very favorably, to Dalí's mustache and Picasso's bare chest. Also Al Capone.

Mim had asked, Will you please think of titles that are not so blind? I mean something more descriptive.

I said, No.

I think the titles should be rethought, she said.

No, I said again, and that was that.

The vernissage ran from six to eight, a full bar and a buffet table crowded with canapés. I suppose at the height of it a hundred people were in the room, young and old, North Side and South Side, and my parents as well, at first ill at ease in a room full of strangers and then more relaxed when June Nieman took them in hand. Harold took great pleasure in introducing me to his downtown friends, the ones whom I had never seen at Sunday lunch. Many of these were bankers and brokers, and I learned then that Harold was a director of one of the small downtown banks, a position he took seriously. He was one of the few Chicago economists asked to join a bank's board, his specific task to explain the present in order to forecast the future. I attempted affability but my eyes always wandered to the marbles to see who was looking at them and I tried to judge from the expressions on their faces whether they were intrigued or bored. In the beginning this was discouraging. I saw weary, puzzled faces, fingers scratching chins. The weariest face of all belonged to Dr. Petitbon, who stood with a glass of scotch in his hand looking skeptically at Number One; and then he turned and saw me and gave a wintry smile, more grimace than smile, and I was left to wonder whether it was a comment on me, my work, or the company he found himself in. But he had thought to come, and when I sent him the invitation I was doubtful that he would.

Then, sometime around seven-thirty, the first red star went up. That was followed in a few moments by another, and a third. The room was aroar with conversation and laughter, two bartenders doing their dance behind the long table, Mim and Jason Alvarez in continual discussion with one or another client. A fourth and fifth red star went up. Number One was still unclaimed, but in a few minutes it too was sold. I shouldered my way through the crowd to my parents, to see how they were getting on.

My father asked, What do the red stars mean?

Sales, I said.

They're buying them? Your sculptures?

It seems they are, I said.

My God, Lee, these things of yours are expensive.

I think so too. But I guess it doesn't matter.

Congratulations, my mother said. They're lovely, your marbles.

And then I was swept away again by Harold Nieman, who wanted me to meet the woman who had bought Number One. She wanted to know my life story and I had to explain that I didn't have much of a life story, or if I did, the plot had yet to reveal itself. I was engaged to Harold's daughter. My father was a judge. I went to the university but neglected my studies. When she said she occasionally wrote articles on art and artists and intended to write one about me now that she had possession of Number One, I said sure, any time. This must be a proud moment for you, she said, you've had a great success at your debut. Yes, I said, very, and the only event comparable was when I was eighteen and a member of an undefeated football team, their first time ever. That was a good day too. She laughed at that and said, What school?

Ogden Hall, I said.

Ogden Hall, she repeated without enthusiasm. She said, My parents knew Tommy Ogden and his frau.

I met him once, I said.

I did also, more than once.

Tell me about him, I said.

You're lucky to have gotten out of Ogden Hall alive, she said. Bad spirits in that house. Bad all around.

Ogden Hall was okay, I said loyally.

Tommy Ogden wasn't okay, she said. He was a bully.

I'm sorry, I said. I didn't get your name.

Trish van Horne, she said.

I smiled at Laura across the room. A number of our friends were there, Jill from Fifteen Hundred, the Indian graduate student Anand, my schoolmate Hopkins. Charles Fford had sent a telegram. I waved at Dr. Petitbon, who was gathering his coat from the rack at the doorway, a glass in his hand. The doctor had told me that the clinic was finished, kaput, and he was returning to Louisiana "where I belong." Now he waved back and disappeared through the door. When I turned to say another word to Trish van Horne she was gone too, vanished into the crowd that had collected around the bar.

Someone had opened a window to clear the cigarette smoke and the room was suddenly chilly. I saw another red star appear, next to Number Nine, and self-consciously turned my back and stepped to the open window. A line had formed at the movie house down the street, *An American in Paris*. Georges Guétary's version of "I'll Build a Stairway to Paradise" drifted up from a loudspeaker. The street was crowded with people going to dinner or the movie. I looked left, past the movie house and beyond Michigan Avenue to the lake, a black void in the darkness. Rain was in the air. A limousine was stalled in traffic and I remembered Tommy Ogden, his open Cadillac and his chauffeur, his whiskey flask and his sneer, his disdain of the Great Books, and his advice on the way of the world. You don't learn a god damned thing from defeat, a chain around your neck. Win always. Keep it to yourself. The world doesn't give a shit. Surely Tommy Ogden would be pleased at my success this evening. But as I stared at the lake-void I remembered Augustus Allprice and his *Omoo* lecture, life below decks, a life of uncertainty and sudden peril, all of it supervised by an unreliable navigator. But these were the ingredients of a well-lived life. I had no idea what had happened to the headmaster and his beautiful Anjelica; surely there was something beyond Patagonia. One could not live in Patagonia forever. People were always moving on, looking for a place to belong to, Dr. Petitbon going home to Louisiana, my mother abandoning New Jesper for the North Shore. Why not Patagonia forever? In its self-sufficiency, its apartness, its occasional violence, Patagonia bore some relation to Hyde Park. I raised my glass in the direction of the lake-void and wished Gus Allprice well. *Gus Gus Gus.*

Then Laura was at my side, her arm through mine. I looked around and found the guests beginning to disperse. Someone came by and patted me on the shoulder and said, Well done. A photographer was circling the room, the first time I had seen him. He was dressed in a well-worn black suit and a fedora, an unlit cigar in his fist. He maneuvered us in the direction of my marbles and took two quick shots, his flashbulbs blinding. I turned to Laura and asked when she thought we could decently leave, maybe go down the street for a drink and a light dinner.

I'm worn out, I said.

She said, Harold and June want to take us and your parents to dinner.

Can't we just slip out?

They're proud of you, darling. They want to celebrate.

What do you think?

It's your night, she said. Enjoy it. You don't look as if you're enjoying it.

I'm enjoying it. That's why I want to slip out for a drink.

We can do that after dinner, she said.

The photographer was suddenly in our faces, asking us to smile nicely for the newspaper. I forced one and he went away after writing our names and ages in the little black book he carried in his pocket.

It'll be fun, she said.

I thought of the photographer and then of Tommy Ogden and his prescription for happiness, or anyway dominance, and the decision was made. Tell Harold and June okay, I said. The sooner the better.

That was quick, she said.

I laughed sourly and said I had good advice. I had decided to cast against type.

But in the event, I was not much good at dinner, even though my father and Harold got into a spirited argument over the election, darkened when Harold referred to General Eisenhower as Bubblehead. My father took offense and inquired whether Harold would have preferred Adlai to supervise D-day. Adlai was an egghead. Adlai would not know how to end the war in Korea because he did not understand the worldwide communist threat, whereas the general, with the reliable Nixon at his side, understood the Asian situation root and branch, to which Harold replied that Nixon was a scoundrel and a threat to the Republic— and June intervened to raise her glass and propose a toast to Laura and her successful dissertation and to me and my successful marbles and to our marriage which would be more successful still, especially when there were grandchildren.

Meanwhile, a summer storm lashed at the windows of the restaurant on Rush Street. I was distracted and bone-tired, as if the strain of all the work of the past years—laborious, shadowed always by doubt—had settled upon me all at once. I was not accustomed to attention. I was not accustomed to praise except for the periodic pep talks I gave myself and Laura's evident confidence. Now and again I did look back to the final game of the undefeated season, walking alone on the football field in a state of the purest satisfaction. I was bone-tired then too, but fully focused and looking to the future. I was not now looking to the future. I wanted only that the marriage ceremony be over and done with so that Laura and I could begin a normal life. The truth was, I was rattled and wanted to go home with Laura. Even Mumm's champagne did not ease my torpor as I listened to Harold and my father disagree amiably on the shape of the Eisenhower foreign policy until my father observed that John Foster Dulles, the general's principal adviser, was unsound. New York lawyers were fundamentally unsound, owing to their allegiance to Wall Street and to Europe. Democrats or Republicans, it made no difference, to which Harold said he couldn't agree more except for the Europe part; and that left them in a quandary. Minutes went by without my saying one word, and my father noticed and asked me if anything was wrong, and I said no, of course not, only a mild postpartum depression that would disappear as soon as I got back to work. Laura and I left early for Hyde Park and I fell asleep in the cab.

I am bound to say that the newspaper reviews, both of them, were merciless. They know how to do that in Chicago, a jackboot to the kneecap without remorse, indeed with a sort of civic glee. Another impostor exposed, Chicago saved from an obscurantist arriviste. I was badly wounded but not destroyed, and in due course went back to work as before.

ONE MONTH LATER Laura and I were married by my father in the university chapel. The old man's judicial baritone was never put to better use; and yes, he did have a pompous quality but I found him endearing. June insisted on the reception being held at home instead of at Harold's downtown club. This is a Hyde Park affair, she said. It has nothing to do with the city. June also had the idea of hiring the pianist from the Blue Note, who arrived with a drummer and a bassist and played the most supple blues. Improbably, the pianist was Russian by birth and before long had a devoted following from members of the Russian department at the university, all talking Russian while requesting the usual standards. He struggled to keep up his end. I remember fondly my parents dancing to the music with something like abandon until my father tired and had to be assisted to a chair and handed a glass of champagne. He and my mother were elated and she kept pulling at his arm to return to the dance floor and at last he did, with a helpless shrug and a wide smile, his cheeks as red as tomatoes. I had never seen them so affectionate with each other and when at last they switched partners with

Harold and June my father was in a state of happy collapse, but even so, he managed an athletic two-step to the pianist's signature solo, "Sweet Georgia Brown." I watched the pianist's fingers dancing left and right, his head nodding like a metronome, and I thought his economical style somehow reminiscent of Chekhov rather than, say, the turbulent Dostoevsky. But that may have been simply more wretched obscurantism from an arriviste impostor. I decided it would be a great thing to be a musician with a signature piece, no version identical. That was what I tried to do with my marbles, all recognizable members of the same family but each with a unique personality, and probably the musician would believe the same thing, each melody delivering a different emotion or a different definition of the same emotion, "Sweet Georgia Brown" played as a march or a dirge or a plink-plink of happy popular music, depending on the tempo and the mood of the musician. He was playing it now as it might be played at a debutante's cotillion, without a debutante in sight except for Jill of Fifteen Hundred, doing a frantic Charleston with Anand. Other dancers made way for them, and it was then that I noticed Alfred Swan looking on with an expression of the utmost alarm as if he were witnessing the prelude to something unseemly, a bacchanal or an orgy, perhaps a coup d'état. Near the bar, a glass in hand, Dr. Petitbon listened to the music with his customary expression of anxiety. He had explained to me that he did not care for jazz music, blues in particular. He had French blood and preferred cabaret, Piaf and Jacqueline François. The blues inspired unhappy memories whereas cabaret offered consolation.

Laura and I cut the cake and moved to the dance floor as the pianist swung into *Fidelio* as Jelly Roll Morton might have played it. I danced with June, Laura danced with my father, and then the floor came alive with dancing friends and family, even Alfred Swan with portly Mrs. Swan. The trio played until nine, when they hurriedly packed their instruments and departed for the Blue Note to begin their evening engagement. Everyone clapped and cheered when they finished their final set and Laura gave the pianist a red rose from one of the vases on the buffet table. The company was momentarily bereft without the piano, the drums, and the bass. The room went silent, then someone rapped a spoon against a glass and the toasts began—Harold, then June, my father, my mother. I had never heard my mother give a toast or speak in any public way but she spoke fluently and affectionately about her new daughter-in-law and when she finished everyone cheered. Professor Altschuler delivered a witty tour of philosophers on the subject of marriage, beginning with Wittgenstein and the *Tractatus* and ending with Vico, the Neapolitan philosopher and jurist, Laura's particular favorite for his theory of "ideal eternal history." Vico's great subject was justice, so Professor Altschuler expatiated on justice as it related to marriage and of course vice versa. Laura grinned all the way through and when the professor finished there seemed nothing to add, but the additions came nevertheless, from Anand and Professor James James and Jill of Fifteen Hundred and my old schoolmate Hopkins, who offered a sarcastic version of the married life, not neglecting the erotic. Alfred Swan contributed a gruff commentary on the virtues of small-town sentiments and the preparation they gave for civic engagement, notably the presence of a community newspaper of conscience, publishing always without fear or favor. The Hyde Park professoriate appeared puzzled by the theme but applauded with enthusiasm, even as it noted the little Ike button in the publisher's lapel. But what could you expect from an Illinois newspaper publisher, reactionary almost by definition? And Ike wasn't all bad—not very bright and a soldier but accustomed to command. Things could have been much, much worse. The nominee could have been the hopeless Taft.

Laura and I managed to steal away for a moment or two in Harold's study. We sat on the window seat and looked at the elms across the street, now in full leaf. The night was calm but very dark. From far away we heard a police siren. Laura said, Is it going to be all right? Yes, I said. Fabulous. She meant our honeymoon. The following day we were booked on the Twentieth Century Limited to New York and a ship bound for Naples. Laura was eager to visit the birthplace of Giovanni Battista Vico, assuming it still existed and could be located. Vico had been dead for two hundred years. This would be Laura's first trip abroad, and mine too. My idea: I thought we should see something of the world before we settled down in Hyde Park. It was easy to believe that Hyde Park was the world, but it wasn't really. Laura was dubious at first. She had always wanted to visit New York and Boston for the museums and symphony orchestras, though the orchestras would be inferior to the Chicago Symphony. But she agreed at last and I engaged a travel agent to make the bookings, the train and the ship and more trains in Italy and the accommodations.

The travel agent warned me that the war was still present in Italy, not literally but figuratively, and to expect communist demonstrations wherever we went—the hatred of the government was palpable and since the government changed every week or so the hatred only increased and the violence with it. Do not expect anything truly first class. The trains were unreliable. Naples was dangerous. Rome was more dangerous. Tuscany was least dangerous, and of course we would want to see the Uffizi and the many palaces and churches not only in Florence but in Siena and Lucca. For that you will need a reliable car. The roads are appalling. The streets are filthy. The people could be warm but they were sly also and always expecting a handout. There is a word you must know. *Chiuso.* That means closed, and you will find that shops are often *chiuso* at exactly the time you want to shop. In addition, you must be vigilant at all times owing to the many pickpockets who stalk American tourists. The travel agent said she did not understand why we wished to travel to Italy. Have you thought about Paris? Paris was not subject to the fas-

cist boot, in the manner of Italy and the operatic Benito Musso-
lini, and despite what you may have heard or read, the trains do
not run on time in Italy. They also say that Rome is the Eternal
City. Rome is not the Eternal City and it never was. Paris is the
Eternal City. You will eat well in Paris whereas in Naples and
Rome you may starve.

I told Laura none of this. We talked about our Italian plans
as we sat on the window seat and looked into the street and the
lights of the houses opposite. We agreed we had had a mem-
orable wedding and reception and how miraculous it was that
everyone had gotten along so well together, not a single argument
save for the professor's wife who had challenged Alfred Swan's
Ike button, Swan not giving an inch until the professor's wife
gave it up with the remark that she wished the Republicans well,
undeserving though they were. It had been so long since they
had run a country, she hoped they had not forgotten how to do
it. *Wilkommen* Herbert Hoover. Poor Adlai. Laura laughed then
and remarked that there were so many toasts of such duration
that we had not thought of our own and no one brought it up.

Laura and I returned to the living room where the party was
in its last moments. Anand and Jill had departed. Hopkins was
gone. Dr. Petitbon was long gone. Those who remained were
conspicuously tipsy, including Harold and June and my parents.
Laura went off to say goodbye to someone, leaving me to cast
an eye around the room, which always seemed to me like one of
those reconstructed rooms you saw in museums. This one was
filled with Bauhaus furniture, all wood and leather and here and
there a chrome lamp. One of the chairs had been conceived and
constructed by Marcel Breuer himself. The walls were crowded
with German and French art and on a little table next to the fireplace my own Number Nine. It seemed more or less at home on
the table. Absent the jazz trio, Harold had put Gustav Mahler's
fifth symphony on the phonograph. All in all, the room had a
between-the-wars feel to it, meaning a sense of apprehension, a

provisional room consistent with the ambiance of Hyde Park. I watched Laura as she talked to Professor Altschuler, the old man blushing slightly at whatever she was saying to him. Harold and my father were in close conversation, gesticulating so that champagne spilled from their glasses. This was all too much. I was eager to get away with Laura, go back to our apartment and pack for the long day and night ahead. One of Laura's friends came to say goodbye and thanks and what a marvelous time she had had, none better, and good luck. That struck a false note—what did luck have to do with anything?—but I thanked her for coming. She said, *Ciao.*

Then my father was at my elbow, breathing hard. His hair was mussed.

I said, You had a good time.

He put his hand on my shoulder. Time of my life, he said. Where have you been?

Laura and I had a moment alone.

Time enough for that, he said.

I guess there will be.

I had a nice chat with your friend Petitbon. Nice fellow.

What did Petitbon say?

He told me about your work at his clinic. I didn't know you worked at a clinic.

It wasn't a particular success, I said.

He thought it was. He thought you'd learned something.

I suppose I did, I said. I don't remember what.

My father smiled and handed me an envelope. He said, For Italy. Have fun.

We will, for sure. Thank you.

Lee, he said and paused a moment. Call me right away when you get back.

WE DOCKED AT NAPLES in a fierce rainstorm and heavy wind from the Tyrrhenian Sea. Laura and I went at once to the hotel, situated in a narrow street near the port. The hotel dated from the nineteenth century and looked as if it had had a bad war, perhaps more than one. The carpet on the floor of the reception room was threadbare. A steep marble staircase led to the upper floors, rising and disappearing into the gloom of forty-watt lightbulbs. The woman at the desk was voluble, remarking on the filthy weather and advising that the rain would last three days. It always did, owing to the merciless west wind. The Tyrrhenian Sea was merciless also, and had been since antiquity. Yet how fortunate you are to be in Naples as opposed to Rome and its self-regard. There are those who disagree but I believe we have a lighter spirit in Naples. We are accustomed to adversity. We are continually discriminated against in Naples! They think we are peasants. Bah! she said. The reception room smelled of old wood and tobacco and, unaccountably, peaches. In an armchair in the corner an old man snoozed. Alas, the woman said, the lift was out of order but she had put us into a fine room but one flight up. She offered a brilliant smile as she pointed to the stairs. You are honeymooners, she said. Laura agreed that we were. There have been many honeymooners in room twelve, she said. None have complained!

We managed to wrestle our luggage up the treacherous staircase but when we reached the room we were enchanted. It was very large with a high ceiling and a window that looked out on a tiny piazza. A bottle of Prosecco was chilling in a bucket. I opened the window to give us air and also to listen to the rain drumming on the flagstones of the piazza. In its utter privacy and strangeness, its breadth and height, its atmosphere of twilight, its great age and sense of occasion, the room was erotic. Laura felt it too. From one of the windows above the piazza we heard a burst of song and someone laughing. I poured two glasses of Prosecco and we undressed and sat on the windowsill and watched the rain fall and collect into puddles on the flagstones below. We were alone on our honeymoon in a place unspeakably exotic, remote as the farthest star in the heavens. We knew no one here and no one knew us. Laura and I tumbled into bed and did not leave the room for twenty-four hours, ordering dinner in that night and lunch the next day, the desk woman remarking each time how pleased she was that we liked our room; and we were not the first. There was no good reason to leave it, at least not until the afternoon, when the rain ceased and the sun arrived and we thought we owed it to ourselves to see a church or a palace. Debt paid, we found an open-air restaurant near the Piazza Dante and dined wonderfully on fish and two bottles of Prosecco. The stone horseman across the street from the restaurant was pockmarked from bullets and shrapnel from Allied bombing, all of it vividly described by the woman at the hotel. The Italian campaign, she said sourly, graveyard of the reputations of American generals. Our graveyard also, she went on, including her own niece and nephew, killed when bombs fell on their apartment. Naples was badly wounded in the Italian campaign, a useless enterprise, but war in general was a useless enterprise, would we not agree? When she asked us where we were from in America, and we said Chicago, she laughed and imitated a hoodlum firing a machine gun; Chicago's lurid reputation always preceded us. I remembered the war games I had played as a boy, never for a moment thinking of the Italian campaign or a pockmarked horseman or dead nieces or nephews.

The next day we went in search of Vico's birthplace but never found it, waylaid as we were by two churches and a long lunch followed by a visit to the archaeological museum. Laura said she didn't care about our Vico failure. Vico seemed far away, even from Naples. Vico could wait until our next visit. The following day we departed for Rome on an ancient train that arrived exactly on schedule. We shared a compartment with two priests who chatted merrily for the entire journey, laughing frequently and rolling their eyes. I was convinced they were talking about girls, but of course that was most unlikely.

Ten days later we found ourselves in Florence, Laura down with a nasty summer cold. She waved her hand feebly: Go away. See the sights. Report back. I wandered across the river to look at the Boboli Gardens, then strolled back again to the Piazza del Duomo. Everywhere I went I scrutinized the statuary and the interiors of churches, thinking they might give me an idea for a fresh project when I returned to my studio in Hyde Park. I photographed constantly with my Kodak but tried to keep what I saw in my memory too. I was trying to retain all of Italy and failing badly, the nation concealed behind the hedges of an unfamiliar language and an ambiance that was at once approachable and enigmatic, not unlike my marbles.

I found a shapely square with a café and stopped for a Prosecco and a double espresso. The hotel was close by and I wished Laura were with me. I liked listening to Italian voices all around me, understanding little but the enthusiasm of their speech. The day was bright, a Wednesday, three in the afternoon. The square was crowded and I wondered if anyone actually worked in Italy besides cooks and waiters. Bus drivers. The policeman directing traffic and the tobacco vendors. Many of the shops round and about were *chiuso*. I lit a cigarette and sat back with my Prosecco, quite content in idleness and anonymity. Across the square was a very old building that looked to contain apartments, its windows as blank as the entrances to caves. I looked at it a long time, a building six stories high, chimney pots at the top. It seemed to have the dimensions of a perfect square, of wooden construction. The door looked heavy enough to withstand a battering ram. No one was visible at the windows. The interior appeared to be as still as the square was lively, its stern face signaling a seigneurial disapproval. The people at the tables took no notice. The apartment building had been there for centuries and, I reckoned, had become more or less invisible, as invisible as I was, a lone American on his first voyage abroad attempting and mostly succeeding in becoming one with the surroundings. Not speaking the language was an advantage because I had no desire for conversation.

Then I felt a hand on my arm, the girl at the next table asking me in English if I could spare a cigarette for her and her friend. I passed them two cigarettes and a box of matches and when she said *grazie* and asked if I was American, and I said yes, the Canadian portion. She lost interest and after a brief smile returned to her tête-à-tête. I did notice her eyes blink when she saw my scar, but it may have been the mime, bone-white face and red stocking cap, moving among the tables and stopping every few moments to strike a pose. He carried a cup for the coins anyone wished to give him. I returned to my contemplation of the apartment building, thinking that Canadians were luckier than they knew. Now I had the idea that the apartment building was in fact a private house, a palace no less, and I guessed the family fortune had disappeared many years before. Probably it had not survived the first war. The building was in need of serious repair, the slatted shutters of the windows on the upper floors hanging drunkenly. I imagined the rooms crowded with artworks and every few years one would be put up for auction, here a Titian, there a Tintoretto, the proceeds from the auction allowing the family to maintain itself from one decade to the next. A daughter might marry an American millionaire and the millionaire would carry them for a while until he got tired of it or tired of the daughter or she with him. I made two photographs with my Kodak and ordered another Prosecco and meantime sipped my coffee.

My neighbors at the next table departed with an amiable *ciao*. The girl and her friend floated through the tables in a stride so languid and unforced that they reminded me of cats, and at the last moment they executed a little sidestep to elude the mime, whose arm had suddenly barred their way. America had never seemed so far away, Hyde Park as remote as Ultima Thule, New

Jesper the far side of the moon. I had difficulty recollecting the American ambiance, not that I was trying very hard. I thought of myself witnessing an avant-garde theater production where the audience was part of the show. All this was soon to disappear: our boat was due to sail in three days. Laura was already fretting about the freshman class she was teaching, her syllabus now in the hands of Professor Altschuler. They would teach the class together and that gave Laura the jitters. I grew drowsy in the bright sunlight. The door of the palace across the street opened to reveal a nun in full habit, looking cautiously around the square, locking the door with an enormous key and scuttling off, but not before she had glanced at the red-hatted mime standing statue-still a few feet away. It occurred to me that I had never seen a nun on the streets of Hyde Park, nor a mime. And then I heard a low laugh and a soft voice.

I knew I would find you here, Laura said.

I kissed her and said she looked better.

Am better, she said. And I'm tired of staying in my room.

The waiter arrived with my Prosecco. I gave it to Laura and asked the waiter for one more and two espressos. We sat a moment in affectionate silence and then I explained my speculations concerning the palace that I had first identified as an apartment house and turned out to be a nunnery. Unless I was mistaken once again. I pointed out the mime, who now appeared to be imitating the Statue of Liberty. Laura extracted a handkerchief from her purse and blew her nose. She said, I'm ready to go now.

You haven't touched your drink. And I have one on the way.

No, she said. I mean, I'm ready to go home to Hyde Park. I wish we were leaving tonight. I've had a wonderful time in Italy with you. But I've seen enough. I can't look at unfamiliar things anymore, the churches, the galleries. I'm tired of being among strangers. Don't you miss it? Our apartment, your studio. The grit and bang of Chicago? That's where we belong. Italy is an interlude.

Well, yes, I said.

We've had a great time but it's over now. Don't you agree?

I did not reply right away. I supposed I did agree but I wasn't sure. I had been an observer my whole life and there was plenty to look at in sunny Italy. I liked the idea of a nation in decline for two thousand years and not caring. I liked the idea of the mime and the nun. But Italy wasn't going anywhere. It would be here tomorrow and the next day and the day after.

I said, We could take the night train to Naples and stay at our old hotel. God knows there are plenty of unoccupied rooms. Maybe we could get our old one back. I looked up as the waiter deposited my Prosecco and two espressos. I asked for the check.

That was quick, she said. We clinked glasses and Laura took a long swallow.

She said, Are you sure you want to?

I didn't think I did. But I do now.

You don't mind changing plans?

They're our plans, I said, and we can change them if we want to.

I'd like to spend our last days in Naples. Naples is familiar.

It surely is, I said. And we can take an afternoon in Pompeii.

THIS WAS A PATTERN that would repeat itself habitually during our long life together. It didn't matter if we were staying somewhere for a week or a month; two or three days before we were due to depart we had had enough and began to yearn for home, meaning Hyde Park. This happened in Paris and Athens and St. Petersburg and Vienna and Bucharest and Los Angeles and, much later, in China. China seemed much larger and more populous than any nation had a right to be. The journey was exhausting. In Xi'an, looking at the terracotta warriors, Laura assigned each of them the name of a faculty member at the university. She got to fifty or so before she ran out of names. That was the signal that we were done in Xi'an, done with China, done with unfamiliar food and strangers swarming wherever we looked. China was fabulous but the true pulse of life eluded us. At any event, we were always happy leaving Chicago and even happier returning.

LAURA AND LEE arrived at their apartment in Hyde Park late on a sultry August afternoon. Laura ran off at once to visit her parents and tell them about Italy and the stormy voyages to and fro. Lee stowed their luggage in the bedroom and took a stroll in the neighborhood to stretch his legs. The day was sweltering, the temperature near one hundred degrees. He walked through empty streets to the dangerous neighborhood to assure himself that his studio was as he left it, and, aside from a family of mice in the closet, it was. He wondered about the empty streets and realized that of course everyone was at the lakefront. When he walked back to the apartment he thought to stop in at the liquor store to buy a bottle of Prosecco, a souvenir for Laura. The manager had none. He had never had a call for Prosecco. Italian, isn't it? Lee bought a bottle of scotch instead and returned to the apartment mildly let down. He wished he had bought a bottle of gin and some Schweppes and a fresh lime. The day was too warm for whiskey.

He made a drink and called his parents, retailing adventures in Italy, Naples and Rome and Florence. The museums, the galleries, the hotels, the food, the scenery. Lee said he had acquired a new outlook on things but what that outlook was he could not precisely say. Italians had a different way of life. Industriousness did not seem to play any part in it. But they were a cheerful and voluble people and had suffered greatly during the war. Alas, he and Laura had not seen any communist demonstrations and, truth to tell, revolution did not seem to be in the air. What was in the air? his father asked. Ardor, Lee said after a moment's pause. He had shot six rolls of photographs and when he had them developed he would send a few along, give you an idea of the look of things. Lee attempted to describe the encounter between the nun and the mime but the story did not hang together. I guess you had to have been there, he said at last. But aren't you happy to be home? his mother asked. Oh, yes, Lee said, Laura missed Hyde Park terribly. His mother rang off then. She had something on the stove. Please come see us as soon as you can, she said, and Lee replied that they would.

I'm glad you had a good time, his father said.

Is everything all right? Lee said. You sound subdued.

Remember last summer, Magda Serra and her mother were in New Jesper. They came to see me, not a productive conversation as I recall. Well, Magda's back. She insists on speaking to you and left a number.

She does?

She does. I'm afraid she was a little bit suspicious when I said you were about to leave on your honeymoon. She seemed to think I was keeping you from her. I said you would call her as soon as you got back and I gave her the date. I told her you went to Italy. I admit I was rushed, she called me in chambers while I was reading a difficult brief. I must say I did not care for her manner. She was curt. So it would be good if you called her right away. Will you do that?

Of course, Lee said.

I think she wants to talk about her life, his father said.

MAGDA AND LEE agreed to meet at a restaurant on the harbor at New Jesper, a family-owned place that specialized in whitefish and lake perch. Magda's voice sounded thin on the telephone, watery, certainly not curt. Lee came up from Chicago on the train and walked the six blocks to the restaurant, Carl's Seafood, fishnets and creels hanging on the interior walls, and beyond the windows one ancient scow from Carl's fleet tied up at the pier. The bar was noisy with lawyers from the courthouse but the dining room was not crowded. Magda was seated alone at a table in the corner of the room and looked up when Lee approached. She was dressed in a white shirt and blue skirt, a scarab necklace at her throat, as if she were meeting a prospective employer. Magda's hair was freshly done.

Oh, Lee, she said. He took both her hands in his and they embraced awkwardly. Thanks so much for coming. She smiled tentatively and Lee saw few reminders of her childhood self. She had been heavy but now she was as his father had said, slender and self-possessed where she had been self-conscious, always eager to please. Magda had been a girl from the wrong side of the tracks and knew it and wanted somehow to make amends. He tried to remember the name of the boy she went to the movies with, the lawyer's son, but could not. He did remember his eyeglasses and clownishness and her apple cheeks and high giggle, but there was no sign of them now. Lee was uncomfortably aware that he knew much more of Magda Serra's life than she knew of his and that put her at a disadvantage. When she asked him about his honeymoon he told her about Laura, how they met, her attachment to Hyde Park and the university, her father's work as a professor of economics, her mother's career in law. Laura was on track to become a professor of philosophy. Magda listened quietly, asking no questions. Lee knew he had gone too far in one direction and not far enough in another, speaking to her as if reciting an entry from *Who's Who*. He lamely described his studio and the work he did there, his marbles.

She said, Where did you get the scar?

A rumble, he said. My studio is in a dangerous neighborhood.

No, really, she said. I want to know.

I stepped outside to have a smoke and two boys jumped me.

What happened to them?

You know Chicago. It was a crime filed and forgotten.

They went free?

They were never caught. They went away, came back, and that was that. Lee opened his mouth to tell her about the clinic and Topper but decided against it. Magda looked at him most intently and seemed disappointed when he said nothing further. Lee had always been reticent, with a manner older than his years. He was friendly but there was always something withheld. Also, he was part of the system and she wasn't. He'd said to her, You know Chicago. But she didn't know Chicago. She had been to Chicago only once, years before, when she was a little girl. Her mother took her to see the Christmas windows of Field's and Carson Pirie Scott, brilliantly decorated in red and green and white, all manner of gifts in the windows. They did not go into the stores. They had lunch at a cafeteria in the Loop and went to a movie and then they went home. Magda remembered the sidewalks crowded with beautifully dressed women carrying festive packages from the department stores.

Their whitefish arrived, french fries and coleslaw on the side, iced tea in frosted glasses.

And you, Magda. You've come back to New Jesper.

I had to, she said.

I don't understand, Lee said.

I'm not sure I do myself, said Magda. There's so much I don't understand. That awful day and everything that followed. I am here but I feel I am looking at a blackboard where everything is written in a foreign language. I can read nothing on it. Nothing is familiar. I'm sure you have no idea what I am talking about. She smiled and said, You were always so nice to me, Lee. Do you remember helping me with my math?

Yes, I do.

I never got numbers. I never understood them and still don't. Magda looked up to see if Lee was listening. She pushed the whitefish here and there on her plate and took a nervous sip of iced tea. You were always good with explanations, Lee. Sometimes I felt you should be teaching the class. I always felt outside of things at our school, as if I was on probation. I didn't know what was expected of me. I felt shunned. My mother was always working so I came home to an empty house. My father had left us, God knows where. My mother thought he left for Puerto Rico with a woman but she never knew for sure. I still don't know if he's living or dead. Isn't that something?

Magda, Lee said, I had no idea. I knew there was trouble at home—

You knew? How did you know?

People talked, Lee said.

They talked about my family? she said.

Everyone was upset, after, Lee said.

After? she said.

You were hurt, Lee said.

I wasn't aware anyone cared, Magda said. She was silent then. The dining room had begun to empty but the bar business was brisk. The waiter took away their plates and asked if they wanted dessert, and Magda shook her head and said, Coffee, and Lee said, Two. When the waiter went away, Lee said, You didn't like your whitefish.

I have no memory of that day, Magda said. None. I don't remember going to school in the morning and I don't remember my classes. I don't remember lunch. I don't remember where I was or what I was doing when I was—attacked. I don't remember him. I can remember a Christmas window of a department store on State Street when I was eight years old but I can't remember *this*. I have a friend who's told me it's better off gone, this memory, but I'm not so sure. I tried hypnosis without result, although I don't think the hypnotist was much good. Her specialty was more voodoo than hypnosis. My mother said I didn't speak for months. I think I slept most of the time. That whole period is a blur, including the weeks in the hospital, one operation after another, bright lights in my eyes. The masked faces of doctors. Pain. I was so ashamed.

I understand, Lee said.

No, Lee. You don't.

I'm sorry, he said. Stupid of me.

Tell me this. Have you ever been ashamed in your life?

He thought a moment and shrugged. Then he said, Yes.

Maybe men don't get ashamed, Magda said.

The waiter arrived with coffee and the check, placed carelessly at Lee's elbow.

I thought it was my fault, she said. I had done something, said something, I didn't know what. I had brought this terrible thing on myself, yet I had no memory of it. I knew what had happened to me because I looked at my own body. I was frightened. My mother told me later that no one came to see me in the hospital except a policeman who wanted to ask questions and when he saw I was unable to answer them, he went away and did not return. I wanted to die but was afraid I would. When you were cut, did it hurt badly?

Yes, he said.

Deep pain, she said.

Yes, he said again.

Magda nodded and was silent once again, sipping her coffee and staring off into the empty dining room. The bar crowd was gathered around the entrance, an expectant hush as they listened to a joke and when the punch line came, a blast of laughter. Magda dropped two lumps of sugar into her coffee, stirred the sugar, and waited.

Magda, I'm so sorry. What an ordeal.

I am trying to rid myself of a blank space. How do you do that?

I don't know, Magda.

You've never had one?

No, I never have.

That's why I came back to New Jesper. I had to talk to someone, and I chose you.

Lee leaned across the table and said, I'm glad you did. I wish I could be of some help. He waited a moment, looking around the dining room, which now seemed to him unspeakably oppressive. All this time he had been remembering the meeting of the Committee, his father, Alfred Swan, the police chief and the banker and Walter Bing and the others, worried about the report in the newspaper. Worried, as he remembered so clearly, about the equilibrium of the town, its reputation. Lee said, I'm wondering if you'd like to take a walk. I've not been back to New Jesper in years. Would you like that?

All right, she said. It's awfully hot, though.

We can finish our coffee, Lee said.

Magda seemed to blush and said, I don't want to meet anyone. I don't know what I'd say to them or they to me. Whatever it would be, I don't think I want to hear it. But everybody's probably forgotten. Do you suppose they have?

Lee thought a moment and said, Not everybody.

I suppose not, she said. She toyed with her napkin, then threw it down. I wish he were dead. I want him dead. It's unfair that he's not, that he's walking around free like anyone else. And I'm the only one who could accuse him. Only me. And my memory is gone. I'm no help at all.

Magda, Lee began, and her eyes widened and she seemed to shrink from the table. A voice behind him said, Lee? Lee Goodell? When he turned he saw Joel Dexter—that was his name, the lawyer's son, the boy who had movie dates with Magda when they were in school and the suspect who had been briefly detained by the police following the assault, though no one believed he had anything to do with it. The police chief refused even to speak his name. Joel looked now much as he did then, short of stature, overweight, heavy eyeglasses, and evidently still the class clown. He had been the one telling jokes. Lee rose and shook hands, and when Joel looked inquiringly at Magda, Lee turned to introduce them, as unnecessary as that would seem. But Magda spoke first.

Hello, Joel.

He was flustered and it was obvious he had not the least idea of who she was, this slender young woman dressed as if she had just come from an office somewhere. Magda was much changed since their schooldays.

It's Magda, she said.

My goodness, Joel said and took a step back. His hand flew to his mouth and the little fuzzy mustache, new-grown from the look of it. Joel said nothing more and Lee noticed a deep flush of—it was either fear or embarrassment, perhaps some of both, and something more besides. After a long moment, Joel said, I didn't recognize you. Gosh, let me catch my breath. What a surprise. You look very well, Magda.

With a ghost of a smile, Magda said, You haven't changed a bit, Joel.

Joel Dexter smiled crookedly, an attempt at charm. Lee had the idea he had drunk too much at lunch and that would be the normal thing for him, a martini before and one during and something to finish up. Joel said, How long have you been here, New Jesper? Are you back for good? It's been such a long time, you'll find our town's changed, and not for the better . . .

I'm only here on a visit, Magda said.

Dexter! someone called from the entrance. Get your ass in gear. We've got business at the office.

My law partner, Joel said apologetically. I have to go. It's good seeing you again, Magda. I remember the good times we had before . . . And he did not finish the sentence, embarrassed again. He said, And you too, Lee. I've heard you're living in Chicago.

I saw your father the other day at Probate, he looked well, all business as usual . . . Joel reached into a pocket for his wallet, extracted a business card, and handed it to Magda. If there's anything I can do, please call me . . . And with that he was gone, hurrying from the room and through the double doors with his law partner.

She watched him go with a tired smile. They're always like that, Magda said. Men, women too. If they know about the rape of me they're embarrassed, as if it's a disease they might catch. They stammer. They fumble for words. They make false smiles. They don't finish sentences and they don't look you in the eye. In some ways the women are the worst because I know exactly what they're thinking. And they can't wait to get away from me. Magda dropped another lump of sugar into her coffee cup and stirred. Poor Joel, she said. So—at a loss. He was a nice boy. She looked at the business card front and back and put it in the ashtray.

They sat in silence. The waiter had gone away and they were alone in the big room, empty tables set with fresh linen and flatware. The afternoon sun cast sharp yellow stripes on the walls and Lee felt a fugitive breeze from the open windows. Lee watched the old scow move away from the dock, the deckhand winding stern lines as the vessel made way from the harbor to open water, its chevron wake bubbling behind. Carl's scows had been at dockside for as long as he could remember. Lee lit a cigarette and watched the smoke curl in the stillness.

I've taken too much of your time, Magda said.

No, you haven't, Lee replied.

I haven't been to this restaurant ever, all the years I lived in New Jesper.

As you can see, you haven't missed much.

But there's one last thing, Magda said. I want to know what you think of this. My mother and I went to the library to find the files of the *World*. I thought if I read the account of the rape

of me the memory of it might come back, some word or phrase
might—rouse it. And then I would know the identity of the man
and he would be arrested and punished. The search took us a
while. And when we finally located the article we could hardly
make sense of the words. "An incident," the story said, but never
described the incident. The story was written in a strange sort
of code, almost a stammer, fumbling for words. Do you remember it?

I certainly do.

Well, then, what was it about, Lee?

They were embarrassed, Lee said.

The man who wrote the story was embarrassed?

Alfred Swan wrote the story. They did not want to embarrass
the town.

The *town?*

They had many of the details, clinical details. Exactly what
was done to you. Those were suppressed. They were afraid—

Afraid of what?

Afraid of alarming people. Afraid the town would be overrun
with Chicago reporters. Afraid that the story was too lurid, too
frightful, and that reputations would be ruined, yours included.
They did not believe that publication of the whole truth would
serve anyone's interest. And that was why the story was written
as it was. Sanitized. Chaste, I would call it. Lee thought a moment before he added one last thought. He said, You. What happened to you was too heavy a burden.

The man who raped me, was he a heavy burden also?

They had no idea who it was, Lee said. They still don't. They
had the crime but not the criminal. The victim had no memory
of it. That was you. No witnesses, no evidence. They had nothing. No leads.

Did they try?

They did try, Lee said. They were frightened too. A maniac in
their midst.

You keep saying "they." Who's "they"?

The people who run things in New Jesper, Lee said. The mayor, the banker, Walter Bing, Alfred Swan, a few others. My father.

They decide, Magda said. What is known, what is not known.

Not always, Lee said. In your case, yes. They see themselves as lawyers with the town as their client. It's pro bono work. No charge.

I know what pro bono means, Lee.

They sat in silence. Magda dropped another lump of sugar into her cup, a sharp clink. She said, Do you think we could get more coffee?

Lee rose from the table and walked into the barroom, where the waiter was reading baseball scores in the sports section of the *World*. When he asked for coffee the waiter replied that the kitchen was closed. Open it, Lee said. It's closed, the waiter repeated and went back to the paper. Lee bent close to his ear, suddenly unreasonably angry. He said, Do your job. Get the lady a cup of coffee. Do it now. The waiter put the newspaper down and hurried off. Lee returned to the dining room, where he saw Magda standing at the window looking into the harbor, a few small sailboats resting at their moorings, motionless in the airless heat. In the sunlight the water was the color of mercury, oily white. Lee noticed a sweat stain on the back of Magda's white blouse.

She said, I was such a terrible student and not only math. I thought of myself as stupid. But when my mother and I went away and my wounds healed my attitude changed. I began to take my studies seriously. I knew that I had to make my own way. We were in St. Louis, my mother and I. I went to parochial schools, taught by nuns. They were no-nonsense nuns. Mean, some of them. Very mean. But I was not rebellious, as I am sure you can understand. Rebellion was the furthest thing from my mind. I did well at school and later in the small Catholic college.

I converted to the Church and it's become an important part of my life. Even so, you have to make your own way. As for this, all you have told me, I don't know what to think. Magda hesitated, and when she resumed her voice had acquired an unfamiliar tone, hard-edged and caustic. She said, I feel like a piece of merchandise. The stuff in the cut-rate bin at the Dry Goods that's been pawed by a hundred hands. Picked up. Put back. What were they thinking? No one was supposed to know but everyone knew. My story was not worth printing. And the man who did it went free. This awful thing has meant everything to me. I am two people, everything I was up to the age of fifteen and something else since. I am unable to connect the two. I am celibate, you know. I always will be. We teach forgiveness in my church but I am not forgiving. In my school I am not a popular teacher. My students find me strict. A disciplinarian. A tough grader. Unsympathetic. Every day of my life I have a ghost at my elbow. And I want him to go away. I want him dead, whoever he is. I would kill him myself. I'm trying to make sense of this, Lee. I had not thought of being a burden to New Jesper or to anybody. The idea of it I cannot grasp. It's New Jesper that's a burden to me. It was a mistake to come back.

Lee heard a noise behind them and turned to see the waiter with two fresh cups of coffee. He put them on the table and hurried away. Lee motioned to Magda, but Magda did not move from the window. An old man and a young boy perhaps six years old were standing in shade on the pier, fishing with bamboo poles. The old man was smoking a corncob pipe, the smoke from it hanging in the heavy air. When the boy moved to the edge of the pier in order to look closely at the water, the old man stepped sideways to stand protectively behind him, his hand on the boy's shoulder. Lee smiled at the physical similarity between them and the protectiveness of the old man, a moment that would make a sentimental cover for a magazine or a calendar. Summer, New Jesper. The old man and the boy stood motionless waiting for a

fish, but there was hardly a ripple on the surface of the water and
no birds either, and what fish there were in deep siesta.

Magda said, I looked at the police reports. I went to the station house and spoke to the desk sergeant, who refused to let me
see them. When I saw the name on his uniform I spoke to him
in Spanish. He knew who I was all right and after a moment
he went into another room. I heard him on the telephone. In a
little while he came back with a folder and handed it to me and
said I could read it there, in the waiting room. Then, after another moment, he said I could come with him and he would find
a place for me to read in private. The reports are as you say. No
evidence at all beyond me. I was evidence. No leads. I was surprised to find the attack occurred in a room off the gym. I didn't
know there was a room off the gym. I had only been in the gym
once or twice. So that was new. Fresh information, for whatever
it's worth. When I returned the file to him, he said he was sorry.
He said, I'm sorry for what happened to you. He wanted me to
know that the case was still open. I thanked him and said I was
happy to meet him. I was, too. He was simpatico.

Lee said, Do you want your coffee?

No, Magda said. I think I'll go now.

Lee said, I'm glad you called me.

It's good seeing you again, Lee.

I'm afraid I wasn't much help.

No, no, she said. I understand things I didn't understand before. I have more to think about now.

I've told you what I know. I hope I haven't upset you.

I'm always upset. It's how I live.

I hope things work out for you, Magda.

Tell me this, she said. Has your life worked out the way you
thought it would?

Lee hesitated and did not speak for a full minute. He hardly
knew how to reply; his life had been so very fortunate. He had
never been amnesiac and wondered now if his life would be dif-

ferent if he remembered nothing about the scar on his face. But it was only a scar, nothing resembling Magda's ordeal. A minor mystery. He said, I never imagined myself living in Hyde Park. My horizons did not extend to Hyde Park. I didn't know where Hyde Park was. When I was in school I thought that if things broke a certain way I could make a living at sculpture. Whether or not I could make a living at it, sculpture was what I intended to do. Maybe I would have to make a living at something else but I would always work at sculpture. I did know that much. It's where I find the truth of things, and once you know that you'll never give it up.

Sculpture, Magda said with a smile. Has that held you back?

Not so far, he said.

THEY WERE ON THE SIDEWALK in the afternoon glare. The old man and his grandson were walking ahead of them, each with a bamboo pole on his shoulder. The boy was lagging behind. His grandfather said, Come along, Willy. The boy turned suddenly and smiled at Magda, announcing that they had caught no fish. Magda said, Maybe next time, all the fish you can eat. The boy said, I hope so. Magda said, Goodbye, Willy, and then added under her breath, You darling boy.

Lee and Magda walked in the direction of the train station, but when they reached New Jesper Street Magda said she was going the other way. She kissed Lee shyly on the cheek and said she hoped they would meet again sometime, as unlikely as that was. She was returning to St. Louis in the morning. As Magda spoke she watched the old man and his grandson cross the street hand in hand, Willy chattering on about fishing, wondering if they needed new bamboo poles or different bait. The old man nodded but did not answer, unless his chuckle was a kind of answer.

Maybe I can be a third person, Magda said suddenly. I have the before and the after but who knows if there's another waiting in the wings, a year or so from now. A later-still Magda. Later-still will be my new life. Wouldn't that be something? Wouldn't that be a gift?

That's a good thought, Magda. Keep it.

I will, she said. It's out of reach now.

Do you think, Magda, Lee said, giving voice at last to the thought that had been with him all afternoon, from the moment she asked him where he got his scar. Do you think it's possible that you're fortunate having no memory of what was done to you? You're living with an unknown and have done for all these years. As you said to my father, your memory is asleep. It may never wake up. And so your imagination has taken charge, and yours is vivid. I know that without being told.

You mean, A thing's better not known than known.

It depends on what you fear most, the known or the unknown.

She offered a ghost of a smile. Do you have to choose?

I imagine it's chosen for you, Lee said.

That's what I think too.

You must have thought about this a hundred times, Lee said.

More than that, Magda said and gave a little wave and walked off down Sac Street, the Victorian eaves of the courthouse visible in the distance. There were few pedestrians in the heat of midafternoon. Ahead of Magda was the *World* building with its brass Elgin clock that gave the date and the time and beyond that the First National Bank of New Jesper. The Dry Goods was a little farther on. Magda walked slowly in the heat, the damp spot on her blouse revealing the straps of her bra. Had she known that, she would have been embarrassed. Mortified.

THEY CORRESPONDED FOR A TIME, Christmas cards at first and then letters, two or three a year. He never went back to New Jesper after the lunch at Carl's so he had no news from there. Lee always sent Magda invitations to his Chicago openings, and she always replied that she would try to come, but never did. Magda replied to his letters with news of her own, written in the smallest script he had ever seen. She had a new apartment that overlooked a park near the river. In her school she had moved on from the classroom to become an administrator, assistant principal. She enjoyed the work. Also, she was a daily communicant at Mass. Her church gave her solace. She had come to love the music and the Latin prayers, the communion and the profound privacy of faith and the essential mystery of it. At one time she had considered joining a holy order, but in the end, on reflection, she did not pursue the matter. Lee tried to read between the lines but was unsuccessful. Of course he considered the obvious reason, but the obvious reason was not always the true reason, so he remained in the dark. He hoped she had not had a crisis of faith and wrote a letter to that effect but when she replied, some months later, she avoided the issue. She wrote that she had found a cat at the local shelter and she and the cat had become great friends. Lee was fearful that he had been too direct, a meddler. Her faith was not his business.

At length the letters both ways became fewer and finally stopped altogether and their only contact now were the cards at Christmastime, hers a religious card depicting the Virgin Mary and the child, and his a color photograph of him, Laura, and their two boys on vacation—Cape Cod, Williamsburg, London, Naples. Magda signed her card "Love and Prayers, Magda Serra." Lee decided to take the card as evidence that her faith was intact.

One Christmas there was no card from her. Lee worried that she had met with misfortune, so he called Information in St. Louis but she was not listed. He called the St. Louis newspaper to see if there had been an obituary or death notice but there was nothing. Magda Serra was not in their files. On a sudden inspiration he called Information in New Jesper but there was no listing there, either. So she had vanished, moved away somewhere in Missouri or elsewhere, no forwarding address. Was the cause the weight of memory or its absence? He knew in his heart he would not hear from her again. He had the idea she was on the run, a step ahead of the shadow that would be with her always. Lee wanted to believe that she was living simply in a place of repose where her prayers, whatever they were, would be answered.

HE HAD GIVEN UP the basement studio in the dangerous neighborhood and was now located in Hyde Park proper, not far from the Midway, the top floor of a building that housed a delicatessen and a bicycle repair shop on the ground floor and a dentist's office on the second. Lee's studio was on the third floor, the windows facing north, admitting a hard wilderness light filled with Chicago dust. Lee had never been a fast worker but over the years had become ever more deliberate, long hours devoted to scrutiny of his wood blocks. He had exhausted the possibilities of marble, or the marble had exhausted him, he was never sure which. At some point he would return to it but for the time being he was in thrall to the internal enigma of wood, wooden torsos, wooden faces. It was there on a Wednesday morning in the au-

tumn of 1963 that the telephone rang, one sharp ring and a few
seconds of silence before a ringing in earnest. That was Laura's
emergency signal, so seldom used that Lee looked up in alarm
and answered at once. However, the caller was not his wife but
his old schoolmate Hopkins, saying he had gotten the number
and the signal from Laura and sorry for the interruption but he
knew Lee would want to hear the news. Lee, angry at being disturbed, said impatiently, What news?

Hopkins said, Ogden Hall has burned to the ground. Total
loss. Nothing left except a few of the outbuildings.

My God, Lee said. When did this happen?

Last night, Hopkins said. No injuries. As you'll remember, the
Hall is basically vacant at night, not even a watchman. Apparently the blaze could be seen for miles around. The Jesper firemen
took forever to arrive, and when they did arrive there was nothing for them to do except stand around and watch. The fire was
too hot to approach. It's early days but they think it was the wir-
ing. Most of it has been around since before the turn of the century. The place went up like kindling. So it's a hell of a mess and
my question is: Shall we go and take a look at the wreckage?

THEY AGREED TO MEET at Ogden Hall at three, while afternoon light remained. The day was warm enough that Lee could
smell the acrid odor of charred wood through the open windows
of his car miles before he got to the school's entrance. He had not
been back in years, his school days not lost in his memory but
much neglected. And they returned in a rush when he saw the
railroad trestle and the stand of white pines and the football field
with its goalposts and bleachers. He remembered the exact spot
where Tommy Ogden sat in his open Cadillac drinking whiskey
from a silver flask. Their conversation returned to him word for
word. He wondered if anyone remembered the undefeated season. That too returned vividly, but he did not dwell on it.

Lee pulled his car off the road and turned off the engine, looking at the football field's white stripes and the goalposts and the big scoreboard beyond the goalposts. The scoreboard and the bleachers were in need of paint. Lee had no idea how the team was doing this year or any of the recent years. He did not follow football at Ogden Hall or anywhere else. He wondered if old Svenson was still alive and living in Fish Creek, caretaker of a country house. Lee had heard a strange story involving Gus Allprice, an accident at sea. The waters were calm but Gus fell overboard and was rescued by the athletic Anjelica. Which sea, northern or southern, was not specified. But Gus was said to be unharmed. This was some years back. Lee had no idea if Gus Allprice and his Anjelica were still together in Patagonia or some other place. The Marquesas. Cape Cod. Maybe they were in Tahiti reading *Omoo* together. Surely wherever they were, *Omoo* was with them. If something untoward had happened to them he would have heard, though on second thought perhaps not. So many faculty had come and gone over the years and four headmasters since Gus. The alumni bulletin, published at irregular intervals over the years, was routinely inattentive and uninformative, mostly concerning itself with appeals for money and unspecified "support." Under a program called Continue the Legacy, alumni were urged to enroll their children at birth, acceptance virtually assured. Now and then in the bulletin there were indications that the school was succeeding, enrollment steady year to year with graduates often going on to respectable colleges and universities, though Chicago was never one of them. The year before, one of the senior boys had won a national science prize, a first for Ogden Hall. Still, the money appeals were so abject that Lee wondered if the Ogden millions had dried up at last, lacking Tommy Ogden's magic touch and Bert Marks's supervision. Lee was conscious of being pressed on all sides by ghosts.

He watched two boys wander onto the field and begin throwing a football, long spiral passes thrown lazily into the damp and sour air. They were decent athletes, skylarking, throwing high and low, leaping for the catch. One of them reminded Lee of Hopkins, a rangy boy, conscious of form, drifting forward as graceful as a dancer. Then Lee noticed two girls sitting in the top row of the bleachers. A few years before, Ogden Hall had gone coed, to the indignation of the alumni, if letters to the editor of the bulletin were any guide. Preposterous. Unacceptable. Unmanly. I am revising my will at once. And Lee remembered thinking that it took some confidence to publish the letters, all but one of them negative. The girls were dressed in red sweaters, a splash of color against the gray of the sky and the shabby bleachers. They were laughing as they watched the boys at play, a scene that could have been replicated at any school in the country except for the foul smell of smoke that hung in the air. Lee found reassurance in the quietness of the moment, an ordinary autumn day when time stopped. He waited awhile, watching the boys play throw and catch as the red-sweatered girls looked on. They paid him no attention whatever. He could have been invisible.

Lee put his car in gear and drove away slowly through the stand of white pines toward the Hall. Smoke in the air thickened and he could feel the heat. There were a dozen or more cars parked off the road and people standing in groups looking at the rubble, and a vast pile of rubble it was, with a free-standing brick chimney to announce the location of the library and its treasure of books and their guardian, Rodin's Chicago debutante. Lee wondered if any of the Ogden books had remained uncut and guessed that there were quite a few. Ogden's was a library from the century before, after all. No one read Robert Louis Stevenson anymore, or Balzac or Melville either, especially *Omoo*. One glance at Tommy Ogden's domain gave the verdict: a total loss, nothing salvageable. Then Lee noticed fumaroles amid the debris, as if a near-extinct volcano lay deep in the earth. Beyond the smoke Lee could see the tennis courts, the nets melted into crispy spaghetti. The great oak back of the courts was scorched and its bony branches still smoldered. Ogden Hall looked as if it had been hit by a bomb, some sort of incendiary device dropped at low altitude with malice aforethought. London, Hamburg, Dresden. Unless you were familiar with the size and shape of the building you would have no idea what had been there. It could have been a barn or a warehouse or anything else. It occurred to Lee that Ogden Hall School for Boys was not yet fifty years old.

With the charred hulk of an automobile as the backdrop, a television crew was setting up for an interview. The lights were garish in the smoke, the scene itself similar to a film set. A four-man hook-and-ladder was stationed nearby, two firemen sitting on the running board smoking cigarettes. All of this was framed in the camera. Lee saw to his surprise that Hopkins was the one being interviewed, the camera five feet from his face and the microphone up close too. Hopkins was speaking casually, as if to a personal friend, as practiced as an actor. The interviewer was wearing a safari jacket and desert boots, as though he had only now emerged from the bush somewhere. The interviewer looked less practiced than Hopkins, his expression moving from funereal to vivacious and back again. Hopkins worked at one of the Chicago exchanges and was sometimes called upon to comment on price fluctuations of commodities like corn and soybeans, wheat and gold. He was difficult to understand sometimes but always fluent and optimistic, except when discussing government regulations. Now Hopkins went on and on, explaining something, the interviewer nodding sympathetically. And then the lights went out and the interviewer put the microphone aside and shook hands with Hopkins, himself incongruous in a dark business suit and striped tie. Meanwhile, the cameraman reloaded film. Then Hopkins stepped away and the interviewer consulted his notes. In a moment the lights blinked on, the camera rolled, and the interviewer commenced his summing up.

Lee and Hopkins shook hands and Lee said, Where did you find him?

He found me, Hopkins said. I told him a little bit about the history of the school and what a tragedy this is. He wanted to know about my feelings, so I said something about them. Boo-hoo. He asked me about prominent alumni, so I mentioned Peter Price, our downstate judge, and Pirelli, the restaurant guy in Wheaton, and you. He drew a blank on all three—sorry about that. It's the lead of the evening news, according to him.

Say anything about Tommy Ogden?

He wanted to know about Ogden but I brushed him off. He's done his homework, so my guess is that he'll mention Ogden, Great White Hunter, blah blah blah. Damned if I was going to help him out. Ogden's a distraction.

Lee gestured around him. He said, What a mess.

Hopkins said, It's only a building. Buildings can be rebuilt.

They spent some time pointing here and there, identifying the dining hall and the kitchen and the various offices, the headmaster's and the dean's and the others. They were pointing at vacant spaces. Hopkins told the story of being called before Gus Allprice and warned that he was on thin ice, *thin ice, Hopkins,* Gus barely able to suppress a smile. Hopkins couldn't remember the infraction, whatever it was, probably drinking or absent without leave. Maybe something to do with Willa. He said, The only way to get thrown out of Ogden Hall was to commit murder with an ax. But that's finished. We don't do business that way now. There's no more of *that.* That's yesterday.

What a shame, Lee said.

Back then, you said Ogden Hall and you were laughed at. I didn't like it. I still don't.

They began a slow transit around the Hall, taking particular note of the space where the garden room was, floor-to-ceiling windows on three sides, boiling hot in summer and frigid in winter. Hopkins remembered the garden room was occupied by the librarian, the woman who always wore her hair in a bun and a rose in the lapel of her jacket. She was a human Dewey Decimal

System, knew the location of every book in the library. She'd never read one but she knew where they were.

She liked Virginia Woolf, Lee said.

Nonsense, Hopkins said.

And Victor Hugo, Lee said.

I doubt that very much, Hopkins said.

Mrs. Haines, Lee said. Mrs. Haines liked to quote Hugo to the effect that a just government encouraged the rich and protected the poor. A line from one of his novels. She was quite well read, actually.

They walked on in uncomfortable silence, and when Lee wondered if it was worth the effort to rebuild Ogden Hall, that perhaps its day had come and gone, Hopkins snorted. He said, Think again. Fund-raising begins tomorrow, a full-court press on the alumni. We'll expect you to ante up, Goodell.

What will it take?

Look around you. Millions. Two million at least to get things squared away.

Hopkins was a member of the board of trustees, much the youngest member but the most active. He described the board meetings, always held at the Tavern Club downtown. Fine group of fellows, lawyers, property developers, advertising executives. Substantial men, Hopkins said. He had been on the telephone— "the blower"—all morning, gathering support. That was one of the things I told that idiot with the microphone. Rebuilding begins right now. The truth is, this fire is a blessing in disguise. The buildings needed renovation and we're short on the sports facilities that parents expect now, swimming pools and the like. Squash courts, a decent infirmary, and it would be good too if the girls had a locker room of their own. The place is rundown, neglected. And your next question is: What happened to Ogden's endowment? And the answer is: Bad investments. Instead of airlines they bought rails. Refused to trade in commodities. We got rid of the old board two years ago, a nicely orchestrated coup d'état. All of them were friends of the mouthpiece Bert Marks. They were Marks's people. Too old, stuck in the past. Gus All-price thought Ogden Hall had a curse on it and maybe he had a point. Something was out of whack all right. You'll not be sur-prised to learn that they all remembered our undefeated season. They all remember the final game. They remember you. They remember me. They even remember old Svenson—he's part of the mythology too. That seemed to have been the high point of Ogden Hall. Nothing before, nothing much since. They liked it that way. Also, they all knew Tommy Ogden when they were more or less middle-aged and he was very old. They told stories about him. Everyone had a story. They liked him. But that's fin-ished now. We're in charge.

I liked him too, Lee said.

You never met him.

Oh, but I did.

Nonsense, Hopkins said.

I met him near the football field, the final game. The one everyone seems to remember. He watched the game from his car and that's where I met him. He and his chauffeur Edgar. He gave me some pointers on life. I can't think what they were, but there were a lot of them. It was Tommy Ogden who sent the silver cups.

Hopkins shrugged, eager to be gone. Tommy Ogden bored him. He had heard all too much of Tommy Ogden over the years, a rake and a gambler, altogether reckless. He was unsavory, never worked a day. Only worthwhile thing he ever did in his sorry life was to found Ogden Hall, and that was because he lost a bet to his wife and was forced to pay up. The bust in the library was part of the settlement and now the bust was gone for good, en-tombed in the rubble, and good riddance to it, an unwholesome legend. Well, Hopkins said, there was every possibility that they would be unable to raise the two million. The trustees agreed to make best efforts. But if best efforts failed they would sell the land. Two trustees, property developers, thought it would fetch a good price. Why, they themselves might be interested. Form a consortium, keep the deal in-house. But first, best efforts . . .

HOPKINS WENT AWAY. The TV crew gathered its gear and vanished. Dusk came on and soon Lee was the only spectator save for the firemen who had retreated to the truck's cab and a few boys gathered around the burnt-out car, suitcases and athletic gear gathered at their feet, waiting for a ride home. Authority was nowhere visible and the boys were passing around cigarettes. Lee stepped closer to the heat of the rubble, fumaroles secreting gray smoke. Debris seemed to extend to the limits of Lee's eyesight, in places ten feet high and more. Sparks collected and spun like fireflies. He moved as close to the free-standing chimney as was safe to do and remembered that the fireplace was big enough for a man to stand full height. Lee stepped back, his eyes burning from the smoke. They would never rebuild Ogden Hall. Ogden Hall was a vanished civilization. Somewhere in the incinerated ruins were homely items from the kitchen and dining hall and the transcripts of a thousand students and the remains of two thousand leather-bound books and deep in the ashes Rodin's beautiful debutante, the marble scorched but surely intact. Lee imagined her excavated years from now, sometime late in the next century, recognizably a bust from Rodin's hand—and the story would end there. Lee remained the longest time, remembering the Chicago girl in the alcove as the Illinois seasons changed, dark to light to dark once again.